THERE WAS NO MISTAKING THE DRIVER'S INTENTION

A panel truck came roaring out of a side street and sped directly at the Turkish secret service vehicle. The driver was using the truck as a guided missile. And the target was Phoenix Force and Agent Kartal.

If the SUV had been stationary the impact would have been worse, but Kartal managed to boost the power, stamping on the gas and sending the SUV lurching forward. The truck slammed into the rear quarter of the SUV instead of full-on. Still, the impact spun the SUV in a half circle, glass shattering and spraying inside the passenger compartment as the car rocked violently, wheels lifting off the road for seconds. The impact drove the lower section of the wheel well into the vehicle's tire.

"Two inside," she called out. "They're showing weapons."

"Move," McCarter ordered. "Everyone out. Fast!"

DON PENDLETON'S

STONY

AMERICA'S ULTRA-COVERT INTELLIGENCE AGENCY

MAN®

DOUBLE BLINDSIDE

A GOLD EAGLE BOOK FROM

W@RLDWIDE®

TORONTO • NEW YORK • LONDON
AMSTERDAM • PARIS • SYDNEY • HAMBURG
STOCKHOLM • ATHENS • TOKYO • MILAN
MADRID • WARSAW • BUDAPEST • AUCKLAND

Recycling programs
for this product may
not exist in your area.

First edition April 2015

ISBN-13: 978-0-373-80450-4

Double Blindside

Special thanks and acknowledgment to
Mike Linaker for his contribution to this work.

Printed in U.S.A.

DOUBLE BLINDSIDE

PROLOGUE

Istanbul, Turkey

Phil Makerson slowly made his way along an empty street awash with rain. The sky was so dark with clouds it might have been midnight rather than early evening. The downpour was so intense the drains could not keep pace and there were sections of the sidewalk where the water overflowed. There was no air movement, so the rain fell in vertical sheets. Rainstorms in Istanbul were rare, especially at this time of year, but this one had come swiftly and with a vengeance.

With no protective clothing, Makerson's suit was soaked. He didn't seem to notice as he made his way along the uneven pavement. Thoughts spinning inside his head, his mind was on other things. So much had happened in the past few hours that he was having trouble keeping it all in some kind of order. And on top of that he was hurting. His body was aching from his encounter with the man he knew as Axos; the son of a bitch had been trying to kill him. Makerson was sure of that. He might have succeeded if Makerson hadn't landed that lucky—and he considered it lucky—blow with the heavy lamp he had managed to grasp. He had lashed out, catching Axos a solid blow across the side of his skull. Thinking back, Makerson was sure he had heard something crack when the lamp connected with

Axos's head. The moment Axos went down, Makerson had vacated the run-down apartment, making his exit out onto the street.

His head was all over the place as he struggled to make sense of the recent events. Axos had been trying to kill him; Makerson had no doubts about that. The blood and bruises on his face and throat, the ache in his ribs, proved the point. Axos's unprovoked attack had taken Makerson completely off guard, and he was convinced he would have ended up dead if he had not fought back.

The only reason for the attack had to be that his cover had been exposed. Makerson had been undercover for a couple of months and, contrary to his usual care, he had somehow let his guard slip. He had become too comfortable in his role and now he was paying for it.

Makerson took that on board. He needed to get clear so he could pass along the information he had gathered. He was hoping that Berna Kartal, the female Turkish agent he had been working alongside, had managed to stay safe. Between them they had gathered a dossier of information on their target. Though Kartal had assured Makerson it was safe, he had backed up their findings by sending data to his laptop in his New York apartment. It had been a way of getting the data away from Özgürlük, the Turkish group under investigation.

Makerson had decided not to contact Kartal. He didn't want to put her in danger. All he wanted now was to escape before Axos's partner, Kristos, recovered and set off in pursuit.

He was unfamiliar with his location. Istanbul was a sprawling city that transitioned between the ancient and modern. And he had not had the time to become too familiar with the metropolis. All he knew for certain was his proximity to the water. In the hazy distance he could make out the lights of the port area.

Images of his dead partner forced their way into his mind. Jerry Callender was a good man who had been slaughtered and left in a pool of his own blood. Gutted like fish on a slab. Callender had been killed in the same room where he had been held. The image refused to fade. Makerson could still see the shock on Callender's bloody face. Those pictures would be with him for a long time.

Only if you get clear, he told himself. So quit feeling sorry for yourself and keep moving.

He sheltered under the sagging awning of a closed store and pulled out his sat phone. He knew there was plenty of power. He just hoped the signal was strong enough to reach the man he was calling. From Turkey to the U.S. He picked up the sound of the line engaging, heard the tone and then a familiar voice.

"Makerson? *What the hell...?*" The voice belonged to Redman, Makerson's contact. Not the most diplomatic of men.

"Callender's dead," Makerson said. "I managed to get out, but I have a feeling I won't be alone for long."

Redman, for once, was out of words.

"They made us," Makerson said. "I don't know how, but they knew all about us. Wanted to find out how much we knew."

"Where are you? Let me send a retrieval team. Get you to a safe place."

"Right now I wouldn't know who to trust, and I have a feeling those bastards are close. Just listen. Our intel was sound. The group is working on something that will affect our assets in Turkey and the U.S. They have something planned. We didn't have time to get any more details before they hit us. I put everything I had in a text on my cell and sent it to my personal laptop in New York."

"Phil," Redman said, "let us bring you in."

Makerson heard the soft growl of a powerful engine close by. He glanced back over his shoulder and saw a high-end SUV crawling along the shadowed, rain-swept street. For a brief instant he felt panic, then a sensation of calm washed over him.

"No time," he said. "No more time."

The SUV accelerated, bearing down on him like a gleaming black monster.

"Phil?"

"Özgürlük," Makerson said. "They call themselves Özgürlük. And I think they might have nukes."

Makerson broke into a run. He was unarmed, his weapon having been taken when Kristos had overpowered him. His cell had been taken, too, but he had managed to snatch it from the table as he'd made his escape. He had to get rid of the phone. It would hold the details of his call. If Kristos took it he would know Makerson had called America.

He crossed the street, heading for the far side where the black waters of the Med shone in the near darkness. As he ran he fumbled open the phone and stripped out the SIM card. He snapped it in two and stood on the edge of the quay. Throwing the broken SIM out into the water, he tossed the rest of the cell.

He heard the rising howl of the SUV's engine as it picked him up in its headlamps. The high bulk of the vehicle bore down on him with such speed Makerson stood no chance. The solid front of the SUV slammed into him, the impact taking Makerson off his feet and flinging his shattered body into the air. He landed with brutal force, unable to move as the SUV came on and ran over him, leaving his crushed body lifeless on the rain-sodden ground.

CHAPTER ONE

David McCarter, the commander of Phoenix Force, was already seated at the conference table in the War Room when the rest of the team entered. The lean, tanned Briton, casually dressed as usual when off duty, set a chilled bottle of Classic Coke in front of him. He watched as the group filed in and took their places at the table.

Hal Brognola, the director of Stony Man Farm, placed a stack of folders on the table as he sat. He had a resigned expression on his face that warned the assembly they were not about to be overjoyed at what he had to tell them. Last into the room was Aaron Kurtzman, the Stony Man cyber boss.

"This doesn't suggest we're about to play happy families," McCarter said.

Barbara Price, the honey-blonde, attractive mission controller, said, "On the button as usual, David."

"Comes naturally." McCarter grinned. "Like second sight. I know what's coming."

Since stepping up to take command of Phoenix Force, the Briton had maintained a confident, often brash character. Out in the field, when the time came for holding a team together, there was no one better than David McCarter. He knew Brognola was about to spell out the upcoming mission and, as always, McCarter was more than ready to take it on board. That didn't stop the irrepressible man from making his flip comments. The former SAS officer had a forceful personality that was hard to ignore. His irreverent humor vanished when Phoenix Force became involved in official business; then he became a skilled fighter with few equals.

With everyone settled, Brognola distributed the folders, sliding one along the table to each man. With that done, he leaned back in his seat and unwrapped one of his trademark cigars and clamped it between his teeth. No one could recall the last time he'd actually smoked one of them. He simply chewed on the cigar, using it like a tobacco-based worry bead. As head of the Farm, Harold Brognola had plenty to be worried about.

Silence reigned for the next few minutes as the teams absorbed the contents of the files.

"Two undercover agents killed?" Carl Lyons, the Able Team commander, queried. Powerfully built, the blond former LAPD cop was a full-on, no-nonsense fighter who seldom took prisoners unless there was a good reason to keep them alive. "In Turkey?"

Rosario Blancanales, Able Team's infiltration specialist, followed up. "Both teamed on the same investigation?" Nicknamed "the Politician," Blancanales had the skills and confidence of a negotiator coupled with his enduring combat qualifications.

Calvin James added, "Hell of a security breach." The black Phoenix Force warrior was tall and leanly powerful. A former Navy SEAL, the Chicago-raised man was also the Phoenix Force medic. James was ferocious in battle, never giving an inch, yet in the aftermath would give as much of himself again to tend to a wounded individual— friend or foe alike.

"The President feels the same way," Brognola said.

"He's already had talks with the Turkish president. There's a lot at stake here, people. So he's passed it along to us. Wants to keep it under the radar, if possible, until it's sorted."

"Nice of him," McCarter said. "Question is why?"

"The bottom line seems to indicate a conspiracy aimed at disturbing the U.S.-Turkish alliance," Rafael Encizo said, tapping his copy of the file. "No definite proof but an overall suggestion. And we can't ignore the reference to possible nuclear ordnance mentioned in the reports. Some kind of blackmail threat."

The Cuban had an earned reputation as being one of the most skilled knife-fighters around and had a fertile, probing mind. He was tenacious, a relentless fighter who never backed down. He still bore the scars from a term in Cuba's infamous Principe prison before he made his break for freedom to the U.S.A. He had never forgotten his imprisonment, the memory still in his mind and the physical scars on his body. One of Encizo's proudest moments was when he became an American citizen. His commitment to Phoenix Force was one of the ways he offered his thanks.

"Nor should you," Brognola said. "Turkey has been a U.S. ally for a long time. That relationship has come under attack on a number of occasions. Their location puts them in a delicate position and the U.S. doesn't want to lose that advantage. However, certain groups in the country don't like the closeness to us. They make their feelings known whenever the opportunity comes up. But the suggestions in the report veer toward more than just protest groups and staged rallies. Top of their agenda has been the removal of our base at Incirlik."

"By nuclear blackmail?" Thomas Jackson Hawkins

said. "That seems to be coming through pretty damn strong."

"Trouble with threats is they can end up turning into the real thing," James noted. "Especially if they're in the hands of extremists."

"So are we taking direct action?" Hawkins asked. A Texan, the youngest Phoenix Force member was former Delta Force and was rapidly developing into a seasoned veteran. He still had moments of unrestrained enthusiasm that got the better of him, but his military experience and fighting skills had made him a valuable asset to Phoenix Force.

"Rein it in, cowboy," Gary Manning quipped. The brawny Canadian fighter held the distinction of being Phoenix Force's demolitions expert. Former RCMP, Manning had extensive knowledge of global terrorist groups. "Your time will come."

"From the little intel we've received, there's a group organizing itself for some kind of extreme protest," Brognola continued. "There was a name in the transcripts that came up a number of times. Kadir Polat is a Turkish national. He's a guy who wants to be counted when it comes to opposition against our presence in the country."

Brognola glanced down the table to where Aaron Kurtzman, head of Stony Man's dedicated cyber team, sat quietly in his motorized wheelchair. The big man had been crippled from the waist down a number of years back when Stony Man Farm had been hit for the first and only time. Despite his disability, Kurtzman had proved himself countless times by providing information that assisted the Stony Man field teams. His ongoing mission was to maintain his department as the best around, and to offer the Stony Man teams the ultimate in backup.

Kurtzman was never more at home than when presented with a complex technical problem. If there was a need for something, Kurtzman would find the solution. His understanding of the internet was matched only by his innate curiosity and the need to keep learning.

"Getting into Makerson's laptop gave us the opening we needed," Kurtzman said. "That guy had put down everything he'd sourced—names and locations and images he'd captured on his cell. He's left us a hell of a legacy."

Kurtzman used the remote he held to bring up the information on the wall-mounted plasma screen. The data Makerson had gathered had been assembled into understandable order and the Stony Man teams were able to follow it clearly.

"The first image is Kadir Polat himself." Another image flashed on-screen. "Then we have this guy—Hakan Kaplan. Polat's second in command and lifelong personal friend. Makerson has him down as the harder man of the two. Both these guys are part of Özgürlük. Pretty well are Özgürlük. It's Turkish for *freedom*, for those interested. Nice little choice of words. Their politics are well-known, and on the surface they appear as people with grievances concerning Turkey's involvement with the U.S. and NATO. Makerson had tracked them both to meetings with other activist individuals."

Kurtzman clicked to a second image of Polat. It showed a close-up of the strong-faced, good-looking man, his dark eyes seeming to actually stare at everyone in the room. The effect was unsettling. The man had a head of thick black hair and a neatly trimmed goatee. The set of his lips showed a hint of a smile.

"Polat. Early forties. A devout advocate of Turkish withdrawal from NATO and involvement with the U.S. His opposition is on record and he openly defies the elected government. He's highly visible. He criticizes the elected government for being a sycophantic ally of the U.S. He is," Kurtzman added, "an extremely popular guy. Has an immense following and the backing of influential people in business and politics."

Barbara Price studied the face, admitting to herself that Polat was more than just good-looking. There was something in his dark eyes that could easily have been tantalizing. Maybe it was the light olive complexion. His black hair. The way he stared into the camera lens. The mesmerizing expression in the deep pupils...

The Stony Man mission controller mentally shook herself, hoping her brief lapse had not been noticed. Price was no giddy schoolgirl. What the hell was she thinking? A faint warmth crept across her cheeks. She was a woman dedicated to her work and not the kind to be easily seduced by a simple photograph of an attractive man. She became aware again of Kurtzman's voice as he explained more about Polat. She realized she had zoned out for a few moments and pulled herself back to the present.

"Polat's background tells us he comes from a wealthy family. Extremely wealthy. And I emphasize *wealthy*. The Polat dynasty goes back decades. Very traditional Turkish. They own businesses around the country, including a shipping line. They have homes in Turkey. A villa on the Costa Brava. Run aircraft like normal people run cars. And there's an ocean-going cruiser Kadir keeps moored in the harbor outside Istanbul."

"Married?" McCarter asked casually.

It was an innocent question on the surface, but when Price caught the Briton's gaze she could see a thin smile edging his lips.

"Just filling in the background."

Dammit, she thought, had he noticed?

"No," Brognola said. "Though he has been linked with some well-known women."

"Interesting," McCarter said. "Quite a bloke, then."

Price felt a flash of anger at his remark. She pushed it out of her mind instantly. She realized McCarter was simply teasing. He was well-known for his dry wit and the pointed way he could deliver his sly retorts.

"So what's Polat done that gets him in this report?" McCarter asked, his attention back on Brognola. "Is he suspected of being involved in the deaths of the agents?"

"Lots of suspicion," Brognola said. "No hard proof. But Polat is smart enough to stay in the background and surround himself with people to make his history interesting.

"Polat has a younger brother who is involved with Özgürlük. Amal Polat. He has the family money behind him and a rep as a hothead. He's twenty-four years old but still has the willful attitude of a teenager."

They went over the files again, taking in the data that applied to each team.

"This is one of the good guys," Brognola said, nodding at the cyber boss. "To be politically correct, one of the good girls."

Kurtzman brought up another image on the plasma. This time a young female. She was strikingly attractive. Her fall of thick black hair framed an oval, mobile face. She had large brown eyes and a full mouth, light brown skin and dark brows.

"Now, she *is* interesting," Encizo said. "And she's on the side of the good guys?"

"Agent Berna Kartal," Brognola said. "And, yes, she is. Kartal is an agent with the NIO—the Turkish National

Intelligence Organization, aka secret service. Early thirties. Did a couple of years in active military service when she was eligible. Her current assignment is investigating Özgürlük. She had the local contact with Makerson and his partner until they disappeared. The next time she saw them was in the morgue. Dead agents push this a step up the ladder."

"So what's the bottom line here?" Lyons said.

"Polat is suspected of having a desire to push his group further along the dissent road. Behind the outer charm he's funded rallies expressing dissatisfaction with American presence on Turkish soil. He has the ear of powerful Turkish groups who also have big money behind them. Industrialists. Old-time Turkish families, like his own, who would prefer nothing better than for the country to be free from foreign influence. And there are groups within the Turkish government who have the same feelings. Kartal believes there may also be some military backing coming via General Demir Marangol."

The next photo showed a thickset man in a Turkish military uniform bedecked with ribbons. The man's broad face stared out of the picture with a belligerent scowl. His dark eyes and thick mustache gave him a powerful expression.

"Marangol. Old family friend of the Polat dynasty. Also extremely pro–Turkish independence. Makes no bones about his feelings. Wants his country independent of foreign influence. Has a lot of power behind him in the military."

"So no solid evidence of anything except hot air?" Lyons growled.

As always the Able Team leader was not shy about expressing his opinion. Carl "Ironman" Lyons saw everything in black and white; there was good and there was bad. It was advisable to remain in the good guys' camp if Lyons was on your case; he tended to subscribe to the school of "shoot first, worry about the questions later."

Lyons had little concern over criminals' rights. He was fair, but had no time for tolerating bad behavior. He'd undergone paramilitary training in preparation for antiterrorist missions. Though he had not had any military service, Lyons had worked in the LAPD as a detective sergeant. Since becoming the leader of Able Team, Lyons had gained on-the-job experience in the fight against terrorism.

"No. Speculation by the carload, but no positive proof. Until recently," Brognola said. "Kartal's report backs up what the dead agent, Makerson, sent to his home laptop. The first time there's been anything except a great deal of hearsay."

"Enough to move on?" Encizo inquired.

"When an investigation ends up with two agents dead, it becomes a possible threat we can't afford to ignore. Enough that the President has called in Stony Man and sanctioned a mission to follow through on what he's been made privy to. His advisers have given him background on the Turkish unrest. The President has taken it on board and told his people to keep an eye on the situation. But behind closed doors he felt there was enough to give Stony Man a mandate to investigate further without the State Department blocking his way. He considered all the options and there was enough to cause him concern. It seems that at one point his advisory briefings postulated at the hint of some actual physical strike against U.S. interests in Turkey."

Brognola looked around the table. "And a veiled hint that a similar incident could take place here, on U.S. soil, to back up what Özgürlük is threatening. Now, this may be nothing more than some Turkish half-assed bullying. But when U.S. agents are murdered—agents investigating Turkish agitators advocating the removal of our base at Incirlik—it all starts to take on a shadow of reality. The deaths have been kept out of the spotlight. No point in allowing press hype to muddy the waters."

"With the background of NATO and the American presence in Turkey," James said, "I have to say we do need to follow through."

"The President doesn't want to be caught on the back foot if something does happen," Brognola said. "Turkish stability needs to be maintained. There's a lot at stake with our base at Incirlik and the NATO alliance. Anything that might upset it at all needs to be eliminated. These days there are too many groups wrangling for position. And U.S. influence is constantly under fire from various involved parties."

"These alleged strikes…" McCarter said. "Do we have any idea how they might be formulated?"

"At this point we're guessing in the dark. That's why we need Phoenix Force presence on two fronts. Turkey and London."

"What's in London?" McCarter asked.

Brognola slid a sheet of paper across for him to read.

"Kartal picked up on some mention of Özgürlük's banker in London. The guy who collects money. Passes it out when the organization needs funds. Makerson had the NSA run some phone intercepts and he liaised with Kartal. Between them they got a location for this guy, Aziz Makar. And phone transmissions from another London address. Could be a safehouse. It's a starting point for a look-see while the Turkish end is being checked out at the same time."

"We ran the address. Tracked it down through local

admin for property tax they pay in the UK. House is owned by a guy called Stanley Rimmer. His bio has him down as a landlord on a few properties. Tracking back through his transactions, we came to a dead stop with the real owner of the house."

"The Polat group?" McCarter said.

"Way down the chain," Kurtzman said. "A long chain, but if you're in there, the truth will come out."

"More to it, though?" McCarter said.

Brognola smiled at the Briton's grasp of the detail.

"Money in the deal was paid via Aziz Makar. Our Özgürlük paymaster."

Brognola waited to see if anyone registered the word and was not disappointed when Hawkins tapped the file in front of him.

"It's in the file," he said. "The organization fronting the opposition to the U.S. in Turkey and the hinted-at American strike—Özgürlük—keeps showing."

"Based on intel from Makerson and Berna Kartal's own file, I had my people run a deep trawl across the internet," Kurtzman said, joining the ongoing conversation again.

Deep trawling was Kurtzman's way of saying his team had dug their way into sites both open and secret. In Kurtzman's eyes, if information was available, whether he got it by fair means or foul, the need was there. It was seldom the Stony Man cyber team failed to come up with the goods. When Stony Man got caught up in missions where lives and security were the main factors, Kurtzman threw rule books out the window. He hated protocols that might deter weaker individuals. They were knocked aside by Kurtzman and his people. To him the protection of America, the SOG teams and that often sneered-at word *justice* were more important. Aaron Kurtzman dedicated every waking hour to maintaining the integrity of his department and his people.

"The NSA has picked up recent phone chatter involving Özgürlük. This group might have money behind them," Kurtzman said, "but they don't have a monopoly on staying totally undercover. They are not very sophisticated when it comes to covering their tracks. We picked up traces of communication between various individuals. Once we located cell phones from the numbers Kartal and Makerson identified, it wasn't all that difficult to expand our lists and start tracking messages."

He put the text messages on-screen—most of the originals had been in Turkish, so Kurtzman had pulled in Erika Dukas, one of the translators Stony Man occasionally consulted. She had taken the messages and fed them through her computer, translating and creating English versions. Passed back to Kurtzman, the messages had been incorporated into his files.

"Lots of talk back and forth," Kurtzman said. "All about logistics. Supply. Locations. This last one will interest Able. You people may recall the late Jack Regan. Arms dealer who was killed a while back. Now we have his successor, a Mexican named Pablo Gutierrez. He's picked up some of Regan's old clients. The Echelon listening device picked up some vague chatter with Gutierrez's name attached to a couple of emails from our Turkish dissidents. Something about a deal with a Russian—Gennadi Antonov. Vague. No specifics, but Antonov is suspected of ties to former Russian military."

"Where does he hang out? This Regan clone?" Hermann "Gadgets" Schwarz, Able Team's electronics expert who had been silent for most of the meeting, asked.

"Miami."

Blancanales scanned the messages on the plasma screen.

"That damn name again," he said. "Özgürlük. It's like a secret handshake for these guys. But unfortunately for them, not *too* secret."

Brognola said, "Okay, people, time to saddle up. Look into it. If it doesn't pan out, no harm done. But if there's solid evidence, you know what to do. We don't dare miss this in case it is real."

There was a brief silence as everyone around the conference table had a final run through their files. A few more questions were put forward until they were all satisfied for the moment.

"Anyone like to hear an idle thought?" McCarter said as everyone started to move.

Brognola turned his attention to the Phoenix Force leader. McCarter never had *idle* thoughts.

"Go ahead, David."

"This is just rambling. If Özgürlük does turn out to be really running this threat to blackmail us and it doesn't work and they set off a nuke close enough to damage the Incirlik base—what about the nukes already stockpiled there?"

"Ouch," Hawkins said. "Damn, how would that work? I mean would they go off, as well?"

Manning said, "If they're not actually armed, maybe not. But radioactive material could be leaked."

"I'll get my team to look into that," Kurtzman said.

Lyons said, "Time to update the President, Hal. He'll need to take some kind of action over this."

"Alerting the base would be in the cards," McCarter said.

As the teams filed out, Brognola watched them go,

his mind already turning over what McCarter had said. The Briton had been right on the button. If the suggestions about nukes were true, with the bottom line being a detonation, the situation would go quickly from bad to worse. Apart from anything else, a strike against Incirlik would make a hell of a statement. It would hit the U.S. hard, dent its pride and take out a strategic factor in the area. The anti-U.S. brigade would get what it had wanted for a long time and Özgürlük would strengthen its position.

If a dissident group wanted maximum publicity for their aims, a high-profile strike against a major target would be the way to go. Small incidents were not very productive, but a massive hit would focus attention. It would focus in on U.S. military presence across the globe. And collateral damage didn't bother the perpetrators any longer—9/11 had set the benchmark.

"So we have to work out whether this Özgürlük deal is a scare tactic or the real thing," Encizo said as he exited the room. "We need to understand if these people are just faking or genuinely willing to set off a nuke on an American base in Turkey."

"And on U.S. soil," Lyons said.

BARBARA PRICE, IN HER usual efficient fashion, went about organizing travel arrangements for the teams. Able Team's was an easy option—simply having one of the on-site vehicles prepared while Lyons and his partners gathered their weapons and IDs. Fixing things for Phoenix Force took the bulk of her work. Via Brognola's clout with the President, travel for McCarter and company was arranged on an Air Force transport on a regular flight across the Atlantic to the UK, then a switch to a similar flight from Lakenheath across to Incirlik,

Turkey. For once, the odds were in her favor and the influence of the Commander in Chief allowed her to complete the arrangements within a short time. She was not made aware of any persuasive arguments the President might have used, and in truth she didn't care. Price only wanted the end result for her people.

If fate had decreed a different direction for her, Barbara Price could have made her living as a model, even a movie star. She had the looks: honey-blonde, with an athletic, slim figure and penetrating blue eyes. Behind the glamorous appearance, she had a keen, insightful brain that had led her to a position within the NSA, where she was in charge of analyzing SIGINT and HUMINT data. Her skills with the reclusive signals and human intelligence arm of the NSA had kept Price busy, but not exclusively satisfied.

As he'd worked at selecting personnel for the newly created Stony Man, Hal Brognola had met the young woman and was so impressed with her intellect that he considered her as a replacement for the deceased April Rose, the Farm's original mission controller. When Brognola approached her and offered her the job, Price, who was disillusioned with NSA internal political squabbling, was intrigued by his offer. It hadn't taken her long to realize she was being given the opportunity to join a special department.

Once on board, Price became aware of the Special Operation Group's unique setup. It was ultrasecret, manned by the best in every field, from Brognola down to the operatives who ran the day-to-day workings of Stony Man. The secret nature of the unit meant Price's personal life became almost nonexistent. It didn't put her off. The people she came to see as her family were enough to satisfy her. The job kept her involved day and night. She built strong relationships with the teams who roved the globe fighting all kinds of threats and menaces. In truth, Price's life was full. She was committed to it, and committed to having her concerns over Phoenix and Able. She fully understood the situations they found themselves in and had made it her responsibility to ensure they received the best backup she could offer.

McCarter had assigned Manning and Hawkins to the UK detail, while he, Encizo and James would go on to Turkey to head up that end of the assignment. Manning and Hawkins would join up with the rest of the group if their part of the mission could be completed in time.

It wasn't a regular contrivance to split Phoenix Force, but given how the information had come through, a two-pronged investigation would be appropriate for the initial probe.

As Phoenix Force was being flown in by the USAF, they were able to travel with their weapons. Once they left the Incirlik base, matters might be different and they would have to check with the Turkish Secret Service, with whom they would be working, on the ability to retain their arms.

Price handed out documentation packs with her usual operational ability.

"And don't go spending your pocket money all in one go," she said lightly. "I expect receipts for everything. They will be checked."

It was her usual banter, part joke, part serious because she worried about them once they were in the field and, as professional as she was, Price had more than a passing concern for their safety. It didn't matter how many times the Stony Man combat teams departed, she experienced the same feelings and would not be settled until they all returned safely from their missions.

On this mission the results of failure were almost beyond belief. Barbara Price had been with Stony Man long enough to accept the reckless behavior of extremist groups. They took on board what they wanted to express and disregarded the wider impact of the damage they might create. In this case, Özgürlük appeared to be playing an extremely dangerous game. One that involved the possible detonation of a nuclear device on their own soil.

Would they do it?

Could they risk affecting a part of Turkey with radioactive poison simply to gain their demands? From past experience, Price knew the answer. The madness of extreme threats had no limits. It had been postulated before. And it would be again if the Turkish fanatics—and Price had no hesitation using the word—went to the logical conclusion of their game.

Nuclear bombs in Turkey and even in the U.S.

A double threat.

One that could easily come true if the Stony Man teams didn't neutralize it.

CHAPTER TWO

Istanbul, Turkey

Senior Agent Cem Asker of the Turkish National Intelligence Organization—Milli İstihbarat Teşkilati—shook hands with the three members of the American team. He had been advised the Americans were to be afforded all possible courtesies as representatives of U.S. Intelligence. His orders had come down from the highest source possible in the Turkish government. Issued by the president himself. There were to be no questions about the team. No obstacles were to be put in their way as they launched the probe into the suspected security breaches that involved both Turkey and the United States. The courtesy also extended to the weapons the men had brought with them.

Asker was a dapper man in his early forties with a neatly trimmed beard. He gave the impression of being organized and precise. He had arranged for additional seating to be provided for the three men when they were shown into his office. He waited until they were ranged in front of his desk before he sat himself.

"It would appear a little churlish to welcome you to Istanbul so casually," he said. "You are not here to enjoy a vacation."

McCarter said, "And we are not here to override your authority, either, Agent Asker. Our aim is to hopefully stop whatever is going on that might affect Turkish security."

"And American interests, as well," Asker said keenly. "Both countries are involved. And as NATO also has an interest in the matter, there is a further urgency."

"It's complicated," McCarter said.

When Phoenix Force had landed at the American base at Incirlik, it was more than apparent that a terrorist attack on the massive base would have a debilitating effect on the American presence in the country. Apart from the military hardware, there were some 5,000 U.S. personnel and family members stationed at Incirlik. Not to be overlooked was the stockpiled nuclear ordnance, there in case the unthinkable happened and American bombers needed to be launched. The commitment to the protection of U.S. interests and the readiness of the American military had been and still was a matter of much debate.

It didn't take a stretch of the imagination to visualize the damage even a small nuclear device could do. Substantial American and other lives lost. And millions of dollars of equipment destroyed. A big victory for Özgürlük.

"It is complicated indeed," Asker agreed. "Which is partly why I have asked Agent Berna Kartal to join us. Her association with your people has placed her at the forefront of this matter. I am sure she will be able to assist you greatly."

"Any help we can get," McCarter said, "will be welcome."

"Berna Kartal is a very experienced agent."

"Always handy to have experience," Manning said. "If it's the right kind, of course."

"Please do not concern yourself with that," someone

said from behind the seated Phoenix Force operatives. "My experience is extensive."

Phoenix Force turned in unison and saw the young woman who had stepped into Asker's office. She was five foot eight. With her dark hair held back from her face, her high cheekbones and generous mouth only added to her natural beauty. Her eyes scanned across the Phoenix trio, searching and curious; there was an intelligence there that told them this young woman was not making a casual statement about her abilities. She wore all black, shirt and pants, and had a holstered Glock 9 mm pistol on her right hip. As she moved into the office to take a chair beside Asker's desk, a faint smile edged her full lips.

"Do I pass?" she said.

"Not judging," Encizo said graciously. "Just appreciating." The Cuban's easy manner was at its most disarming.

Kartal smiled and placed the folder she was carrying on the desk.

"I'm sure Senior Agent Asker has expressed our condolences over the deaths of your colleagues," she said. Her English was good, with barely an accent. "May I add mine? I knew both of those men, especially Makerson. He was an extremely capable agent."

McCarter nodded. "You shared your information?"

"Yes. We both felt there was something to be concerned about involving Özgürlük. Although we had gathered data, it was… I believe you would say…all up in the air?"

"Difficult to make sense of?" James suggested.

"Exactly. Many individuals and messages. But nothing any more solid than that." Kartal leaned forward and opened the file, turning pages. "I take it you have all read the information?"

"Yes," McCarter said. "Our own people looked into the background and used their own system to dig deeper."

He slipped out the file Kurtzman had prepared and placed it beside Kartal's. She spent a little time going through it, comparing the information with her own, and nodding as she read the data.

"It is extremely extensive. How did you get all this?"

"By using the best facilities around," McCarter said. "Let's just say if it's out there, our people will find it. I can't say any more than that."

"Much of what is in here tallies with what Makerson and I had suspected."

"It seems we are already in your debt," Asker said.

"No point scoring," Encizo said. "All we want is to put a stop to whatever Özgürlük may have planned."

"Do you have any suggestions?" Kartal asked.

"As you know, two of our team have gone directly to London," McCarter said. "They're going to take a look at the lead you offered there. See what they can come up with. In the meantime we need to run down your intelligence here, Agent Kartal."

"Please, my name is Berna. Agent Asker will tell you I am not very strong when it comes to formalities."

Asker managed a strained smile. "That is very true. Agent Kartal, it seems, is more at home with your casual American ways."

"Fine by us," McCarter said.

He quickly offered their cover names and sensed that Kartal seemed more relaxed with that.

"Please make use of Agent Kartal's office," Asker told them. "I am sure you have much to discuss. I am not being inhospitable, but my position means I must divide my time between the many other agents in the department. We have other problems to deal with."

"No need to apologize," McCarter said. "We'll keep you updated."

Kartal led them from Asker's office and through the busy department to her own office at the other end. It proved to be slightly larger than Asker's, with a wide window overlooking the city. A ceiling fan provided a stream of cool air. On a cabinet against one wall a coffeemaker bubbled quietly. As Kartal slid behind her tidy desk she waved a hand at the machine.

"Help yourselves," she said. "I cannot offer you traditionally made Turkish coffee because that has to be prepared by the cup and takes a long time. But the coffee in the machine there is quite acceptable."

James smiled. "We have someone back home who brews coffee so strong it would leave a scorch mark on your desk."

"Mine is strong but not that strong."

James stepped up and poured cups for each of them, passing them around.

Taking one of the cups, Kartal watched with a faintly amused smile on her lips as they each tasted the brew. The reaction was interesting.

"Just remember not to drink too quickly," Kartal said. "In Turkey we prefer the grounds to be quite coarse and they should be allowed to settle in your cup. Try not to swallow them."

"Thanks for the advice," James said.

McCarter and Encizo tried their own cups.

"Tell me the truth," she said.

"Beats instant. I'll give you that," McCarter said.

Getting down to business, Kartal noted, "Makerson and the other agent had gathered background on Özgürlük that details their possible intentions. The information about the chance they are ready to actually use nuclear devices was uncovered shortly before their deaths. My own feelings are that finding that possibility triggered a reaction and pushed Özgürlük to murdering them."

"You have no positive evidence as to who was responsible?" Encizo said.

Kartal glanced at him, her smooth brow furrowing.

"What Constantine suggests," McCarter said, using Encizo's cover name, "is that you have suspicions but not enough to move on."

Kartal agreed. "We have nothing more than, as you say, suspicion. My feeling is Özgürlük is aware we are powerless at this time."

"And?" Encizo said.

"And it makes me angry."

"And...?"

"And it makes me determined to find a way to stop Özgürlük."

"That wasn't hard, was it?" Encizo said.

Kartal smiled. "Are you always so…so…?"

"Irritating?" McCarter said. "Not all the time."

"Just most of the time," James added.

The casual banter helped to break any strain over the meeting, and Kartal relaxed visibly. They spent the next couple of hours going over all the information they had, pooling everything. Kartal was not shy in sharing her own views. She was able to match anything Phoenix Force said.

"In the morning," Kartal said, "we can formulate a plan of action. But now you must be ready to relax after your long journey. Have you somewhere to stay?"

McCarter nodded. "Accommodation has been reserved for us at a hotel in the city."

"Give me a little while and I will drive you there."

CHAPTER THREE

Thirty minutes later Phoenix Force had loaded their luggage into the rear of the large SUV Kartal had been assigned, and she rolled out of the NIO compound.

"It will only take us twenty minutes to reach your hotel," she said. "You do realize where you stay is a very expensive place."

James said, "Our organizer always makes sure we get the best."

"So it seems."

The streets were busy with traffic and the sidewalks congested. Kartal knew a shortcut to the hotel. It took them away from the main stream of traffic, allowing them a relaxing drive as she negotiated the city. She pointed out landmarks as she drove, showing sections of the old city and comparing it to the modern buildings. Istanbul struck Phoenix Force as a city of diverse contrasts.

"A beautiful city," James noted.

"I love it," Kartal said, unashamedly proud of it.

"Is it where you were born?" McCarter asked.

"Yes. I grew up here and spent my childhood in it. And now I am lucky to be working here." She hesitated. "The city is in the stages of bringing in the modern without losing too much of our historical past. It creates difficulties as this is achieved."

Kartal eventually eased off the main route and picked up the side roads she would be using. She plainly knew her way around Istanbul. It was a pleasant enough drive for Phoenix Force after their long flight from the U.S.

Pleasant, that is, until someone decided to use them as target practice.

The panel truck was old, the paintwork faded and the bodywork battered and rusting. It came roaring out of a side street and sped directly at the NIO vehicle. There was no mistaking the driver's intention. He was using the truck as a guided missile—and the target was Phoenix Force and Kartal.

If the SUV had been stationary the impact would have been worse. Kartal managed to boost the power, her foot stamping hard on the gas, sending the SUV lurching forward as she caught sight of the approaching truck. The vehicle slammed into the rear quarter of the SUV instead of full-on. The impact spun the SUV in a half circle, window glass shattering and spraying inside the passenger compartment as the car rocked violently, wheels lifting off the road for seconds. The impact drove the lower section of the wheel well into the vehicle's tire.

"Two inside," she said loudly. "They are showing weapons."

"Move," McCarter ordered. "Everyone out. Fast!"

The rocking SUV began to settle. Phoenix Force exited as quickly as possible, clearing the immediate scene and pulling out their weapons.

Berna Kartal hit the ground running, immediately moving around the SUV, her Glock targeting the truck as she spotted movement behind the cracked windshield.

The truck's passenger door was kicked, the metal protesting where it had been buckled from the impact. A dark figure pushed out through the gap, a subgun clutched in his hands. The guy dropped to a crouch as he cleared the panel truck, the muzzle of the weapon rising. He fired quickly—too quickly to acquire a solid target. His burst of autofire sent 9 mm slugs into the SUV. As the guy altered his stance he fired again and his second burst missed James by inches. The black Phoenix Force member twisted his lean body aside, swinging his own weapon on line, and put two 9 mm slugs into the shooter. They hit high, one punching into the chest area, the second catching the guy in the shoulder. He was turned around by the impact, slamming into the side of the truck, then bouncing off and falling.

McCarter saw the driver emerge from the opposite door, the SMG in his hands rising.

Kartal had already leveled her Glock, triggering a pair of fast shots that punched through the door window, throwing glass fragments into the guy's face. He reacted, still coming, and Kartal fired again. Her shot came a second before both Encizo and James fired. The driver's body jerked under the impact of multiple shots, blood staining his shirt as he fell back and slammed down hard on the road.

McCarter moved toward the stalled panel truck, angling his Hi-Power to line up on the windows. The interior was empty except for the scattered trash that littered the floor. "Clear," he said.

James and Encizo checked the area, weapons held ready. "I think we're good," James confirmed.

The others relaxed.

"Nice shooting," Encizo said to Kartal.

The young woman offered a fleeting smile. "Not my best. Took three shots."

"You got a result," McCarter said. "That's the important part."

Kartal gestured at James and Encizo. "With help. Thank you," she said.

McCarter gestured for Kartal to take a look at the downed men. She stared at their faces, moved, then returned to take a closer inspection of one of them.

"This one is still alive. I will call for assistance. The dead one…you know, he looks familiar to me," she said. "But I can't be certain for the moment who he is. When we get identification, perhaps we can find out who did this."

"Something is already telling me who," McCarter said.

Kartal glanced at him, realization dawning.

"Özgürlük?"

"I don't know anyone else in this town we might be in line to have upset."

McCarter didn't say a great deal more. He would hold his judgment until he had solid facts. Yet he did have the sneaking suspicion that Phoenix Force's presence was already known to unfriendly forces. They had barely set foot on Turkish soil and were already under attack.

It did prove one thing to McCarter. The Özgürlük problem had, for him, just been pushed up the scale. If people were ready to kill them, the probability had just been made a reality.

The short ride to Phoenix Force's hotel had suddenly become a protracted event.

Turkish police arrived in force and a crowd gathered. Before they showed up, Phoenix Force put away their weapons and offered no resistance when the cops did arrive. Kartal took charge, advising McCarter and company to stand down while she used her NIO status to manage the situation. Watching her, McCarter was especially impressed by her management skills. She dealt with the local cops, using her NIO credentials and her not inconsiderable talent for defusing matters.

"Medical help has been summoned," Kartal said. "Recovery vehicles, as well."

Phoenix Force stayed close to the NIO SUV. They remained passive, but every one of them scanned the crowd and watched for any follow-up to the attack. The volatile crowd surged back and forth, held back by armed Istanbul cops who had no problem using force to restrain anyone overstepping the line that had been invisibly drawn. It became noisy and at times there was a feeling of danger in the air.

The Turkish cops displayed an aggressive attitude toward anyone who made any show of resistance. A few arrests were made when passion took over from common sense. A police van was summoned and restrained onlookers were taken away.

"This place is hot," James said, referring as much to the agitated crowd as the weather.

"You got that right," Encizo said. He had spotted more than one raised fist aimed in their direction. Angry faces. Loud voices. As was usual in events such as this, emotion took control and pushed buttons. Calm took a backseat.

Kartal took a moment to rejoin them.

"Not the best introduction to my country," she said. "I apologize."

"No need. Has it occurred to you, the way this attack came so quickly, that our presence is not so secret?" McCarter said.

Kartal nodded. "That is what concerns me most. How you have been identified so easily. This attack was no random incident."

The wail of another siren reached them as a large black SUV nudged its way into view, police having to force the crowd back. It had the NIO symbol on the doors. When it stopped, Senior Agent Cem Asker climbed out and made his way to where Phoenix Force and Kartal stood. His face was grim.

"What happened here? This is not good," he said as he faced them. "How could this have happened?"

"Easily answered," Encizo said. "Someone was in the know about us being here. To the point where they even knew the vehicle we were in."

"Doesn't that suggest something to you, Agent Asker?" McCarter said tautly. "This was supposed to be a covert mission. How the hell did information get out so damn quickly?"

Anger flashed across the man's face. "Are you saying there is a leak within the NIO?"

"I'm saying that it's likely someone else knows we're here. And I can tell you for sure it didn't come from our organization."

Asker bristled. For a moment McCarter thought the man was going lash out. His expression betrayed his thoughts. Then Asker stepped back physically and mentally. His face relaxed.

"Yes, you have a point, Mr. Coyle," he acknowledged, using McCarter's cover name. "A valid point. I apologize for my attitude. The situation is difficult. When I return to NIO I will initiate an investigation into how your being here has been compromised. I am glad none of you was injured in any way. May I say I am impressed at how you handled the situation? And you, Agent Kartal. You displayed your usual competence." He inspected the damage to the NIO vehicle.

"The damage has affected the rear wheel, sir," Kartal said. "It cannot be driven. This vehicle will need to be removed for repair."

"You are certain of this?"

"Pushed the bodywork into the tire," McCarter said, stepping in to back up Kartal. "Cut into the rubber."

Asker peered at the damaged section of the NIO vehicle. His manner indicated he knew very little about the mechanics of them.

"Not going to get us very far," James noted.

"New wheels?" Encizo suggested.

"I can arrange…" Asker said.

"No need," McCarter said quickly. "We can deal with this ourselves."

"You must allow me to help."

"Agent Asker, you have your department to look after, as you told us earlier. We have this covered," McCarter said. "We can organize a rental vehicle to get around in. Less noticeable than one of your official NIO cars. No offence, Agent Asker, but we try to work without too much fanfare. A vehicle with the NIO brand on it doesn't help."

Asker seemed ready to resist and for a moment McCarter felt the man was going to argue. He seemed to be having a problem controlling his emotions.

"Very well," he said finally, his voice tight as he held himself under stress. "If you insist. My orders were to accommodate you, so I will. Agent Kartal will be able to help you to find a suitable vehicle."

"Of course, sir. I am sure Mr. Coyle has made the right decision."

A frown darkened Asker's face before he regained his composure. He seemed to be having a troubled moment.

"Yes, well, of course. I will leave you to your new team. Please keep me informed of your progress," Asker said to McCarter.

"Oh, you'll be hearing from us," McCarter said forcibly.

Asker went to speak to the attending Turkish police officers before returning to his own SUV and driving away.

"That was tense there for a moment," Encizo said. "Asker got a little uptight."

"That he did," McCarter said.

He glanced across to where Kartal was checking the panel damage to their SUV. He noticed the way she had been watching Asker, and the tight set of her face suggested there was a lot going on inside her head.

"I hope I did right," she said, crossing to join him.

"Just fine," McCarter said. He couldn't hold back a grin. "You catch on quick."

"I believe I understand. You do not want any more vehicles from the NIO."

"We leave the NIO, pick up a shortcut and that truck still found us," James said.

"Too bloody easily for my liking," McCarter said. "Found us like they knew exactly where we were."

"Tracked us?" Encizo offered.

Kartal's face paled as she became aware of the implications. "But we never stopped once after we left the department. Are you saying a device was planted at NIO?"

"Tell us different, Berna, and we'll listen," James said.

They waited until the tow trucks showed up to remove the two vehicles. The ambulance had arrived and was dealing with the casualties. By this time the crowd had had its fill of rubbernecking and most of them had moved on. One police cruiser remained.

An empty passing taxi had been flagged and Phoenix Force transferred its bags to the trunk. Kartal told the driver to wait. He didn't mind as they were already on the clock.

McCarter strolled casually across to take a look at the

damaged NIO vehicle as it was being hoisted onto the tow truck. He made a show of inspecting the damage, peering beneath the SUV.

Kartal had a final few words with the local cops before they climbed into their cruiser and drove off.

"I will have so much paperwork to complete," Kartal said.

"Cops are the same wherever you go," James said. "They have a thing for statements."

"And when you get down to it," McCarter said, "just don't mention this."

He opened his hand to show them the three-inch-square black box he had located under the SUV.

"A tracker," James said.

"Sends out a signal to a locator unit," Encizo said. "Tells them where you are."

McCarter took it and turned it over. A red indicator light was blinking. He flicked a small plastic switch and the light shut off.

"Magnetic base," he said. "Sticks to any metal surface. There will probably be a locator unit in that panel truck they towed away."

"This was on the side of our fuel tank," McCarter said.

Kartal's expression revealed her thoughts. "You are saying this was placed at NIO?"

"Couldn't have been anywhere else. The minute we drove out of the gate we never stopped moving," James said. "Had to have been already in place."

"Not your fault, love." McCarter smiled. "But it tells me we have enemies closer than we thought."

"You were with us, too," James said. "In the same danger we were."

"Part of the package," Encizo said. "You are now officially on the hit list."

"We should go," Kartal said moments later. "It will be a little more peaceful at your hotel."

"You think?" James said. "Let's hope there isn't a welcoming committee waiting there, as well."

McCarter said, "Hold that thought."

He took out his sat phone and called up Stony Man. When Price answered, he quickly brought her up to date with the current events.

Price listened in patient silence.

"And how long have you been in Turkey?" she said when he had finished.

"I know. Fast turnaround on this one."

"You sure you're all okay?"

"Fine, love, but I have a little job for you. Cancel our current hotel. Find us another and book us in."

"You think the opposition might know where you were going to stay?"

"They found our car. So I'd rather not find out if they had our hotel under surveillance, as well."

THE STONY MAN call came less than twenty minutes later, Price updating McCarter on their accommodation status.

"You're booked in," she said, offering McCarter the hotel details. "Unless your Turkish sparring partners have access to Stony Man, you should be clear."

"Good," McCarter said. "Efficient as ever. We'll keep in touch."

"Make sure you do."

McCarter beckoned and they all piled into the taxi. He told Kartal the new address. She relayed this to the driver and they drove away from the scene.

"Can you find out where the wounded guy was taken?" McCarter asked. "In case we need to talk to him later."

"Yes, I can do that. Do you believe he will give you anything useful?"

"It's always worth a try," McCarter said. "If you don't ask questions, you won't get answers."

"A logical line of thought, boss," James said in a tone reminiscent of Mr. Spock.

"Star Trek," Kartal said lightly.

"Ah," Encizo said, "the global reach of American culture."

"How does it sound in Turkish?" James said.

"If you check your hotel TV, it could be showing."

CHAPTER FOUR

The hotel was large and close to the water. Part of a global chain, it was the sort of place that had lots of rooms and guests. The taxi pulled up to the entrance and the three Phoenix Force men hauled out their luggage and followed Kartal inside. She confirmed the rate and McCarter handed her the cash to pay.

"Perhaps I should call back later," Kartal said once they'd checked in. "Allow you to settle. It will give me the chance to change into something a little less dramatic."

She left them, picking up one of the taxis waiting outside.

"I don't have any objections to the way she dresses," Encizo said as they made their way to their rooms.

"This thing you have about women in uniform, carrying guns…" McCarter said. "I think we need to talk about it."

They took the stairs to their floor, parting company as they located their individual rooms. Even in the comparative safety of the hotel, the Phoenix Force commandos made sure security was on their minds, each keeping a handgun close. They had agreed to meet up in the cafeteria after freshening up.

After a quick shower and a change into fresh clothing, McCarter used his sat phone to contact Stony Man again and spoke to Brognola.

"Hell of an introduction to Turkey," the big Fed said.

"Not the first time we've had a warm welcome," McCarter reminded him.

"So, what happened?" Brognola asked. "You got any suspects?"

McCarter laughed. "How about the NIO? They're the only ones who knew we were here. As far as we're aware."

"They were supposed to be the only ones aware of your presence in Turkey. Big agency. But it's not unknown to have leaks in large organizations. We should know about that. This Özgürlük deal is a Turkish phenomenon. Nationalistic fervor can turn up in surprising places. And so can prying eyes and ears."

"That supposed to make me feel better?"

"Not really. Just aware."

"Hal, I'm already aware we are in a tricky position here."

"Just saying stay alert, David."

"Concern noted."

"Any doubts about your Turkish lady cop?"

"I think she was as surprised as we were when it happened. I'm just glad she's on our side. She handles herself pretty well."

"My suspicious nature warns me to remind you to keep watch until you're one hundred and one percent sure."

"Don't worry, Mother, we will. You have any results from Gary and T.J. yet?"

"Still waiting."

"Okay, talk to you if and when something happens," McCarter said, knowing that sooner or later something would.

CHAPTER FIVE

Sea of Marmara

"There is no easy way to tell you this," Hakan Kaplan said. "Amal is dead. He was killed by the Americans when his team attempted to neutralize them. Salan was wounded and taken prisoner."

Kaplan waited for Kadir Polat's reaction and was surprised when the man failed to do or say anything.

Sitting at his desk on his cruiser, Polat shifted his gaze to look beyond the open window to the glittering sea. Sunlight danced across the waves. He saw nothing but emptiness. The death of his younger brother had affected him more than any outward sign might show.

Like a movie played in reverse, he saw the images that took Amal from manhood to his teen years, then beyond to when he was a child. Always at Kadir's side. The tie between them had strengthened as they'd grown. Amal had always been the impulsive one. Always ready to take risks. His older brother had been forced to step in on many occasions to pull Amal out of dangerous situations. Amal's recklessness was part of his character and no matter how many times he placed himself in danger he would do the same thing again and again.

WITH THEIR PARENTS having died while both Kadir and Amal were young, it had been the elder brother's responsibility to look out for Amal. Being the heir to the Polat dynasty had made it easier. There were always advisers around, people to watch over the young brothers. As the years passed and Kadir assumed full control over the family businesses, he remained aware of his family responsibilities. Family was important in Turkey. Kadir never forgot that.

He'd spent time with Amal. He'd indulged the young man. He knew he'd taken that indulgence too far at times, but his love for his younger sibling had been too great. There were times he'd had to bail Amal out, rescue him from the escapades of youth. If it wasn't the fast cars Amal drove, it was the young women he always seemed to hang on his arm. No matter how many times problems came along, Kadir had cleared the way for Amal.

It helped that as well as being ultrawealthy, Polat was a well-liked man. His power and influence had grown over the years and he'd used his position to get Amal out of his various scrapes. Living in such luxury as the Polat dynasty offered, Amal had grown into a good-looking, intelligent young man. But he'd never moved on from adolescence. He'd simply enjoyed the good life. The money. The trappings of wealth and the lack of responsibility.

With Kadir involved in the growing Özgürlük organization, Amal had found himself being pushed aside to a greater degree. Özgürlük had become Kadir Polat's passion. His need to free Turkey from the grip of America and the base at Incirlik increasingly devoured his life. For the first time since childhood, Amal had felt himself being pushed into the shadows.

He'd realized that to regain his brother's attention, Amal had to insert himself into Özgürlük. He might not have fully understood his brother's politics but he quickly grasped that Kadir was becoming a national figure. The rallies and the constant meetings with important people appealed to Amal. He'd understood the meaning of celebrity. He'd joined in with Kadir's new obsession. He met the people involved.

And he'd allowed himself to be caught up in the heady atmosphere of the crowds. The eager men who wanted to become part of Kadir's army, the willing participants clamoring to use affirmative action on behalf of Özgürlük. He'd allied himself to the cause, finding this new experience liberating, and he'd understood Kadir's anger when it was learned a team of Americans had been assigned to work with the NIO in an attempt to disrupt Özgürlük's plans.

The Özgürlük inside man at the NIO had given out details of the arrival of the Americans, and Amal had put himself forward as part of the hit team preparing to strike at them.

The operation had been devised in haste. The moment the Americans arrived at the NIO, the Özgürlük insider had planted a tracking device on the official vehicle assigned to the team. Amal and his partner had waited in their battered pickup until the Americans were driven out of the NIO building. With the tracking unit working, it was not difficult to pick up the NIO vehicle's location.

It had seemed such an easy operation. They would trail the NIO vehicle until a moment presented itself. They would ram the vehicle and fire on the Americans.

It had been a poorly conceived plan, Kadir knew, badly executed, and this time Amal's cavalier disregard for his own safety had cost him his life.

AT TWENTY-FOUR years old he was gone. Everything taken away. And his older brother was left with a yawning chasm of blackness. No more Amal. No smiling, handsome young man with a wild enthusiasm for life—and the loyalty to Özgürlük that had taken him to his death.

Özgürlük. Freedom.

Amal had achieved his own freedom in a perverse way. He no longer had to suffer the denials of Turkey's political and military alliance with the Americans. His passion to sever the links binding the country to U.S. needs had cost him his life, and Kadir Polat would not allow that to go unavenged.

"How did you find out about this?"

"I spoke to some of the others. The younger ones Amal was friendly with. They told me he had volunteered when the operation was planned. Amal was eager to prove himself to you. To show he was not worthless. The younger recruits kept everything to themselves. I think it was a group effort to show their loyalty to Özgürlük."

"Amal had no need to prove himself," Polat said. "He was my brother. That was all I needed to know."

"He was young, Kadir. He thought he needed to take that step," Kaplan said. "I know that was not what you wanted. But you know how he was. Impulsive. Ready to go ahead and show you how smart he was."

Polat understood. His younger brother had lived in his shadow for so long. Always eager to please Kadir by doing something reckless.

That wild streak had never left him. It had stayed with him all through his young life, and in the end it had killed him.

"Will you bring Amal home for me?" Polat said quietly. "Arrange things quietly?"

Kaplan nodded slowly.

Polat knew he would not need to ask again. His mind was still coming to terms with his loss. The full force would come later. Most likely when he was alone at night. The time when resistance was low. When the shadows held a thousand images and the silence the whispers of lost voices.

One thing Polat knew for certain. His brother's death would not be forgotten. He would see to that. The Americans would pay a heavy price. Their interference in Özgürlük's plans had to be stopped. Too much had already been invested in the program. Many people and a great deal of money. The whole thing had a momentum of its own now. Piece by piece, matters were coming together. Özgürlük was close to initiating its strike. A plan that would play havoc with Turkey and its relationship with the U.S. He had a meeting that day with other members of Özgürlük's committee. That meeting would put into motion critical operations. Operations that would start the countdown…and once that was done, nothing would be allowed to interfere.

Özgürlük took precedence over all other considerations. Even the death of his brother would be sidelined until such time as it became acceptable. Polat struggled to push Amal's death to the back of his mind. He wanted his revenge against the people who had killed Amal. He understood that in time he would have that revenge. But first the operation had to be carried forward regardless of personal grievances.

Polat reflected how swiftly life could change. How with a single act the tracks of existence could be wiped away. Earlier that day Amal had been alive and obviously eager to take on his covert mission. Now, hours later, that young life had ended and Polat had to carry on as if it had not taken place.

"See to it Amal is taken somewhere safe and looked after. Do this for me."

"Of course. It will be done, my friend."

"And find out about these Americans. The ones who murdered him. Be assured it *was* murder. I will accept no other explanation."

Kaplan nodded. "I understand. Our people within the police department will help. I will arrange it. I will inform you as soon as I have anything useful."

Polat stood, moving from behind his desk. He clasped Kaplan to him, the contact solid.

"Always at my side, Hakan. With advice and friendship. Now I need your strength more than ever."

"And you will have it. Go about your business with the committee. There is a great deal to finalize. Much to coordinate with our friends in America. I understand this will be hard for you, but it needs to be done, Kadir. If we lose our timing now, it may be too much for us to regain the balance."

Polat did not need telling. He understood the implications of failure at this time. His personal feelings had to be put aside. His people and his country were the most important considerations right now. The long-term planning could not be compromised. As things began to slip into place, keeping the momentum was vital.

"You go," Polat said. "Use whoever you need. Recruit if you have to. And do not worry about money. It is there for you to take."

POLAT'S CAR WAS waiting at the quayside when he left the cruiser. He sat in the rear, his hands resting on his lap. He looked out the side window, seeing very little as the car eased out through the gates and picked up speed. In the front sat the driver and an armed bodyguard. They had a twenty-minute drive ahead of them. During the drive no one spoke.

Thoughts rolled back and forth inside Polat's head.

What he would say at the meeting. The logistics of the merchandise to be moved into place. How he would arrange the funeral of his brother... Polat could not quell those thoughts. No matter how much of the burden Kaplan handled, Amal had been his brother and the active memories refused to go away. Those thoughts plagued Polat to the point where he almost missed the sound of his cell phone. He pulled it from his pocket, glancing briefly at the caller ID as he activated the call.

It was General Demir Marangol, a member of the Turkish military, and one of the high-ranking Özgürlük group members.

"I learned about your brother's death a little time ago," Marangol said. "Accept my sympathies."

"Thank you, General."

With that out of the way, Marangol moved on quickly to the reason he had called.

"Is it true one of our people was wounded and taken prisoner?"

"Unfortunately, yes. Salan."

"He must not be allowed to give away any information. This is understood? At this stage that is vital. We must protect ourselves. Can you have arrangements made that he will be silenced?"

"It will be done, General."

"Good. Remember I can step in if need be."

Polat knew Marangol meant every word. The man was strictly military. Down the line. There was no left and right in Marangol's world. He walked the center. Polat felt a momentary pang of jealousy, wishing he could maintain such a posture himself.

"The offer is appreciated."

"We will meet on your boat later to review matters," Marangol said. "No mistakes, Kadir."

The cell went dead. Polat had been dismissed. Marangol had the unfortunate habit of treating everyone as if they were one of his lowly military recruits. It seemed he was never off duty. There were times he forgot who Polat was and spoke to him with familiar contempt.

Polat pushed the thought away. He had too much to concern himself with to be overly worried about Marangol and his ego.

CHAPTER SIX

The truck pulled in at the service entrance to the hospital, and two figures dressed in the standard green uniform of ancillary workers climbed out. They both had identification cards hanging around their necks and were wearing latex gloves. They opened the rear of the truck and maneuvered a large wicker basket on wheels to the ground. It contained piles of folded towels and sheets. They pushed the basket in through the rubber doors leading to the ancillary department.

It was late, almost nine o'clock at night, and the department was quiet. They rolled the basket through the department unchallenged and entered a service elevator that accessed all floors. The men talked between themselves as they emerged onto the floor they wanted. At the reception desk they asked for the linen supply section and were directed along the corridor. They carried on until they reached the section they wanted and pushed through the swing doors.

Once inside, they reached into the basket and threw the sheets and towels to the floor. Resting in the bottom of the basket was a pair of AK-47 autorifles and two canvas bags. The bags were slung across the men's shoulders and the AKs were quickly checked and made ready.

Emerging through the door, the men walked along the semilit corridor until they came to a junction. It was obvious they knew where they were going as they chose the left junction.

They were halfway along the corridor before they encountered anyone. A nurse, studying a patient chart, glanced up as the men appeared. She stared at them, surprised at what she saw. She was given no chance to warn anyone. One of the men produced a handgun from beneath his uniform top; it was a bulky weapon made larger by the suppressor screwed to the end of the barrel. The pistol fired twice, making a comparatively quiet sound. The 9 mm slugs hit the nurse in midchest. She fell back against the wall and slid to the floor, blood blossoming on the front of her uniform top.

The men didn't break stride as they walked by the body. The shooter kept the pistol in his hand in case they encountered anyone else. They saw no one.

The corridor branched off at the end and again the two men changed direction without pause. The man with the pistol put it away so both hands were free to hold his Kalashnikov.

The corridor ahead of them ended after thirty feet. There were doors on each side of the corridor. Midway along, two uniformed city cops stood guard at one of the doors. They reacted when they saw the armed men approaching.

The AK-47s rose and the loud hammering sound of autofire filled the corridor. The cops never stood a chance as twin streams of jacketed slugs ripped into them. They were knocked back by the impact, bodies punctured by the slugs. Their bloody corpses slammed to the floor.

One of the men raised a foot and kicked open the door. The room inside, with a shrouded light, was empty except for the motionless figure in the bed. Monitoring equipment showed lights and a number of tubes were attached to the patient.

Standing side by side, the intruders trained the AK-47s on the figure. They opened fire and triggered their weapons until they snapped empty. Brass casings littered the floor around them. The shooters ejected the empty magazines. They took fresh ones from the shoulder bags and reloaded. While one man guarded the door, the other took out the pistol again, walked to the side of the bed and fired two shots into the head of the man in the bed. It was an entirely unnecessary action; the man on the bed, resting in a spreading wash of blood, had been shot almost to ribbons by the sustained AK-47 overkill.

Together the men left the room. Already alarms were sounding as they moved along the corridor. From their bags they produced smoke canisters. Activating them, they dropped them on the corridor floor. Thick smoke began to rise and fill the corridors. The men dropped more of the canisters as they proceeded to their escape route.

They pushed through the fire escape door, emerging on an iron landing, and made their way down the ladder. When they reached the bottom they made their way to the far corner of the hospital grounds, pausing only long enough for one of them to take out a remote unit. He flicked the power switch and waited for the light to come on. He thumbed the button. The van they had arrived in was suddenly engulfed in an explosion that blew it apart. Flame and smoke rose in a cloud. Pieces of bodywork were thrown into the air.

As the debris fell back to the ground, the two made their way to the trees that edged this section of the hospital grounds and concealed the AK-47 rifles, the pistol and the bags that had held their weapons in the undergrowth; they would eventually be discovered, but by then the assassins would be long gone. The latex gloves and the hospital uniforms were removed and dumped. The men wore casual civilian clothing underneath.

Three streets away a nondescript Fiat sedan sat at the curb outside a closed store. The keys were already in the pocket of one of the men. They climbed in and drove away. Behind them in the distance could be heard police sirens approaching the hospital.

A HALF HOUR LATER Kartal received a call informing her that the man wounded in the attack on Phoenix Force had been killed during an armed strike at the hospital where he was being treated. She was with Phoenix Force at their hotel and immediately passed along the information.

"Great," McCarter said. "These buggers don't waste time. They're bound and determined to keep us in the dark."

"Didn't want anyone talking," Encizo said.

"They are organized," Kartal agreed. "Able to buy whatever they need. People. Weapons."

"Well," McCarter said, "we'll have to see about that. But tomorrow, how about we go take a look at Mr. Polat? Time we sussed out our enemy."

CHAPTER SEVEN

London

Tak Kumad had just shot two men and was on his way to kill a third.

His agenda was firmly set out. It was to clean up matters relating to Özgürlük to make certain nothing could be traced back to the organization and hinder the progress of the operation. His orders had been specific; and Tak Kumad followed his orders for the client he was working for.

It was his job.

He was an assassin. His current assignment was to locate and eliminate the three men who had turned against Özgürlük and betrayed the organization.

Kumad had already visited the apartment where two of the men had been staying. He'd caught them both and placed 9 mm slugs in their skulls before they'd been able to do a thing to prevent it.

With that part of his assignment over, Kumad moved on.

Aziz Makar was Özgürlük's banker. He handled all the money the group used and collected. And, as with a number of terrorist organization bankers, he was based in London.

Makar had decided to go into business for himself by cheating Özgürlük out of millions of dollars. To add to Hakan Kaplan's problems, two of his trusted lieutenants had also joined forces with Makar to work a deal that would give them the chance to fleece the organization out of even more money.

Kaplan's betrayal by Egemen Binice and Bora Terzel had been a bitter blow. He had championed the pair since they had first joined the organization, not realizing their enthusiasm and dedication to Özgürlük had been false from the start.

Binice and Terzel were cousins. In their late twenties, they were minor criminals, having spent most of their teen years committing small crimes for little reward. They considered themselves smart, a cut above the lower Turkish criminal element, and they possessed sharp minds always on the lookout for a chance to make a score. Unfortunately they always seemed to miss the best opportunities.

Until they'd learned about Özgürlük. A drinking friend, himself on the criminal fringe, had made mention of the organization in passing. Binice and Terzel had listened to what he'd had to say, and when they were on their own again, decided it was worth looking into.

They'd picked up on one of the public meetings in the city, went along and afterward made contact with the man they soon found out to be Hakan Kaplan.

Now, one of the many talents the cousins possessed was the ability to be extremely persuasive and willing to commit to a cause. They'd learned about Özgürlük and its aims, though at that stage they were not privy to the underlying intentions of the group. They were willing and eager recruits, listening to the party line and proving themselves by performing the tasks offered to them. Over a few months the cousins had insinuated themselves deeper into Özgürlük.

Anyone who had come in contact with them and lis-

tened to their talk had been convinced of their usefulness to the organization.

Whenever they were in the presence of Özgürlük's
people higher up the ladder, they performed as expected,
and because they showed their compliance with the policy, their involvement became deeper.

While Binice and Terzel professed commitment to
Özgürlük, they were, in truth, simply looking for opportunities to make money.

It hadn't taken them long to see how Özgürlük put
cash out to anyone who showed genuine interest. They'd
realized the organization was pretty well loaded. The top
man, Kadir Polat, had money in spades, to say nothing
of the money being donated by sympathizers. It hadn't
taken the pair long to learn about the man, his business holdings that raked in millions, his property, cars
and planes—even a luxury cruiser he used like a floating HQ.

While maintaining an interest in the organization, the
pair had been gathering intelligence, watching and listening at every opportunity. Hakan Kaplan had taken a
liking to the young recruits and had offered them more
and more responsibility as the weeks went by.

They'd been assigned to Polat's cruiser on a number of
occasions. Their duties consisted of making sure guests
were supplied with food and drink, and keeping things
running smoothly. Their service offered them a chance
to pick up snippets of information as drink often loos-
ened mouths and they learned valuable details.

It was about this time that Hakan Kaplan, convinced
the pair was genuinely part of Özgürlük, had taken them
aside and, in the presence of Polat, filled them in on the
organization's long-term plan. Not to simply create unrest and agitation, but to do something that would throw

the country into confusion and, as the main thrust of the plot, to damage the American presence in Turkey.

Their indoctrination took a couple of weeks and Binice and Terzel, realizing it was becoming deeply involving, had upped their act and made it clear they were on board.

When Kaplan had eventually broached the real reason, despite their act, Binice and Terzel were almost caught off guard.

Polat and Kaplan were proposing to blackmail the Americans by threatening to detonate nuclear devices. One at Incirlik. The other to be transported to America.

After the revelation, Binice and Terzel had readily endorsed and volunteered any and all assistance; they had realized an opportunity presented itself. Hakan Kaplan, by this time convinced of their loyalty to Özgürlük, had enlisted their help in taking control of the nuclear devices being delivered by the Russian, Gennadi Antonov.

This encounter had brought them into contact with Aziz Makar, the moneyman, and the pair, spotting the man's discontent at having to handle so much money, quickly moved in.

Makar might have been in charge of the Özgürlük finances, but he was not personally wealthy. His skill with money had brought him little for himself. Binice and Terzel had spent their lives assessing and playing other people's emotions. And that was how they'd manipulated Aziz Makar.

Their persuasive manner had drawn him in. He'd worked a few small *withdrawals*, and his new partners had taken it and used it to feed a new account, well out of the reach of Özgürlük. The ease of the operation encouraged Makar and he'd devised other ways to move and *lose* donated amounts. With each success Makar began to increase the amounts. Polat and Kaplan were so involved in the main operation they had little time, or opportunity, to be aware of what was happening. Money was coming in and going out on a daily basis, and only Makar, safe in his London office, had any real grasp of how things were. The thousands became hundreds of thousands and then Makar, flushed by his success, had made his major error when he'd earmarked a couple of million for siphoning.

Unbeknown to the duplicitous trio, their scheme to take Özgürlük's money had been discovered and the information passed on to Hakan Kaplan.

Kaplan had initially refused to accept the news, but his source was impeccable. A bank teller loyal to Özgürlük had discovered the cash movements and checked it out. When the discovery was verified, Kaplan was informed. The bank official initiated a full trace and the extent of the theft was revealed. The trail led to accounts opened by Binice, Terzel and Makar. Following disbelief and embarrassment that he had been taken in by the three men, Kaplan had the information kept quiet so he could deal with the three. Loyalty to the cause had taken a backseat, smothered by deceit and pure greed. Ignoring the reason behind Özgürlük's existence, the trio had given in to their base emotions.

Having been put in the picture, Kaplan took control and made the decision that the traitors would not be allowed to escape. He set in motion the means by which he would exact his revenge.

Revenge. Retribution. It had to be done. Betrayal required closure. Allow people to steal from you and it diminished your standing. The scales had to be balanced. With all that was going on, Özgürlük's reputation needed to be put on firm ground—and allowing a pair of petty crooks to sully that reputation was unthinkable.

KAPLAN HAD MET Tak Kumad in a busy Istanbul café. They'd sat at a table, outside, the sun high overhead. They could have been any Turkish customers, drinking small cups of aromatic coffee and discussing anything.

But they were discussing something far deadlier than the price of food or the results of the international football match that had taken place the previous night.

They were arranging how Binice and Terzel would pay for their treachery. The moneyman, Makar, would be dealt with as a separate matter.

"This must be painful for them before the final bullet," Kaplan said. "I am not normally a vengeful man, but those two have manipulated me. Made me look a fool. So my heart seeks a way to make them suffer."

"As God looks down on me, I promise you suffering for them both," Kumad, the assassin, said. "By the end they will welcome my final bullet."

"Should I ask how you will achieve this?"

"Do you recall Alexander Litvinenko? Former Russian SSB officer. He left Russia to avoid being prosecuted for his stand against the Russian Secret Service. He was given asylum in the UK and continued as a journalist writing about the behavior of the Russians. He wrote books condemning their actions. He became ill in November 2006 and died three weeks later. It was confirmed later that he had died from being poisoned by polonium-210. A very lethal radioactive compound. Most likely put in his tea. It is undetectable in that condition, but works very well on the immune system, or so I have been told."

"Is this what you would propose for our friends?"

"I have been able to obtain some. Only a small amount," Kumad said. "That is all it will take."

Kaplan thought it an ideal way to repay Binice and Terzel.

"They would not die immediately?"

Kumad smiled. "No. The full effects would run over a few weeks. But initially they would become extremely ill. Skin affected. Loss of hair. General lassitude."

"How would you give it to them?" Kaplan asked, his interest piqued.

"In a similar fashion," Kumad said. "I have spoken to a friend in the business and he has instructed me how to do this." He smiled at the thought. "A very smart man who has been in the business for a long time."

"And has he used this polonium-210 himself?"

Kumad nodded. "Oh, yes."

When Kaplan picked up his coffee again he hesitated. "It would be as simple as putting it in a cup like this?"

"Don't be concerned. I did not bring a sample with me."

"I want this done quickly."

"Then all I need from you is a timetable of where Binice and Terzel can be found. Once I have that, I can make my arrangements."

They concluded their meeting after finance details were completed.

Kaplan felt satisfied. He had cleared the way for a matter of honor, Turkish-style, to be carried out. With Binice and Terzel dealt with, the episode could be forgotten and he could concentrate on the Özgürlük campaign.

TEN DAYS LATER Kumad received a call from Kaplan.

"It has been reported to me that Makar is becoming a nervous man," Kaplan said. "I believe he may be regretting his involvement with Binice and Terzel. Remember he knows a great deal about Özgürlük. As banker he has been responsible for moving around money. Most important, the payment for the devices from the Russian. We cannot risk anything going wrong at this stage. It's time he was retired. Better that way than risk additional problems. Deal with him but make sure you bring his computer back with you. Understood? Above everything, that computer must be returned into our safekeeping."

"Understood." Kumad brought up the other business he was involved with. "Did you know Binice and Terzel are in London? At one of our emergency apartments?"

"Yes. I sent them there to keep them away from everything here. They believe they are being given a reward for the work they have been doing for the cause. I told them I needed them to oversee a project that is coming off in London. Their arrogance is amazing. They truly believe that while they have stolen money from us I am rewarding their loyalty. I told them to take a break while the project is being set up. Your *treatment* seems to be working well. In the last week they have started to look unwell but have said nothing because they have no idea what is happening. Tak, as much as I would like to have them suffer even more, I think it is time to cut short their suffering. We have enough on our hands with other, more important matters. Would you agree?"

"It would complete our deal and close it nicely."

"See to it."

KUMAD KNEW LONDON WELL. He visited often. He enjoyed the rush of the big city, the busy pace. The fact that for the most part he could come and go as he pleased. Anonymity was a useful thing for someone in his profession. Although security, as in any large city, had been increased, London was still an easy place to get around. The busy streets, full of people going about their business, were comparatively safe. Armed police were in evidence, but with such crowds it was easy to lose himself. He was, on the surface, simply a citizen going about his business. He posed no threat to the watchful eye.

With Binice and Terzel taken care of, all that remained was for him to handle the banker. Kumad saw no problems there. Makar would not offer any kind of resistance. He was just a money mover. Not a trained gunman.

Sitting in a small café that served *real* Turkish coffee, Kumad considered his options. Makar would not be in his office until morning. It was just after nine o'clock in the evening, so he would have to wait until the man came to his office for the next day's business. As he drained his cup, Kumad decided he may as well return to his hotel and get some sleep. Nothing was going to happen until the next day.

At his small hotel in Bayswater he had a shower, cleaned his pistol and made sure the magazine was fully loaded. Then he went to bed and got a solid night's untroubled sleep. He knew that Makar never opened his office before nine thirty.

He was in another café across the street from Makar's building, having breakfast and keeping an eye out for the man, when Makar stepped out of a London cab, paid the driver and went into his building. He carried an attaché case that would most likely contain his laptop. Kumad finished his food and coffee, paid and left the café.

He walked along the street before he crossed it and eased into the alley a few doors along from Makar's building. The rear area was quiet and Kumad made his way to the wooden gate that would lead him to the back of Makar's property. He had been here before and knew all the access and exit points. There was a brick wall with a timber gate. Kumad pulled on a pair of latex gloves, slipped the latch and stepped through, closing the gate behind him. There was a small yard leading to the metal stairs, which in turn led to the upper floor. At the top was a metal door that gave access to the interior. From earlier visits, Kumad knew that Makar kept the door unlocked during the day; the man had a fear of being trapped inside a locked building and turned the key when he arrived each morning. He didn't worry about anyone breaking in to steal because there was never money on the premises. Everything Makar did was via his computer; he brought his expensive laptop with him each day and took it home at night. The office setup was nothing more than a front for Özgürlük.

The door in front of him let Kumad take the short passage to Makar's office. He took out his sound-suppressed pistol and eased off the safety. He could hear Makar on the phone and waited until the man finished his call. The moment Makar replaced the receiver, Kumad pushed open the door and stepped inside. He closed the door behind him and walked across the room to stand at the desk, extending his arm, the pistol inches from Makar.

Makar stared at the black muzzle, then at Kumad.

"Who are you?" He had never met Kuman before and would have no idea he worked for Özgürlük. "What do you want?"

"I'm here to close your account. The same as I've done for your two partners," Kumad said and pulled the trigger.

It was a close shot, the skin around the wound peppered with powder and scorch burns. The back of Makar's head blew open, depositing brain and skull matter on the high seat back. Makar's head bounced against the seat, then forward. The phone rang at that moment. The sound startled Kumad for a second. He recovered, putting away his pistol. He closed the laptop and disconnected the cables. He turned and disturbed items in the office to make it appear as though someone had broken in. He didn't believe the actions would fool the authorities for long but it was no more than a distraction.

The phone stopped ringing

With the laptop under his arm he pulled the office door almost shut, made his way out of the building the way he had come in. A couple of minutes later he slipped back onto the street, walking calmly, and merged with the pedestrians on the sidewalk. He had already removed the latex gloves by then.

Kumad returned to his hotel, packed his carryall, with the laptop under his clothes, and made a quick call.

"Your appointments went well?" Kaplan said. "No difficulties?"

"None."

"You found the laptop?"

"Of course."

"Then I will see you when you return."

"Yes."

Downstairs, Kumad checked out, paying his account in cash, and walked to the nearby multistory car park where his rental sat. He took a pair of leather gloves from his pocket and pulled them on before he unlocked the vehicle, placed his bag in the trunk and slid behind the wheel. He was always careful not to leave any prints behind. There were too many ways to be identified these days, so covering his tracks was something he did as a matter of course.

He started the engine.

And that was when it came to him as he stared at his hands gripping the wheel.

The shell casing.

He had not picked up the spent bullet casing from the floor of Makar's office. The ringing of the phone had distracted him and his mind had been occupied with other matters.

The casing.

A small item in itself, but one that could become important if it was found. Because there would most likely be a print on it from when he had loaded the pistol's magazine. When he loaded his magazines he used bare hands. In the past he had found using latex gloves to be a problem; twice the thin latex had been snagged by the loading slot of a magazine, tearing off a piece of the rubber and becoming jammed in the spring mechanism. Something as small as that could have interfered with the action of the magazine, causing a misfire. Since then, he had always worked barehanded—he compensated for that by never, ever, leaving behind a spent bullet casing.

Until today.

A stupid error on his part. One that could have repercussions if it was found.

Kumad considered the implications of identification that would place him at the scene, making him the number one suspect. He valued his anonymity, but he was not stupid enough to believe he was not on a database on some computer. And via that identification came the possibility he could be linked to Özgürlük.

He sat in the car and considered his options. Foremost in his thoughts was protecting his identity. In his line of work, remaining anonymous was vitally important. He needed that status to stay as it was. If he was identified as the man who had assassinated Makar, then his usefulness in the future would be compromised.

Kumad turned off the engine and took a fresh pair of latex gloves from the glove box. He climbed out and locked the car. He exited the car park and began the return journey to Makar's office building. It would take him about a half hour. He did not hurry.

First he would check out the area. See if there seemed to be any unusual activity around the building. If the police were there he would walk away. By then it would be too late for him to recover the casing and he would need to leave London as he had planned, and as quickly as possible.

He realized there was no other way he could handle this. If the police found the casing, which they undoubtedly would, the process would begin. It would take time, and during that time Kumad needed to get as far from the UK as he could. There were many places he could go. Give himself time to cover his tracks and establish a new identity. He had the money to do it; his profession paid him well, and Kumad had always been prudent when it came to spending the contract fees he gathered. With money he could purchase any of the documents he needed. Some minor cosmetic enhancement would also help. His fingerprints were another matter—but that was something he had been thinking about for some time. He could not change them but he could have them removed so that problems such as this would not occur again.

There were so many ways the authorities could check out evidence nowadays. A fingerprint, any small piece of evidence, could be passed from country to country, logged into electronic search engines. Cooperation between law-enforcement agencies extended globally. A single item could be passed around quickly, checked and rechecked, throwing up answers in a short time.

Kumad needed to retrieve his bullet casing before it was found.

When he walked by the alley to Makar's establishment he didn't stop. He carried on until he was satisfied it was safe. Observation of the street showed no unusual presence in the area. It was a busy London high street, lined with stores and populated by large numbers of people, somewhere unusual activity would be noticeable. And a uniformed police presence would be almost impossible to conceal.

He realized the longer he delayed the more likely Makar's body could be discovered. If he was going to retrieve the shell casing it had to be now. He was aware of the risk but in reality he had no other choice. If the police found the shell casing and a check for fingerprints proved positive, the matter could escalate. Kumad did not underestimate the skill of police procedures. And he could not allow any investigation to tie him to the Turkish organization.

He turned around and calmly walked back to the alley, moving quickly and making for the access stairs to Makar's building. He pulled on the latex gloves as he headed to the stairway.

At the top of the access stairs he opened the door and stepped inside the building.

He moved into the corridor where Makar's office was situated.

And that was when it all went wrong.

CHAPTER EIGHT

London, earlier that day

Gary Manning watched the rain streaking past the window of the USAF transport as it touched down at RAF Lakenheath and rolled along the runway. The base was host to a large American contingent. Strings had been pulled to get Manning and Hawkins onto British soil without fanfare. The presence of the Stony Man operatives had not caused much of a ripple on the aircraft, which was making one of its regular supply runs.

The President had spoken to the echelon of the Air Force, requesting their assistance in a security matter that touched on NATO safety and an overspill into Turkey. There might have been a collective intake of Air Force breath because of the President's involvement, but in the end his request was agreed to.

And that found Manning and Hawkins, with their carry-on bags, enduring the flight on canvas seats fixed to the side of the big transport plane.

On arrival the Phoenix pair were met by their Air Force liaison and directed to the civilian SUV rented for them. They dropped their meager luggage into the back and Manning took the driving position.

"Glad you're doing the driving," Hawkins said. "I'd never feel comfortable on the wrong side of the road."

The Canadian smiled at that. He knew T.J. was as good a foreign driver as he was.

"You, my brother, are just getting lazy," he said as they exited Lakenheath.

"Damn," Hawkins said, "you saw right through my little ploy."

Manning punched in the coordinates for their destination and let the SUV roll.

Lakenheath was roughly seventy miles northwest of London. Manning observed the speed limits as he followed the sat nav's directions. The satellite navigation system had speed camera alert capacity, so the audible sounds that informed Manning were a help in avoiding any of the cameras.

Halfway along their journey Hawkins pointed out a roadside café where they stopped. He went inside and purchased two cups of takeout coffee. Back in the vehicle he slipped the cups into the provided holders.

"I'll bring you along again next time," Manning said, "if you keep this up."

They downed the coffee as Manning drove. It was close to midday when the SUV cruised the final stretch. They had left the rain behind them and pale sunlight had broken through the clouds. Traffic was building now as they reached the busy London inner roads. As with any large city, traffic congestion was a standard feature of the UK capital. Manning followed the sat nav directions and, busy traffic aside, reached the street where the apartment building was located.

The street was midmarket. It might have been smarter during its prime, but now it was just one of dozens dotted around the London map. The place was ready for a facelift. Manning didn't figure that was going to happen soon. He spotted an empty space close to the building and eased the SUV against the curb. Before they exited the SUV, both Phoenix commandos equipped themselves with a Beretta 92FS from their hand luggage. They made sure the handguns were hidden under their coats in belt holsters as they crossed the sidewalk and entered the building.

"Two floors up," Manning said.

"Why do these places smell the same wherever you go?" Hawkins said as they climbed the stairs. "You think they bottle it?"

The corridor stretching ahead of them was gloomy, the carpet underfoot dull and worn. The walls had been painted in a beige color that had an unhealthy sheen to it. Faint music could be heard from somewhere along the corridor.

Manning indicated the door they wanted.

"We announce ourselves," Hawkins said, "or do we just bust in?"

Manning reached to check the door and found it was not locked. He glanced at his partner.

"Let's do this, T.J.," he said.

Manning pushed the door partway open and peered inside. He scanned the room, holding a hand up to stop Hawkins from moving past.

"You don't want to go in there, partner," he said. "Believe me…"

AN HOUR LATER Manning called David McCarter via his sat phone.

"You're not going to like this," Manning said.

"Well, don't bloody wrap it up. Just tell me."

"That Turkish cell in London? We found two guys there. They looked odd—just lying on the floor of the apartment. I saw the condition of their flesh from the door so T.J. and I stayed clear."

"How bad are these blokes?"

"They're dead. We called in the British hazmat people and they're dealing with the site right now. Sealed off the whole apartment block and evacuated the residents. But the sickness hadn't killed them. They'd both been shot in the head. Single bullet."

"Execution?"

"That's what the medical examiner figured."

"You two okay?"

"Had ourselves checked out. No problem. Like I said, we didn't step inside once I saw those two."

"Let's hope the locals get some ID on them. Why London?" McCarter queried. "Our intel was hinting Özgürlük planned strikes in Turkey and the U.S. No mention of the UK. Bloody hell, Gary, I hope have we haven't missed something here."

"Could be London is just a midbase. We know Özgürlük's banker is here. We have his name. T.J. and I will scout around. See if we can dig up anything."

"You catching any flak from the authorities?"

"No. I called your old mate Doug Henning at that number you gave me before we left. He cleared a path for us. It's like we're a couple of heroes who saved the day."

McCarter laughed. "Well, don't let it go your heads. Hey, tell Doug I said hello and thanks. Keep me updated. Something tells me this isn't going to go away quietly."

Manning shut down his cell.

Hawkins said, "Hey, that's your serious face you're wearing."

Manning detailed what he had been discussing with McCarter.

"I think we might be spending a little more time here than we expected."

"Okay," Hawkins said. "So where do we start?"

"Let's talk to Henning. Then we'll go find that Özgürlük banker."

CHAPTER NINE

Aziz Makar had an office on a busy London street. It stood between a pair of local businesses—one was a property broker, the other a travel agency. Makar Investments was identified by the inscribed plate on the door. Inside was a small reception area, not too tidy, with worn furniture and a rack holding wilting brochures offering the building's services. From the information on the wall sign, Makar was the sole occupant. At the far end of the reception area stood a flight of stairs. There was a desolate air to the place.

"We sure we got the right place?" Hawkins asked.

"They're not going to advertise what they're really doing," Manning said, loosening his jacket so he could reach his pistol if he needed to.

They went up the stairs to a small landing with a door on each side and one at the end.

"Is this place quiet or what?" Hawkins observed.

"You said it."

Manning stood at the door that bore the inscription Aziz Makar Financial Services on a plastic strip. The door was not fully closed. Manning started to experience an uneasy feeling as he reached to gently push the door open. It swung wide and he looked into the office.

Desk. Filing cabinets. Couple of chairs. One on its side. Behind the desk a high-backed office swivel chair.

In the chair, leaning to one side was a slight figure,

the dark eyes seeming to stare at Manning across the office. Only they were not seeing anything.

The man in the chair was dead.

There was a swollen, puckered hole in his forehead where someone had fired a bullet at close range. There were powder burns around the wound and his open eyes bulged from the sockets. The back of the man's head had burst open where the bullet had emerged and plowed into the chair back. Bloody brain matter and shards of bone had been sprayed against the leather seat. The lingering smell of the gunshot was still there.

"You don't think this guy is in the same condition as the others?" Hawkins said.

"No sign of any skin discoloration," Manning said. "Apart from the bullet hole, he looks clean."

He still had reservations. After the earlier discovery, Manning wasn't taking any chances.

Manning pulled his Beretta even though he was certain he and Hawkins were alone. Hawkins did the same. It was a reflex action. He lowered the weapon as he scanned the office. Now he could smell the sour odor of death in the room from where the dead man had voided his bowels.

Hawkins stood beside the Canadian, checking the room himself. Someone had gone through the contents. Not too tidily. There were documents on the floor. A file cabinet drawer was half open. He saw cables on the desktop where something had been disconnected.

"Took his computer," he said. He scanned the room again. "I'd guess this was more than just a burglary."

"More like somebody cleaning house. Covering themselves because their...whatever it is, their operation, has started to go off the tracks?"

"Took the computer because Makar would have data on it about his accounts," Hawkins said.

"The guy was the banker. Had to have details somewhere."

Manning took a last look around the office. There was nothing in the room that was going to help them… He paused, noticing something on the floor a couple feet to one side of the door. A small object that caught the light. Manning pulled a pen from his inside pocket, crouched and slid the pen into the open end of the object. He showed it to Hawkins.

"Somebody didn't police his brass," Hawkins said, examining the 9 mm bullet casing his partner was holding.

"Clumsy. Or in a hurry," Manning said. "Find me something we can use to hold this bad boy."

Hawkins pulled out a pair of latex gloves. He'd almost forgotten he was carrying them. Manning laid the casing in the folds of the gloves and placed them in his pocket.

"Maybe Henning can get a print off this," he said. "Now let's get out of here."

They backed into the hall, Manning closing the office door.

He took out his phone and contacted Henning. When the man came on the line Manning told him what they had found. He gave the address.

"You need to get your hazmat people down here. Check this guy out in case he's infected."

"Every time you blokes come to town, life gets complicated," Henning said. "Just stay put. I'll be with you soon as I can. I'll have Hazmat with you on the double."

Manning called Stony Man to update Brognola. He wasn't available, so he got Price.

"I don't expect this is just to say, 'hi, how are you?'" Price said.

"Just an update."

"Ominous."

"That's a suspicious mind you have, Miss Price."

"Comes from working with you guys."

"We located the Özgürlük apartment here in London. Only the two guys we found were suffering from what might be some kind of radiation poisoning. The local hazmat team has dealt with them and the location is being cleaned up. Add to that by telling Hal the men we found had also been shot. I'm guessing to make sure they couldn't talk if they were discovered."

"Hal will want to update the President."

"Tell him we found the local moneyman for the group…"

Manning's pause was enough to alert Price there was more to come.

"Don't tell me he was affected by this *radiation*, as well."

"We won't know until he's been looked at. But we do know he has a case of lead poisoning like the others. A bullet to the head in his own office, and it looks as if the place had been searched. His computer's gone."

"The two you found earlier shot. Now this guy," Price said. "Somebody panicking? Or just cleaning up loose ends?"

"The guy was shot in the head with a 9 mm. Not what your average burglar uses, and the searched office looks staged to me. All that was taken was a computer. This was done in broad daylight, too. On a busy street. Guy must have used a suppressor. Barbara, make sure this all gets to Hal. Could be things are speeding up. We just sent a picture of the dead man to Aaron. Let me know if he gets an ID."

"What next for you and T.J.?"

"Until the cops arrive we just wait."

TAK KUMAD EASED open the building's rear door and slipped inside. He had already drawn his pistol. As he entered the corridor he saw the two men standing at Makar's office door.

They were both holding autopistols.

Instinctively, Kumad raised his own weapon. The men's presence meant only one thing. They had already seen or were about to discover Makar's body.

One of the men registered Kumad's presence and saw the pistol in his hand.

Both men fired.

The pair of shots filled the passage with sound.

Kumad saw his slug punch plaster from the wall next to the other man.

Something hard slammed into his left shoulder. He felt no immediate pain as he slumped back against the wall, but when he tried to brace his pistol with his left hand he couldn't raise it. His arm was numb. He fired anyway, triggering the pistol in a reflex action.

T. J. HAWKINS FELT a tug of something on his right sleeve. He dropped to a crouch, angling his 92FS up at the armed man facing him, and triggered a fast trio of shots that hammered into the guy's torso. The other man's pistol fired as his hand jerked, the slug passing harmlessly over Hawkins's head. The Stony Man operative responded and burned off a number of follow-up shots that forced his attacker to slide down the passage wall, leaving a bloody trail from exit wounds.

Manning's Beretta tracked in on the bloodied form rolling to the floor.

"You hit?"

Hawkins shook his head. The only damage was a tear

in his jacket sleeve where the shooter's slug had sheered the material.

"You wouldn't like to put a few more in him by any chance?" Manning said, seeing the number of bullet holes in the man's body.

"No. I don't want to overdo it," Hawkins said.

"Henning is going to love this," Manning said. "We've only just showed up and already London is turning into Dodge City."

DOUG HENNING AND A couple of his team arrived twenty minutes later. The hazmat contingent was right on his heels. One of the techs ran his handheld counter over Manning and Hawkins, declared them clean, and ordered everyone to vacate the area.

Henning viewed the attacker's blood-soaked body without saying a word as he followed the Phoenix pair outside, knowing that before the team entered the office they'd wait until Manning, Hawkins and Henning were outside on the sidewalk.

The street was already cordoned off with police cars and the hazmat vehicle. A wide area had been cleared of people, leaving the street empty. Even the surrounding shops had been emptied.

"You guys must love us showing up," Hawkins said.

"Think so?" Henning sighed. "Gives us something to do instead of sitting around on our arses."

"Told you he likes us," Hawkins said.

"Tell me your story," Henning said. "I'll need something for my bloody report."

Manning told it the way it had happened.

"So you believe this bloke came back to search for his missed shell casing?"

"Didn't want to leave fingerprints. He needed to pick up his brass because there could be a trace on it."

"Hoping he could do it before Makar's body was discovered."

Hawkins said, "I expect the slugs from the other bodies will match the one from here."

Henning nodded. He turned to one of his team, a stocky, blond-haired young man.

"Marsh, make sure everything is cross-checked. I want the bullet from that man in the office looked at against the ones from those bodies in that flat. Check everything. It's starting to look as if this *is* all tied together. And I don't want any grief from anyone about contaminating the crime scene. It's too late for that." He turned back to Manning and Hawkins. "I think it's time we had a chat about this whole bloody mess. Marsh, call me if you hear anything. I'm going back to the office with our witnesses."

Leaving his man to monitor the scene, Henning followed Manning and Hawkins to their rental. With Manning behind the wheel, Henning directed them across London to his base. On their way to his office Henning dropped off the shell casing at the forensic department. Through the glass wall they could see the rest of the department at work.

Inside his office, Henning poured mugs of coffee, sat and faced Manning and Hawkins from across his desk. He waved a hand at the overflow of paperwork.

"I can do without any further complicated incidents," he said. "Three dead already today. God, I'll be writing this up for days."

"We'll tell you what we have," Manning said.

He outlined the overall mission, Henning sitting back and not interrupting until the Canadian had finished.

"So this Turkish bunch is in the process of making some kind of protest against American presence in their country?"

"It looks that way. A blackmail threat that might turn into the real thing."

"*Nuclear?* How the hell do they expect to get away with that? By setting off a device in Turkey—against their own people?"

"We think the Turkish attack might be against the U.S. base at Incirlik," Manning said. "If I was planning this, it's the way I'd do it. Take down the base and a large number of Americans with it. You guys have a right to know because the RAF has a contingent there."

"Scarier by the minute," Henning said. "That's one hell of a way to make a statement."

"Our intel indicates there might be a follow-up attack in the U.S., as well," Hawkins told him.

Henning drained his coffee in a long swallow, stood and poured himself a second one. He digested what he'd just been told, and Manning, watching him, saw a question forming.

"Even if you're certain about this attack and considering the things that have gone wrong…"

"Do we still believe it will take place?" Manning said.

"Yes."

"The group behind it is dedicated in their beliefs. They want America out of Turkey. Our weapons gone, too. They see NATO as a continuing presence and seem willing to disrupt the alliance as much as they can."

"If this first phase doesn't work?"

"They'll regroup and try again," Hawkins said. "These people don't pack up and walk away."

"Right now you don't have enough to go in and finish them?"

"Working on it," Manning said. "But they're not going to make it easy for us. Knowing and proving are two sides of the coin."

"Anything more I can do?"

"Push that fingerprint through. It might give us something. We already sent pictures of the two perps through to our base, hoping they might be able to give us some good news."

"That's something we could do with," Henning said.

He picked up one of the phones on his desk and connected to another department. When he failed to get the response he was expecting, he made his feelings clear. His impatience overrode any considerations toward the feelings of the person on the other end of the line.

"Call the damned head of every department you want. I'll tell them exactly the same thing. This request—no, this demand—goes to the top of the priority list. Enter the prints in your system and run them. Is that so bloody hard to do? When you've done that you can go and have your mug of tea. Then the minute you get a result you phone me directly. Understand? Do you understand? Do not test me, son, because I know where you work and I will come down there and show you the true meaning of being an utter bastard."

Henning replaced the receiver very gently.

"Feeling better?" Hawkins said.

Henning leaned back in his chair. "Definitely better."

HENNING RECEIVED HIS CALL less than an hour later from the technician he'd had words with. He listened to what the man had to say, pulling a pad to him and writing quickly.

"Fine, Collins," he said. "Your help is appreciated. Now do me one more favor. Print off the data, plus photos, and get them sent to my office. Right now. Give yourself a pat on the back. It was good work and bloody important. Thanks."

"I'll bet that guy loves you now," Hawkins said.

Henning smiled. "What can I say, I'm just a big, soft teddy bear," he said. "Now, before the pics get here, I can tell you we have ID on two of the dead. One of the blokes in the apartment and your shooter.

"He was Tak Kumad. Turkish national with a background that suggests his killings here in London were not his first. His name and face have popped up before. Nothing detailed. Just that he was considered a paid assassin. Pretty sharp operator by the sounds of it. Suspected but never proved. But when his prints we took today were run against that shell casing, they matched. So we have him for the shooting of the guy in the office. Coming back today for that casing was his first mistake."

"And his last," Hawkins said.

"I'm betting the bullets from all the dead will be the same. We don't have a deal on this bloke Makar. He kept a pretty low profile here. But now that we're digging, it looks as if he was some kind of money manipulator. Records show he didn't have much of a client list."

Henning continued. "The ID we got on one of the men in the flat has him as Egemen Binice. Turkish again. We ran his profile through Interpol and Turkish records. Comes back as a low-scale criminal. No major crimes. All scams and cheap tricks. His record shows he was associated with a long-time partner. Bora Terzel. They were a pair of conmen."

"Looks like they conned their way into our Turkish bunch," Hawkins said. "Wanted to step up the ladder."

Henning flicked his finger over one of the papers in his hand.

"Binice had a cell on him. It was checked. Call list showed a particular number he called a lot over the past week or so." Henning smiled. "It was checked out and found to have belonged to Aziz Makar, our dead money-man."

"Binice and Terzel both capped by Kumad. Then Makar," Manning said. "Maybe they upset someone in the organization. Enough to get them a bullet in the head."

Henning shrugged. "It's a strange one. Same with Makar. Either someone is cleaning house, or settling an old score. And you guys just happened to walk in on the end result."

"What about the sickness those two had?" Hawkins said. "We suspect Özgürlük is working something with nuclear devices. Were those two involved?"

"I'm hoping to have some kind of answer to that later today," Henning said. "I'll let you know."

"You have my number," Manning said. "Once you give us our clearance, we need to get back to the rest of our team. Can't see there being much more for us here, Doug. Hate to have to say it, but this has reached a dead end."

CHAPTER TEN

Miami, Florida

"Let's get this done," Lyons said. "I want to talk to this Gutierrez slimeball. If he's a lead to these creeps, we need to get him to talk."

"He'll have protection," Schwarz said.

"I hope so," Lyons said. The Able Team commander was in a warring mood—never a good thing for anyone he came in contact with.

"This is crazy," Blancanales said. "He supplied Striker with weapons on Barb's say-so. Now we're going after his hide."

"He should have stuck to supplying straight weapons," Lyons said. "You think I'm going to talk nicely when he could be involved in hitting the U.S. with a nuclear device?"

"When you explain it like that…" Schwarz said.

Blancanales rolled the SUV to the sidewalk and parked, switching off the engine. Along with his partner he checked his pistol, while Lyons did the same with his hefty .357 Colt Python.

From where they were parked they could see the apartment building gleaming white under the tropical Florida sun. Off to the other side of the street, palm trees bordered the beach and the blue Atlantic.

"Nice area," Blancanales said. "Pity a piece of garbage like Gutierrez gets to hang out here."

"Bro," Schwarz said, "this is South Beach. Money talks the loudest in this burg. And trash like Gutierrez have plenty of that."

Lyons spun the Python's cylinder. "Money talk is not as loud as this."

"That's scary talk," Schwarz said.

They exited the SUV, Blancanales locking it with the remote. The trio made their way across the sidewalk, heading for the entrance to the apartment block.

"How much rent do you figure they charge here?" Blancanales said.

"More than a poor grunt like you can afford," Lyons growled.

"You hear that?" Blancanales said. "Now we're just grunts."

Schwarz gave a short laugh. "Yes, but special grunts with badges."

"Jesus," Lyons said. "Why don't you pair team up and go on *America's Got Talent*?"

"He could have something there," Schwarz said. "You and me on the comedy circuit."

"No more getting shot at. No more chasing bad guys."

As they neared the entrance Lyons spun around.

"So help me, if the perps upstairs miss, I'll shoot you myself."

Blancanales frowned. "You think our liability insurance would cover something like that?"

"No way we could be so lucky."

A uniformed doorman stepped out from beneath the sun canopy to meet them, barring the way.

"Can I help you?"

Lyons took out his DOJ credentials supplied by Stony Man Farm and thrust them into the man's face. The doorman studied the wallet and the badge attached to it, his tanned face creasing as he digested what he was reading. Blancanales and Schwarz took out their own IDs and added them to the mix.

"You expect me to just let you in because you show me a couple of badges? How do I know they're real?"

Lyons opened the light sport coat he was wearing and exposed his holstered Python. The doorman eyed it with a frown on his face.

"The badge is as real as the gun," Lyons said. "I can demonstrate if you need me to."

"Look, gentlemen, I'm only doing my job."

Blancanales said, "We understand that and we are just doing ours. I'm sure you don't want to get in the way of federal agents, so it would be in your best interest to let us in."

The doorman realized he was on a loser; hampering Feds was not a good idea. So he stepped to one side and keyed in the access number on the pad beside the glass doors. The moment the lock clicked, Able Team walked inside, Blancanales pausing for a final word.

"Your cooperation has been noted, Dennis." The name came from the neat badge pinned to the doorman's coat. "Hopefully we won't be here long."

"There isn't going to be shooting, is there?" Dennis asked. "It could upset the other tenants. If they get upset they keep calling me to deal with it."

"If we have to, we'll keep the shooting to a minimum," Lyons said.

They made their way across the wide lobby, Dennis

staring after them, and aimed for the stairs, ignoring the elevator.

"Top floor," Schwarz said. "This guy lives the dream."

"Maybe we can turn it into a bad one," Lyons said.

The Farm had provided the team with satellite data from the Zero platform. Photo imagery of the area had detailed the building from above, showing the presence of a rooftop swimming pool belonging to the apartment Gutierrez was using. Emerging from the stairs, they pushed through an access door and stepped into a twenty-foot-long corridor that took them to the apartment entrance.

Blancanales had spotted the camera mounted over the door, monitoring their approach, and signaled the others. They kept their weapons holstered under their coats as they walked up to the door casually. Lyons thumbed the bell. Then they waited. When the double doors opened they were faced with a tall guy in a flowered shirt and light-colored chinos. He held an HK MP5 in his broad hands.

"Private apartment," he said. "You look like cops to me. Now I don't give a damn if you have a warrant or a Gold American Express card. Nobody comes in here without Mr. Gutierrez saying okay. I don't remember him saying okay."

"Man has a point," Schwarz said. "We didn't ask."

"So let's go see Mr. Gutierrez and do that," Blancanales said.

The big man shook his head. "You jerking me off? I don't like being messed with. And you morons are doing just that."

The HK lifted in a threatening manner. And that was when Lyons pulled out his Python and slammed the heavy revolver across the side of the man's head. The blow was hard enough to put the guy down. He slumped to his knees just inside the door. Blancanales picked up the fallen SMG and reached under the guy's shirt to pull out the holstered autopistol he carried. Schwarz stepped in to jerk the man's arms behind him and loop plastic cuffs around his thick wrists and ankles.

"Never leave home without plastic ties," he said.

Lyons made a snarky sound.

"He does get cranky when people point guns at him," Blancanales said.

"So he does," his partner said.

"Let's go inside," Schwarz said.

Lyons walked by the downed minder and along the hall into the expansive, sunny apartment. Directly ahead of him wide glass doors were open to the flat roof and the swimming pool. Lyons walked across the expensively furnished lounge area and through the open doors. He held his Python behind his back as he stood facing the three men on the patio area fronting the pool.

He heard his partners move up to flank him, both showing their Beretta 92FS autopistols.

The two thugs had reached for their own weapons but the sudden appearance of Able Team had caught them off guard. Aware of the 92FS Berettas already trained on them, they showed sense and held their hands well clear of their own weapons.

Blancanales stepped around them and removed their weapons. He ejected the magazines and cleared the breeches, then tossed each gun into the pool.

"Hey," one guy said.

"Now, this must be embarrassing for you," Blancanales said. He patted each man down to make sure they were not carrying any other weapons. "They're clear."

"Go take a swim," Lyons said. "Do it now. In the pool."

"What if we said no?"

Lyons waggled the Python at them. "I'd just as soon shoot you. Make your damn choice."

"Don't think he won't," Schwarz said.

The thugs looked at each other, shrugged indifferently, turned and stepped off the side and into the pool.

"Keep moving to the center," Blancanales said. He watched the two men wade out to the middle of the wide pool. "I feel safer now."

Lyons turned his attention to the third man sitting on one of the loungers.

Pablo Gutierrez, the lean, sharp-featured Mexican, was watching with a wary expression. He had not moved or spoken during the entire episode. He matched the image Stony Man had forwarded to Lyons's cell.

"No *mi casa su casa*?" Lyons said.

Gutierrez shrugged as if he didn't give a damn. "What do you want?" he said.

"It isn't to be your lifelong buddy," Lyons said.

"I can call my lawyers and you will be in very bad trouble. You know who I am?" Now there was a trace of antagonism in Gutierrez's voice, self-importance that was part of the man's makeup.

Lyons said, "Someone who doesn't impress me? A piece of scum? Get the picture, Gutierrez?"

"You realize I could have you killed for doing this?"

"You know, I think he believes he can do that," Schwarz said.

Gutierrez pushed himself off the lounger and faced Lyons.

"I have connections you people should be aware of. People in your defense community. Your government. Very powerful people."

"Save your breath," Lyons said. "I don't give a damn who you have on your Christmas card list."

"Hombre, you won't frighten us with your threats," Blancanales said. "Quit the tough-guy act. It doesn't work with us."

"And if I find out who you are and put in a complaint?"

"Good luck with that one," Schwarz said. "Some days I forget who we work for myself."

"Who are you? Cops? No. Not cops. Feds maybe? ATF?"

Blancanales said, "He knows all the names."

"That must be because they've all got him on their databases," Lyons said. "This chucklehead is known all down the agency lines, I guess."

"If I was the type to brag," Gutierrez said with a curl of his mouth, "I would say that was so, but…"

Blancanales caught the flash of impatience in Lyons's eyes. It was a bad sign coming from the Able Team leader, and what followed only confirmed the fact.

There was no warning. Lyons simply launched a fist that clipped Gutierrez across his jaw; there was enough power in the punch to drive Gutierrez backward. He caught the edge of the lounger and went over it, sprawling on the pool patio on the far side. Lyons took a long step, grasped the lounger and threw it aside. He towered over the stunned man, the big Colt revolver aimed down at Gutierrez. In the silence that followed the Mexican's falling, the click of the hammer being pulled back was loud and unmistakable.

Gutierrez dragged the back of his hand across his

mouth, smearing the streak of blood from a split lip. He stared up at the towering figure standing over him and saw death staring over his shoulder.

"*¡Por Dios!*" he said. "What is it you want?"

"The deal you brokered for Özgürlük? Who handled it? And don't play dumb. We have evidence you received payment. I want the name you dealt with. A location."

"If I don't tell you, will you shoot me?"

Lyons pressed the muzzle hard against the Mexican's forehead. "You remember Jack Regan, bubba? The guy you like to emulate? He figured he had the world by the balls. Smart guy. But not smart enough to dodge a bullet."

"Maybe you want to go out like your hero," Blanca-nales said. "It'll be quick. All over in a flash."

"One less arms dealer to worry about," Schwarz added.

Lyons watched as Gutierrez's gaze moved from man to man, seeing nothing but the same determination in their eyes. Whatever else he might have been, Pablo Gutierrez was not a fool. Nor was he a man to believe he was immortal. A single bullet from Lyons's Python would end his life as easily as the one that had taken out Jack Regan.

"All right. His name is Gennadi Antonov. A Russian. I introduced him to a contact."

"The buyer. That's the one we would like to know about."

Gutierrez hesitated.

"*Who?*" Lyons insisted.

"A Turkish guy looking for special merchandise."

The Colt's muzzle moved closer to Gutierrez's face.

"Hold off," he said. "Guy was called Kaplan. Hakan Kaplan. Out of Istanbul."

"You'd better have a location for Antonov," Lyons said, waving the .357 in the Mexican's face. "And one that really exists."

The Python stopped in front of Gutierrez again, the cold ring of the muzzle pressed close to his cheek, Lyons's finger against the trigger. He had a rising urge to add that extra pressure. Knowing what he did about the background and, more important, how things might turn out, wiped away any consideration for Gutierrez's comfort. This was more than a few crates of weapons. It was a possible threat to the lives of American citizens. Just that single thought was enough to make Lyons pull the trigger.

"Okay, okay," Gutierrez said. "You want Antonov that bad, I'll give him to you."

The address was noted and Lyons backed off.

"Word of warning, Pablo," he said. "If I find out someone has warned Antonov we're coming, I'll know. I'll find you wherever you are and I promise it will be the worst thing ever to happen to you. I might not have your connections but I promise you'll be doing yourself a big favor if you chalk this up to experience. Believe me, you do not want to get into this."

"If we pass the word you've been dealing to supply weapons of mass destruction that might be used here, on U.S. soil," Blancanales added, "I don't think even your special status will save you. Think about it, *bubba*."

BACK DOWN ON the sidewalk Lyons took out his sat phone and called the Farm.

"Gutierrez is out of the frame. Next up is the contact who dealt with Hakan Kaplan. Gennadi Antonov. Sounds like he's the one who fixed the deal for the Turks. Find the rock he's currently under so we can go talk to him to find out the what and the where."

"Let you know," Price said. "Hey, is it nice and sunny down in Miami? What wouldn't I give for a few days in the sun."

"It's sunny," Lyons said, "except for the big black cloud hanging over Pablo Gutierrez's swimming pool."

CHAPTER ELEVEN

Price had posed the question to Kurtzman. He had taken it to his cyber team and tasked them with locating Gennadi Antonov's current residence. It hadn't taken them long to locate the Russian or for the mission controller to relay the information to Able Team.

As it turned out, Antonov had rented a property in Las Vegas, Nevada, and, having quieted his business dealings for the present, was staying out of the limelight. Unusual for the high-flying Russian dealer.

The house was located off the beaten track in a residential area of the city, but Kurtzman's team had pinpointed the address through their extensive resources. If it was in the cyber universe, the Stony Man team would track it down.

It was Jack Grimaldi, Stony Man Farm's resident pilot, who flew Able Team into an executive charter airport a couple miles off the strip. The three men disembarked and followed Grimaldi across the tarmac to the charter office. The manager greeted the pilot as a long-lost friend and told them the rental car Grimaldi had asked for was ready and waiting.

Grimaldi had contacts like this one across the U.S., having cultivated such relationships over his years as a freelance pilot, his easy manner and genuine friendliness building up a network of contacts in the private aviation business. The flying community was a close-knit one and the people who inhabited it kept in touch.

None of them knew of Grimaldi's connection with Stony Man; no one outside the SOG knew about Stony Man. As far as the world knew, Grimaldi was a freelance pilot who could fly anything with wings and a motor. In reality Grimaldi was a skilled pilot who could handle automatic weapons as well as he handled the controls of a plane.

This trip was a peaceful jaunt for Grimaldi. Once Able Team drove away for their meet with Gennadi Antonov, Grimaldi was on stand-down. All he had to do was wait around until the team returned from their mission. In the comfortable lounge of the charter office, Grimaldi, supplied with coffee and refreshments by his buddy, relaxed and quickly struck up a conversation with an attractive young woman employed there.

ABLE TEAM ALWAYS entered an investigation expecting the worst and were usually presented with exactly that. The situations they encountered—and the people involved— were of a type that usually responded with hostility. People who had something to hide or protect, and who did not respond favorably when confronted.

Always primed to face problems, Able Team was wired to react swiftly, so Lyons was not overly surprised when he was faced by two armed and violence-prone men ready to inflict harm.

They were ready for trouble. More than ready to work their orders, which seemed to push them into preventive action as they came out of the house and confronted the Able Team leader.

Carl Lyons read the intent in the pair the moment he set eyes on them. Lyons possessed a suspicious nature, which allowed him an innate ability to see when trouble was coming almost before it began. It was a lifesaver, and on this particular day it benefited the Able Team leader to the point where he was able to make his advanced play well ahead of the game.

They had parked a few properties down from where Antonov was currently staying. It was a midsize but expensive single-story house with an attached double-car garage. A smooth lawn fronted the property with a plain Ford sedan parked on the paved drive. Lyons had sent his partners to check out the rear of the property via the lane that ran along the back lots of the houses while he made his frontal approach.

As aware as he always was of violent reactions coming quickly, Lyons had to assume the armed men bracing him were overly nervous or had been given prior instructions to react in the way they were.

He slid his hand under his sport coat, closing his fingers around the butt of the holstered Colt Python revolver. Chambered for .357, the big Magnum delivered its six loads with devastating force. In the skilled hands of Carl Lyons they were guaranteed to hit home.

Lyons had an affinity for his Python, often refusing to change to a different weapon. His dogged clinging to the Colt was likened to Phoenix Force's David McCarter, who stayed faithful to his 9 mm Browning Hi-Power, the weapon he had used for decades.

Lyons steadfastly resisted change. It was in his nature to stay with the weapon. He had an ally in the form of Stony Man Farm's resident armorer, John "Cowboy" Kissinger; the weapons master had made it his business to purchase a number of the discontinued pistols, which he kept by for Lyons. Kissinger had a half-dozen Colt Pythons inventoried, plus a stock of spares that kept Lyons happy. In Kissinger's skilled hands any damage that occurred from overuse or by accident could be remedied, or the weapon retooled and brought back into service.

Sliding the Python from leather, Lyons eased it forward in a smooth action that caught the antagonistic pair way behind.

Their autopistols were still rising. It must have occurred to them they were too slow. It was too late to step back. Their commitment to their actions forced them to continue.

In Lyons's big fist the heavy Colt lined up on target. His finger tripped the trigger, sending the first shot. The 145-grain Silvertip slug burst from the Python's bore and streaked forward. It struck with devastating force, penetrating flesh, splintering bone and blowing out the guy's left shoulder in a spray of flesh, bone and blood. The force from the big slug threw shock waves through the guy's torso, and his nervous system initially protected him from pain. The pain would follow. At the moment of impact too much was happening and the man went down in an uncoordinated heap, his weapon springing from his grasp.

Only seconds passed following Lyons's shot. He turned in a lowering crouch and lined up his weapon on the second guy, who'd had that extra time to center his own weapon. Fast as he was, the guy lacked the reflexes that allowed someone to stay ahead in a firefight.

Lyons had no problem. He understood the techniques of facing an armed opponent and his combat-honed responses kept him on line. The Colt boomed as he triggered another pair of shots.

The two Magnum rounds hammered the target's torso, kicking him back a couple of feet as they went in hard, breaking ribs and cleaving through organs. The guy let out a harsh cry as he landed on his back, the severe impact of striking the ground driving air from his lungs. His body arched in protest. Blood pumped from the holes in his body, spreading across his clothing in glistening patches. He kicked a few times, then went still.

Lyons stayed where he was, scanning the area in case the two would-be shooters had partners in the vicinity. When he heard running footsteps he half turned.

It was Blancanales, his Beretta 92FS in his fist. His glance went from his partner to the bodies on the ground, then back to Lyons. When he realized there was no more of a threat he visibly relaxed and lowered his weapon.

"I see you went ahead without us—again," he said.

Lyons shrugged. "Have to seize the moment."

"Very poetic," Schwarz said as he came up to join them, hearing Lyons. "You could put that to music." Schwarz had his sat phone in his hand. "I called for medical help. They're on their way."

"You find anything?" Lyons said.

"Nada," Blancanales said. "Nobody back there. Just the backyard."

"Why the overreaction?" Schwarz asked, holstering his Beretta.

"We can ask him," Lyons said, indicating the guy he'd shot in the shoulder.

Schwarz said, "I don't think he'll be inclined to see that as his priority right now."

Lyons was standing over the wounded gunman, his expression suggesting he was far from happy at the outcome. The guy on the ground, his face creased in pain, flesh glistening with sweat, stared up at him.

"I've three more loaded chambers," Lyons said. "Up to you what happens. Give me what I want to hear and you get a ride to the hospital. Play hardball and you'll still ride in the ambulance, but you'll have a sheet pulled over your face."

Lyons pulled back the Python's hammer, the hard sound loud in the general stillness.

"You…can't do that… I'm hurt… Cops don't shoot unarmed prisoners…"

Lyons grinned unpleasantly. "You need to understand, mister. We are not cops. We don't have *Miranda* tattooed across our foreheads, so forget that crap."

The wounded man's eyes flicked back and forth as he looked at the Able Team trio.

"Who the hell are you?"

"Just some guys who need you to give us some guidance," Blancanales said.

The man clutched at his bloody shoulder, teeth clenched now that the pain was kicking in. He could feel the blood welling up and running between his fingers.

"You blew my shoulder apart," he snapped. "I can lose my arm, goddammit."

"You want nice, go join a sewing circle," Lyons said. "Check his pockets, Comer."

Blancanales crouched beside the moaning man and went through his coat and pants. He produced a cell, holding it up to show Lyons.

"We can have it checked out," Lyons said. "Might give us a location for Antonov. Unless our bleeding friend can help."

Schwarz had checked out the house, slipping in through the open front door. He returned holding his hands apart in a negative gesture. "Place is empty. Nobody home."

The wounded man had closed his eyes. His face was

deathly pale. Lyons took off his jacket and, with Blancanales's help, wrapped it around the wound.

A few of the neighbors had wandered out of the adjoining properties. They stood in groups, necks craning as they stared at the scene. Blancanales wandered over to assure them there was nothing to see. He waved his badge in their faces and made sympathetic noises.

Schwarz called Stony Man to give Price an update. The mission controller knew there would be repercussions, but said she would step in to cover with the local PD.

The approaching sound of an ambulance reached them minutes later. As the vehicle swung to a stop, a pair of medics jumped out and Lyons and Blancanales moved to where Schwarz was standing. The two medics ignored the Able Team trio as they attended to the wounded man.

Schwarz had used his phone to take pictures of both hardmen and transmitted them to the Farm. His short text asked if they could make IDs.

"Who are you guys?" one of the medics asked. Lyons showed his ID. "Okay. So what did you shoot him with? That wound looks big enough to put my hand in."

"A .357 Magnum round," Lyons said matter-of-factly.

The medic shook his head. "What did he do to get that?"

"Does 'he was about to shoot me' count?" Lyons said evenly. "Any more dumb questions?"

The edge to his voice warned Blancanales and Schwarz their leader was not in a cheerful mood.

Blancanales stepped over to where the medics were dealing with the wounded man before they moved him. He showed his ID wallet and badge and jerked a finger in Lyons's direction.

"I suggest you don't piss him off too much. He's still got bullets in that gun."

"Yeah, like he'll shoot us."

The medic chanced a glance at Lyons and something in the blond man's expression warned him to keep quiet.

"That's all down to who we meet up with," Blancanales said. "Kind of roughnecks we get to see have the habit of shooting even before we get to say hello."

Lyons's sigh of exasperation could be heard by everyone.

"I need to talk with your patient before you leave," Lyons said. "This is important."

The medic backed off, realizing he was not going to get the better of the blond man.

"Make it fast. He's stabilized but he needs attention."

The wounded man stared at Lyons as he approached. *"What?"*

"I ask. You answer. Even you should be able to deal with that."

Schwarz felt his phone vibrate. He checked it and read the text from Kurtzman. He sent a response, then pocketed the phone.

"The dead guy is Ritchie Mathias," Schwarz said. "His partner is Nate Brewster. Offer them a wad of cash and they'd do a number on their grandmother. Not very bright guys."

"Yeah?" Lyons said. "Well, Mathias had his bulb switched off for good this time."

"This guy Brewster… Information says he has affiliates with some suspect groups on the Homeland Security list. And guess what—his name comes up as having connections with Antonov."

"Where is he?" Lyons said. "He's not at home, so…?"

Brewster swallowed, clearly intimidated by Lyons and his gun.

"Look, we only been working protection for the guy. He pays us to stay around and keep people away."

Lyons asked, "So why is Antonov so nervous?"

"Since he ran a deal for some Turkish guy, he's been walking on glass. The gear has been taken away but Antonov has a case of the shakes."

"He's figured out he's worked a bad deal," Schwarz concluded.

"You know what the goods were?" Lyons said.

Brewster shook his head. "Antonov handled it all himself. Ritchie and me, all we did was provide his protection. Everything else was kept close."

"No surprise there," Blancanales said.

"What's Antonov been running?" Brewster asked. "I'm not taking the fall for this."

"Isn't loyalty grand," Lyons said.

"When will Antonov be back?" Schwarz said.

"This evening," Brewster told him. "He said he was going to pick up some more protection. Bring them back here."

Lyons moved away, dismissing the wounded man.

"Get him out of here," Blancanales said to the medics.

Brewster was placed on a gurney and wheeled to the ambulance. Once it was secured, one medic stayed with the patient, the other climbed behind the wheel and drove off.

"Hide our wheels," Lyons said. "We'll have to pick up Antonov when he gets back."

"Extra protection," Schwarz said. "Antonov is really worried over this."

"Because he's got himself in one hell of a mess. In over his head and he's jumping at shadows."

"That's what happens when you work a deal like this," Lyons said. "Antonov should have stayed with selling guns. A consignment of nukes is a step too far."

IT WAS ALMOST DUSK before a vehicle appeared and rolled to a stop outside the house. The scene was quiet again. Even the rubberneckers had gone indoors to pick up on their television programs.

Lyons was becoming increasingly restless. His partners knew why, because they were in a similar mood. The possibility of a nuclear device being detonated on U.S. soil was easily enough to put a strain on them.

The car was a current model. High end.

"You know how much one of those costs?" Schwarz said.

"I don't want to know," Blancanales said.

"Let's just agree neither of you can afford one," Lyons rumbled.

The driver and the guy riding shotgun stepped out of the car. They were both large, their bulk apparent even through the cut of their expensive suits.

"Logic says these guys are so muscle-bound they can't move all that fast," Blancanales observed. "What good is a bodyguard who isn't quick on his feet?"

"And who has such a wide chest he can't properly fold his arms," Schwarz added.

"All part of the hardman image for Antonov," Lyons said.

Antonov himself appeared, climbing out of the back of the vehicle. He was well dressed, wore his dark hair thick, and his eyes were hidden behind designer sun shades even at this time of day. As he stood beside the car, his bodyguards moved to shadow him, heads swiveling as they checked the frontage of the house.

"Now they earn their money," Schwarz said.

The Russian said something and followed his protection as they moved toward the front door.

Antonov stopped abruptly, seeing the dried blood patches on the driveway.

Before anyone could react, Lyons moved out from the side of the garage, his Python thrust out in front of him, covering the three men. Schwarz and Blancanales were following, moving to flank the Able Team commander.

"I see a hand reaching under those jackets," Lyons said, "I forget my manners."

"You boys are a little slow," Schwarz said.

Antonov said, "Don't tell me about it. I hired these jokers to protect me, and the first time something happens…" He was attempting to bluster, but it was obvious he was figuring the worst.

Lyons walked up to confront the man.

"It's question time, Antonov. I have a feeling you know what about."

One of the bodyguards, simmering because he had been caught napping on the job, leaned forward. He poked a thick finger at Lyons.

"Leave Mr. Antonov alone, you asshole. If you weren't waving that goddamn gun around…"

Schwarz glanced across at his partner.

"Asshole?"

Lyons turned his head slightly as the bodyguard spoke. He stared at the man for a few seconds before he moved.

Lyons didn't hold back. His left fist snapped forward, connecting with the guy's nose. The force behind the punch was full-on. The man's nose was reduced to a crushed, bloody mass. The pain forced him to pause to wipe his sleeve across the blood pouring down across his lower face. Then he made a wild, uncoordinated swing at Lyons. It was the worst thing he could have done. Lyons swung the hard edge of his left hand in a savage slash that caught the guy below the chin, the blow collapsing his throat and smashing through bone and cartilage. The hardman tried to suck in air but the damage to his throat prevented that. He stumbled away from Lyons, clutching at his ruined throat, gasping for the air denied him.

Schwarz and Blancanales moved in and disarmed both bodyguards.

"I hate unnecessary violence," Lyons said. "But it highlights the seriousness of the situation. You ready to talk, Antonov?"

Antonov said he was. He had quickly realized he had no choice if he wanted to stay upright and unhurt.

"Where did you have the shipment delivered? The one you worked for Hakan Kaplan."

Antonov's gaze flicked back and forth between the Stony Man operatives.

"Don't waste time, Gennadi," Schwarz said. "We know about the deal. The nukes. Where did they go?"

"You have to believe me. I had no idea what was going down."

"You made a deal to supply backpack bombs to Kaplan's organization. To Özgürlük. You know what they're going to do with them?"

"I worked it out from what I'd heard," Antonov said. "If I'd known before the deal I would have backed down. I tried to cancel the deal. Kaplan said no. A deal had been struck and there was no going back. Then he said I was a dead man if he couldn't trust me."

"Where did the bombs go?" Lyons repeated in a low voice.

"They went from my source in Russia to an island off the Turkish coast. Belongs to Kaplan's principal. After that I have no details about where the package went. Kaplan cut me out of the loop after the delivery."

"Still leaves you on the hook," Lyons said. "You figure all the money they paid you was worth it?"

Sweat had formed on Antonov's face. It ran down his cheeks and soaked into the collar of his expensive shirt.

"I helped you people," he said. "Now you have to protect me. Keep that crazy Turkish guy off my back."

"That's nice," Blancanales said. "He wants to be our friend now."

"I didn't think he liked us," Schwarz said. "I suppose being threatened with having your cojones sliced off and fed to you makes a difference."

"We can arrange for you to have a nice long vacation in a federal jail," Lyons said. "Give you plenty of alone time. That suit you?"

Antonov considered that and wasn't too happy.

"I don't want jail. People can get to you even behind bars."

"Looks to me like you're in a mess, Gennadi," Schwarz said.

"Wait…I might have something you can use. Kaplan bought guns from me as part of the deal. Said he needed backup weapons in case their operation turned sour. Automatic weapons. Handguns. Ammunition."

"You deliver those yourself?"

Antonov nodded eagerly. "To a place in Baltimore. A storage facility. Belongs to a company called the Turkish Spice Company."

"Nice down-home name," Lyons said.

He turned away and took out his sat phone to contact Stony Man.

BROGNOLA BIT DOWN on his cold cigar with enough force to cut through it. He took out the cigar and dropped it on the desk in the office he used when at the Farm. His fingers peeled away the shredded tobacco and he shook his head in frustration. Not at the tobacco. At the seemingly never-ending evil of man.

"You still there?" Lyons said, an edge of impatience in his voice.

"I'm here, Carl. Just taking in what you told me. I'll alert the local LEOs and get them down to your location. Damn Özgürlük. Why do these people have to bring their problems to us? Why can't they keep them on their own doorstep?"

"Because doing that isn't going to make as big a statement," Lyons said. "They want to make as much noise as they can. These guys want everyone to know they can challenge us and force a withdrawal of U.S. interests in Turkey. If we don't play their game, they trigger the bombs."

"I don't see the President agreeing to demands."

"Hal, that's his call. But I figure this one is going to be pushed right to the edge."

"Who backs down first, huh?"

"You want us to hang around?"

"Until the Feds show up to take Antonov away, then you can hand over."

"Find out about this Turkish Spice Company in Baltimore. Could be the lead we've been looking for."

"You got it, Carl. Get back to you."

CHAPTER TWELVE

Aaron Kurtzman swung his wheelchair and joined Akira Tokaido at his workstation. The younger cyber tech was pointing at his large monitor where he had punched up the records from the data.

"Took a while because the information was in a mess," he said. "They must have been using it as a day-to-day log. Dude who was inputting used Turkish but Erika deciphered it no problem."

"Break it down for me," Kurtzman said.

Tokaido nodded and worked his keyboard, putting more information on-screen.

"This backs up what Able got from their contact," he said. "I got something that could help the guys. A company in Baltimore. Just like the guy said—the Turkish Spice Company. Based on an industrial estate. It's come up as being a business linked to Polat. Buried deep in layers of shell companies. They tried to hide any connection, but it never really works."

Kurtzman slapped the young tech on the back. "Get this all tidied up. As much detail as you can. Great work, Akira."

Baltimore

THE INDUSTRIAL PARK looked quiet. Of the fifty or so units, about half were empty. The Turkish Spice Company was located in the east section, right in the middle of a double row of mostly empty units.

Blancanales parked the SUV a few rows back and the men of Able Team exited the vehicle. They went in on foot, armed with their handguns, which they kept out of sight in case anyone spotted them.

On the corner of the row they wanted, they paused to make a final weapons check.

"I'll take the rear of the unit," Lyons said. "You two cover the front."

He didn't wait for his partners to comment, but simply moved quickly across the avenue and down to the end of the row to vanish around the far corner.

"Something we said?"

Schwarz shrugged his shoulders. "It's Carl," was all he said.

"Hey, is our timing good or what?"

A medium-size box truck had turned in at the far end of the row.

"If it's the one we want," Schwarz said.

"We'll look pretty stupid if all it's delivering are Turkish pastries," Blancanales said.

Schwarz smiled. "Always time for a snack."

Blancanales felt his sat phone vibrate. He took the call. It was Lyons.

"One guy on watch. He was armed. He's down. Go when you're ready."

"Boss man is way ahead of us," Blancanales said.

So who needed a gun to guard Turkish food? Blancanales thought.

He lowered his cell, meeting Schwarz's questioning glance. He told his partner what Lyons had said.

"Leave him on his own for five minutes," Schwarz said, "and see what happens."

"Can't fault him on the results."

"He's going to make sure we know that."

Blancanales chuckled. "Oh, yes, he will."

They could make out the logo on the side of the truck now.

The Turkish Spice Company.

"Let's hope it's hauling hardware," Schwarz said.

The box truck slowed in front of one of the units. When Blancanales looked up above the shutter door he wasn't surprised to see the unit logo on a long board overhead. It was the same as the one on the truck.

A harmless foodstuff store like many others on similar sites.

Blancanales turned to check their backs again, while Schwarz watched the truck maneuver into position before reversing through the open door. As the truck slid into the unit a figure emerged from where he had been covered by the vehicle, following it inside. He stayed close to the wall, checking up and down the avenue.

What caught Schwarz's attention was the squat SMG the guy was carrying close to his side. He caught sight of it as the gunman vanished inside.

Blancanales, standing back to cover their rear, asked, "What can you see now?"

"Truck moving inside the unit. Watcher following it in. Guy's armed. Looks like an HK MP7."

"They don't skimp on armaments, then."

The MP7 was a Heckler & Koch PDW, a compact but deadly piece of weaponry. It fired a unique HK 4.6 mm bullet at 950 rpm at either semi- or full-auto.

"Looks like we arrived at the right time," Schwarz said. "Snacks and armed guys?"

Blancanales said, "I've heard of protecting your recipe, but this is taking it too far."

The Able Team partners rechecked their Beretta 92FS pistols. The 9 mm autoweapons held 15 rounds in the magazines. They had both used the solid, dependable weapons for a long time. Schwarz and Blancanales each carried extra mags in a side pouch on their belts. With the weapons set, the two men moved quickly out from cover and closed in on the raised shutter door. As they neared it they heard the rattle as the door began to close.

Blancanales sent Lyons a quick heads-up. "Going in now."

They cleared the remaining distance to the unit.

"I'll take left," Schwarz said.

Blancanales nodded, moving to cover the right-hand side.

They ducked under the descending shutter door and were inside before the door rattled to a stop.

Blancanales made first contact as he came into view around the side of the truck and the guy who had been standing outside faced him. Blancanales's appearance had taken the man by surprise, but he brought up his MP7 quickly. The 92FS, double handed in Blancanales's grip, was already centered on the thug. The Beretta snapped out a tight trio of shots, the 9 mm slugs punching into the guy's chest. He went down without a sound, his weapon unfired.

Schwarz heard his partner's shots on his side of the vehicle and saw rapid movement farther inside the unit as others reacted. He increased his pace and as he reached the rear corner of the truck he saw a couple of armed figures ahead of him. One was saying something to his partner, jerking a hand in the direction of the shots. The second guy turned and concentrated his attention on Blancanales's side of the truck. Schwarz eased around the corner of the truck, bringing up his Beretta and putting two shots into the guy before he could confront Blancanales. Both 9 mm slugs hit the guy in the side of his skull, spinning him around and dropping him to the concrete floor of the unit. As he fell he sprayed a burst of red from the holes in his head.

The moment he fired, Schwarz dropped to a crouch. Out the corner of his eye he had seen the third man turn in his direction. The guy's MP7 crackled with autofire, sending a stream of HK 4.6 mm slugs Schwarz's way. The slugs hammered at the aluminum bodywork of the truck over Schwarz's head, tearing ragged holes in the metal and showering the Able Team hotshot with aluminum fragments.

And at that moment Blancanales stepped into view from the other corner of the truck, his Beretta raised. He tracked his target and fired, placing a triple burst into the third man. The guy fell back, his right arm flying loose in a reflex action, spraying a random burst of autofire that blew ragged holes in the unit's metal roof panels.

Schwarz spun around as he picked up on a sound coming from the truck cab. As he turned he saw the passenger door swing open.

The driver.

The guy had still been in the cab as the Able Team pair had breached the unit. In their need to engage the armed crew they had missed him.

The stocky figure, wielding a large handgun, leaned out the door and took a rapid shot at Schwarz. He felt the slug tug at his sleeve and burn across his upper arm. Schwarz leveled the Beretta and returned fire, burning off the rest of his magazine. Some slugs struck the driver's thick torso, others slammed into the cab. Schwarz heard the driver gasp under the impact of the 9 mm slugs tearing into him. He lost his coordination and tumbled forward from the cab. He hit the floor in a loose sprawl.

"Hey, you okay?" Blancanales said as he moved to stand behind Schwarz.

"We're getting sloppy," Schwarz said. "We missed the driver?"

Blancanales glanced at the bloodied corpse. "Only the first time around," he said.

They walked to the rear of the truck and unlatched the doors, swinging them wide.

Lyons appeared from the rear of the unit, still holding his Python. He barely glanced at the bodies on the floor. His attention was on the exposed contents of the truck's load.

The interior was stacked with crates and boxes. Blancanales climbed into the truck and freed the catches on the closest box. He raised the lid and reached inside to lift out an object they were both able to recognize immediately. Brand-new HK MP7s. The smaller boxes held stacks of magazines already loaded with 4.6 mm cartridges.

"These guys were ready for any contingency," Blancanales said.

"Protection," Schwarz said. "Running interference for the main group."

"Not this time," Lyons said. He called Stony Man and relayed the news. "We need local cops to move in and take charge here," he told Price. "The sooner they move this consignment of weapons to a safe place, the sooner I'll breathe easier."

"I'll take care of it. You guys okay?"

Schwarz rubbed his bullet-creased arm.

"Hermann got a little scratch," Lyons said, "but it's nothing serious."

"Hey, I'll decide that," Schwarz said.

"He doesn't sound too traumatized," Brognola said, picking up Schwarz's comment as he came on the line with Price. "I'll give the story to the local LEOs that you guys just busted a bunch of illegal gun runners," Brognola advised. "We don't say anything about the possible nuke threat until we have more on it. Word gets out and we'll have a citywide panic."

"Do that."

"Tell the walking wounded to take it easy."

Lyons was still smiling when he put his phone away.

"Hal telling you jokes now?" Schwarz said.

"He says you should go lie down in a darkened room with a cup of herbal tea."

"Nice he can joke about it," Schwarz said.

While they waited for Baltimore PD to arrive, Able Team searched the unit. The place was stacked with crates of vegetables. Nothing else.

Lyons pushed a pile of empty crates out of his way with a growl of frustration.

"You expecting to find a nuke sitting in there with a notice saying Bomb?" Blancanales quipped.

"Carl likes things tidied up with a big pink bow," Schwarz said.

"Better than a damn mushroom cloud," Lyons said.

Schwarz and Blancanales couldn't disagree with that.

The sound of sirens finally reached them. Raising the shutter door, the three men of Able Team walked out to meet the police, holding their ID badges out in front of them.

Uniformed cops scrambled from the cars and spread around the area. Some went inside to inspect the damage.

"Regular slaughterhouse in there," a uniformed sergeant said after he had been inside.

"Lots of guns, too," Blancanales noted.

"We'll need to call in ATF," the sergeant said. "Weapons are their specialty." He looked Able Team over. "Don't recognize any of you guys. Not local?"

"We tend to move around a great deal," Blancanales said.

"Hope you don't leave bodies everywhere you go."

"Only when they don't play nice," Schwarz said.

"Guys like those in there usually don't if they get caught."

Lyons handed the officer a card. The number on it would put him through to the Farm, though he wouldn't know that, and Price would field any questions needed to clarify the situation.

One of the other cops appeared. "We checked the bodies," he said. "No survivors, Sarge. I called in the wagon to pick them up."

"We need to roll," Lyons said. "We're still on assignment."

"Sounds like you guys are busy."

"You don't know the half," Schwarz said.

"Yeah," Blancanales said. "Right now we have to catch a boat."

The sergeant was still puzzling over that one when Able Team drove off.

CHAPTER THIRTEEN

Turkey

The launch they had rented was a sleek wood-and-aluminum craft propelled by a covered motor that pushed out a great deal of power. McCarter was at the helm. Berna Kartal and the others were gathered in the stern. The Istanbul cityscape lay well behind. Along this stretch of the channel were wide-spaced residences, large house that stood on the shore, each with its own docking jetty for the many expensive boats populating the water.

"Millionaires' Row," Encizo said.

Kartal nodded.

"There is Polat's house," she said, pointing to a stylish, sprawling two-story structure. Moored at the jetty was the sleek, large cruiser Polat owned.

"That guy," James said, "has money. Just take a look at that boat."

"Yes, he has," Kartal said. "The Polat fortune runs into the billions."

"So why devote himself to this Özgürlük group?" James queried. "Why doesn't he just enjoy his wealth?"

"I suppose," Kartal said, "he has found his purpose in life. For some people that is more important than a pocketful of money."

"Polat has ideals that force him to act," Encizo said.

"I'd hazard a guess he'd hand over his fortune to take his country along what he believes is the right road."

"But it should not be at the loss of human life the way he is threatening," Kartal noted.

"That's where he has it wrong," McCarter said. "Way too wrong."

"Özgürlük proved how they want to run with this thing," James said. "They had no concerns about who got hurt during that hospital attack last night. Our witness. A nurse and two cops. We shouldn't forget that."

"We won't," McCarter said.

The powerboat slid easily through the water under McCarter's steady hand. He kept the boat moving slowly as they began to approach.

"We have movement," James said. "Coming out of the house to the jetty."

Kartal raised the binoculars she was holding to take a look at the distant figures.

"Polat. Kaplan. General Marangol. All our principal players."

"What about the fourth guy?" Encizo said.

It took Kartal a moment to focus in on the figure standing a little apart from the others. She took a longer look, then nodded to herself.

"Shukla. Darshan Shukla. Government minister known to have views that do not follow the party line. Very pro–independent Turkey."

"He a buddy of Polat's?" Encizo asked.

"Yes. Why?"

Encizo nodded toward the two men. "That conversation they're having doesn't seem too friendly."

Polat and Shukla were in animated conversation. Shukla was gesturing to emphasize his words. He turned abruptly and walked away, along the jetty and around the drive to where a car was parked. He climbed in and was driven away.

"I wonder what that was about," James said. "Whatever those guys were saying, it wasn't going well."

They continued watching as the three men on the jetty climbed aboard the motor cruiser. One of the crew cast off and the vessel eased away from the jetty and out into the channel.

"Pity we can't hear what they're discussing," McCarter said. He let their powerboat drift along slightly behind Polat's cruiser. "Clever. A floating conference venue. Private. No one to overhear what they're saying."

They moved along the channel, Polat's cruiser cutting the water smoothly.

Encizo said, "Be interesting to find out what Polat and that Shukla guy were arguing about."

"Yes, it would," Kartal admitted. "On such a peaceful day it's hard to imagine the things Polat and his organization are planning."

She didn't realize at that moment how quickly things could change.

SADIK YIGIT LISTENED to the voice on the phone, not making any comment until the speaker finished. He understood his place within the organization and respected the position of Hakan Kaplan. Kaplan was an important man in Özgürlük, second in command under Kadir Polat. As a follower of Polat's policies, Yigit was ready and able to carry out whatever orders he was given. He listened to Kaplan's directives, then realized the man had stopped talking.

"Sadik? Are you still there?"

"Yes."

"Have you understood my instructions?"

"Of course."

"Carry them out. And do not waste time. I want those damned Americans dead."

Yigit turned and indicated to his crews they had been called into action. As they rushed out to the helicopter pad, the pilots were well ahead of them, scrambling into the cockpits to commence the startup procedure. The rest of the crew climbed into a pair of waiting choppers and secured their belts, then began to check their weapons.

Yigit sat in the seat next to the pilot of his machine. He slipped on the headset.

"Our information tells us these Americans have been seen in the vicinity of Mr. Polat's motor cruiser in the channel. The woman, Kartal, is with them. Get us there so we can deal with them." Yigit then spoke to the pilot of the second helicopter. "You make a wide sweep. Come in from the other side, over the bridge."

The pilots worked the controls, lifting the helicopters off the pad and swinging around to cut across the harbor.

Yigit twisted in his seat to speak to his companion.

"Is the machine gun prepared?"

"Yes," the man said.

"Go to it and be ready."

The guy swung the 7.62 mm machine gun on the pintle mechanism that would allow it to be operated via the side hatch when it was opened.

"We can offer them a real Turkish welcome," Yigit said.

"One they would not forget if they were left alive," the man at the machine gun said.

"Let's make sure they don't survive," Yigit said.

The pilot angled the helicopter across the water. Ahead, the gleaming length of Polat's motor cruiser was moving across the channel, turning away from the motor launch.

"There," Yigit said, "is the powerboat. That's our target."

"I see it," the pilot said.

"Let's get the door open and that machine gun set. We can blow that damned thing out of the water."

Behind him, Yigit felt the pull of the air as the side hatch was opened. He turned to see the machine gun being swung out.

He watched the second helicopter make a long sweep over the bridge, then turn around and make its run.

"We will let Badir make the first attack," he said. He spoke to the other helicopter pilot. "You make first run. Now."

"Ever get that feeling you're being followed?" James asked. His tone was serious enough to alert his teammates.

"What?" Encizo said.

"I said…"

"I know what you said. We're on the water. Not an easy place to tail someone."

"Who mentioned water?" James jerked his thumb over his shoulder in the direction of the sky.

A helicopter was coming at them. It was approaching quickly, the outline of the bridge behind it.

McCarter checked and muttered something when he saw the outline of the aircraft James had spotted.

"Told you," James said.

"Doesn't mean it's following us," Encizo said, though he didn't sound too convinced himself.

As the words left his mouth, the chopper dropped and skimmed the water no more than fifteen feet above the surface. The aircraft was dark, with no markings. The pilot knew his business as he maneuvered the helicopter to follow the powerboat's course.

Polat's cruiser had dropped away.

Kartal had spotted an elongated object emerge from an open hatch; it only took her a few seconds to realize it was a rigged 7.62 mm machine gun.

"I believe we could be in trouble," she said.

"I don't believe this…" James said under his breath, then louder to McCarter, "Evasive maneuvers, boss, and don't waste time…"

The guy behind the machine gun pulled his trigger and sent a stream of slugs in their direction.

The heavy chatter of the machine gun punctuated James's warning. The burst hit the water in the power-boat's wake, kicking up spouts that crept closer.

"Bloody hell," McCarter swore.

"Okay, let me have some room," Encizo said.

He slid off the jacket he was wearing, exposing a U.S. Survival AR-7 rifle. It was hanging from his shoulder in a harness rig. Encizo pulled off the stock base and slid out the components. Kartal, who had never seen an AR-7 before, watched as the Cuban locked on the receiver, then attached the barrel and screwed it in place. Encizo's model had a composite barrel with a rifled steel liner.

"How long have you been hauling that around?" James asked.

"Ever since that damn truck rammed us," the Cuban admitted. "Had it in my carryall, so I brought it with me before we boarded the *Titanic* here."

"Great," James said. "The *Titanic* sank."

"You're right," Encizo said, grinning as he worked the mechanism to feed the first load from the 8-round magazine. The rifle would automatically feed each round into the breech with its semiauto function.

"What have you got in the magazine?" James said.

"CCI Velocitor hollow points," Encizo said. The .22-caliber bullets were 40-grain, copper-plated lead.

"Can he do this?" Kartal said.

McCarter nodded. "He's as good as any with a rifle."

The chopper had completed its turn and was coming at them again.

James said, "Hey, we've got another coming from the other direction."

"One at a time," Encizo said. "One at a time."

He was concentrating on the configuration of the approaching helicopter, the AR-7 at his shoulder. The motion of the powerboat didn't help as it swept across the water. Encizo braced himself and let the aircraft swoop in. He was judging when the guy behind the machine gun might ask the pilot to give him a broadside approach; it might allow the machine gunner a better chance, but it would also increase the target area for Encizo. The AR-7 was a limited-range weapon, so the closer he could get to his target, the better.

The helicopter turned sideways.

The machine gunner leaned over his weapon, ready to pull his trigger.

Encizo set his AR-7, held the weapon steady and eased back on the trigger.

The rifle cracked and the .22 slug cleared the muzzle. It struck the side-mounted ammo canister. The machine gun was whipped to the side as the box was torn open by the slug. The box fed the ammo belt and the impact of Encizo's slug split the case open, spilling the linked belt onto the deck.

As the helicopter slid by, Encizo kept firing, the AR-7 pumping the rest of the magazine load into the aircraft fuselage. The projectiles ripped through the aluminum panels over the power plant. Before the bird flew out of range, Encizo had laid his entire magazine into it. As it curved away, streamers of smoke began to show.

"If he doesn't pull up," Encizo said, "he'll hit the bridge."

The chopper seemed incapable of gaining height. It was only yards from the bridge structure when, without warning, it was enveloped in a ball of flame and whirling smoke. The helicopter, engulfed, blew apart and the flaming mass dropped until it struck the water with a heavy splash. Steam mingled with the flame and smoke, mini waves radiating out from where the aircraft had sunk.

"Didn't expect that," Encizo admitted.

"That was spectacular," James said. "Great shooting, but I think we should haul ass because that other damn chopper is coming our way like a bat out of hell."

McCarter spun the wheel, taking the powerboat in a wide arc that caught the second chopper pilot off guard. The helicopter overshot, then began its own turn.

"Be a good idea to get us off the water," James said. "We're not going to outrun him for long."

"I don't have any more shots in this thing," Encizo said, holding up the rifle.

He pulled his Beretta. It was more of a symbolic gesture than a tactical one. Bringing down a high-powered helicopter with a 9 mm handgun was no easy option, but the weight of the handgun made the Cuban feel better.

Kartal observed, "Coming round again."

McCarter took a couple of seconds to check for himself.

"Let me know when he's in position," he said.

The Briton increased the powerboat's speed, his eye flicking to the side where he could see the shoreline.

McCarter laid a free hand on the throttle lever, ready to boost the power. He wasn't going to have much to play with, but he had no intention of ending up in the murky water of the Bosporus.

"Do it!" James yelled. "Now!"

McCarter hauled the wheel around, slamming the throttle wide-open. The powerboat stood on its stern, churning the water to a white foam as it curved around and headed for the shore. Enzico, Kartal and James were forced to take hold of the side rails as the boat canted to one side.

The helicopter made its own turn, falling behind as the powerboat sped off. The second the aircraft was on line again the 7.62 mm machine gun fired. The line of water spouts tracked in. A section of the stern shattered as high-caliber shells ripped into the wood and fiberglass, showering the men of Phoenix Force with fragments. The helicopter flew over the boat, beginning another turn around.

James flinched as a sharp splinter burned across his left hand.

"Now I'm pissed," he said.

Kartal, her Glock clutched in her hand, said, "He's coming back."

McCarter worked the wheel and took a zigzag course across the choppy water. Cold spray swept across the boat, soaking their clothing.

The helicopter dropped to a level that brought it dangerously close to the surface, the downdraft from the rotors whipping up more spray.

"What's he trying to do—drown us?" Enzico shouted.

The chatter of machine gun fire reached them again. The 7.62 mm slugs hacked at the water but fell well short of the bouncing boat.

McCarter spun the craft back and forth, aware of their vulnerable position but unable to shake off the pursuing chopper.

"We are closer to shore now," Kartal said. "If we get off the water we would have a better chance for cover."

"We couldn't be in any worse a position than we are out here," James said.

McCarter felt the shadow of the helicopter as it overshot them again. He couldn't argue against that, so he spun the wheel and directed the boat at the shoreline.

McCarter brought the boat to a jarring stop as it grounded against the shore, the deck canting under their feet as the craft settled.

"Let's get the hell out of here," the Briton said.

They scrambled out of the powerboat, splashing the last couple of feet through the water, and headed for cover.

"This way," Kartal directed, pointing to a jumble of tumbledown huts and overturned boats. Their choice had brought them to an abandoned boatyard cluttered with rotting hulls and maritime debris.

They pounded their way over, aware of the helicopter's beat as the pilot brought it around.

"Persistent bugger," McCarter quipped.

He threw himself down and rested his arms on the upturned curve of a splintered hull, watching the helicopter line itself up. The others joined him.

"Even four of us can't shoot down a chopper," James said.

The helicopter came at them like a bat out of hell, the beat of its rotors loud and growing louder with each second. The 7.62 mm machine gun opened up again, laying down a line of shells as it came. The thump of the shells kicked up dirt and stones.

"Go," McCarter said.

He kicked himself away from the boat, Encizo, James and Kartal following as the barrage hit the hull, exploding rotten wood into the air. The shooter in the chopper had committed himself to the line of fire and was unable to alter it as the helicopter flew over the target area.

"Split up," McCarter said. "Come in from the sides."

Encizo and James separated, leaving McCarter and Kartal together. They all turned to face the helicopter as it maneuvered and made a 360-degree turn. The Phoenix commander eyed the dark bulk of the chopper as the pilot hesitated, unsure which man to go for first.

Ignoring the personal risk, McCarter swung up the Browning and snap aimed, firing off a trio of 9 mm slugs. Two hit the canopy, starring the Perspex shield and making the pilot jerk back on the stick. The chopper lurched sideways. As it moved, the shooter opened up with the machine gun, but his line of sight had vanished as the aircraft yawed. The shells impacted the ground yards away from McCarter and Kartal.

Picking up on the opening McCarter had made, Encizo, James and Kartal triggered their own handguns, peppering the helicopter from both sides. They concentrated on the engine compartment, firing off their entire magazines. The 9 mm fusillade punched holes in the canopies. The smooth beat of the helicopter's engine began to falter. Smoke from leaking oil began to issue from the louvers.

Using the distraction, McCarter ducked low and ran beneath the chopper, reloading as he moved, emerging at the rear. He stepped back and burned off the Browning's clip. His target was the tail rotor and the concentrated fire from the 9 mm took its toll, the slugs chewing at the blades. The helicopter began to veer off course, the tail swinging around, and when the startled pilot tried to gain height the aircraft began to spin out of control.

The rest of team completed swift magazine changes and then repositioned themselves as the stricken chopper sank to the ground, the pilot struggling to maintain stability.

Kartal found she was facing the open hatch and the machine gun. The shooter was hauling the bulk of the weapon around, leaning forward to pick up on James's lean figure. The Turkish agent found her spot and leveled the Glock, working the trigger, and laid a half dozen shots into the head and shoulders of the shooter. Blood flew and the gunner let out a yell, falling back from his position behind the machine gun.

IN THE CABIN, Yigit, his own weapon in his hand, was shaking the pilot's shoulder.

"Take us out of here," he said.

"It's no use," the pilot said.

"Now!" Yigit ordered, jamming the muzzle of his pistol against the pilot's throat. "Fly this accursed machine."

"We have no power. *Understand?* We are going down."

The helicopter lost power and dropped, hitting the ground with a heavy crash.

"I CANNOT BELIEVE we just did that," Kartal said.

"Well, we did," McCarter said as if it was an everyday happening.

The cabin door was flung open, the man in the co-pilot's seat scrambling out. He brought his pistol to bear as he filled the opening.

A wild yell erupted as he angled the pistol at the armed figures.

His move proved the well used phrase that resistance is futile.

He was still yelling when James and Encizo opened fire. His body flopped forward, sliding out of the cabin door. He was dead before he hit the ground.

Kartal and McCarter closed in on the chopper, weapons aimed at the pilot. He stared at them through the bullet-pocked canopy, indecision on his face. Common sense prevailed and he raised his hands. McCarter gestured with his Browning and the pilot reluctantly unbuckled and released his door, climbing out. Kartal spun him around and checked for weapons. She found a shoulder-holstered pistol.

"You speak English?" McCarter asked. The man nodded. "Then understand me, chum. You are deep in the brown stuff. Right now I'm pissed enough to shoot you and walk away. Believe me, I have that idea."

The pilot glanced at Encizo and James. Kartal was watching him closely, her face taut with repressed anger. They all still held their weapons. He had been witness to their ability and willingness to use them, and despite being committed to his cause, he saw no reason to sacrifice himself uselessly.

"I can tell you nothing," he said, "because I know nothing more than what has happened today."

"Odd how you guys always have memory lapses when you get caught," James said. He gestured with his pistol. "Let me shoot out his kneecaps. Might bring his memory back."

"Pretty messy," McCarter said.

"And painful," Encizo added.

James said, "It means we'll have to drag him along with us when he can't walk."

"Your choice," McCarter said to the pilot. "Tell us something useful and maybe we'll just hurt you a little."

"Let me do the knees," James said. "Been a while since I did that."

Kartal listened to the banter, not certain whether or not to believe James's threats. She erred on the side of caution before condemning what she heard. She had seen her new partners in action, and despite the directness of their combat effectiveness, she felt doubt that they would ever indulge in any kind of deliberate physical torture.

The feeling was confirmed when McCarter, turning away from James and the prisoner, gave her a quick grin.

James made sure the pilot could see the Beretta in his hand as he moved across his field of vision.

"You can shoot me," the pilot said. "I am just a pilot. I take Mr. Polat and his friends wherever he wants."

"Yeah," James said. "In a helicopter armed with a machine gun."

"For his protection. He is a wealthy man. Very powerful. And he has enemies."

McCarter said, "The way he's treated us today, he's got some more to add to his list."

Kartal had climbed inside the cabin. Now she came out holding a flight chart.

"These are places you have taken Polat? The ones penciled in?"

"Yes."

The chart bore a number of marked-up sections. McCarter leaned across. He pointed a finger. "This an island?"

The pilot nodded. "It belongs to the family. Has for generations."

"Anything interesting there?"

The pilot became reluctant to say any more. McCarter noted his attitude.

"I still have my gun out," James said.

"There are some of the Özgürlük people on the island. They have been there from time to time. I do not know what they are doing there."

"Interesting," Encizo said.

McCarter left the pilot under the watchful eye of the Cuban Phoenix warrior while he took the others aside.

"Berna, can you arrange to have our cooperative flyboy locked up? Somewhere he can't cause us any problems?"

Kartal nodded. "I will have him detained indefinitely. It will be no problem. Did you find what he had to say helpful?"

"Interesting enough for a visit later to Polat Island. We have no idea how or where this Özgürlük strike is going to happen. Right now we need to go after anything that might point us in the right direction," McCarter said. "But first we should go have a little chat with Minister Shukla. See if he's involved."

CHAPTER FOURTEEN

Kadir Polat's cruiser

"This is not good," Polat said.

He had just received a call informing him of the failure of the helicopter to stop the American force. The Americans had brought the helicopter down, shot and killed Sadik Yigit. The chopper pilot had been handed over to the local police.

Hakan Kaplan said, "Now they have allied themselves to the NIO they will have access to more information."

"Then we must make full use of our contact there," Polat noted. "What's the point of a man on the inside if we don't use him?"

"It does not help," Kaplan pointed out, "that there is an NIO agent assigned to help these men."

From the other side of the cruiser's expensively appointed lounge, General Demir Marangol cleared his throat. "If this NIO officer is causing us problems, why not simply have her taken care of?"

"As easily as that?" Polat said. "All that would do is attract attention. Do not forget instructions came from high up in the government ordering the NIO to assist these Americans."

Marangol found that amusing. "This coming from someone willing to detonate a nuclear device alongside an American base."

"If we draw too much attention our plans may be compromised," Polat said. "Until the American arrangements have been completed, we must try and stay in the shadows."

Kaplan stared out the windows at the dark-clouded sky. "Well, there seem to be plenty of those at the moment."

Polat pressed a bell at the side of his seat, summoning a steward dressed in pristine white.

"Fresh coffee," he said. "And make it strong."

He took a cigar from a sandalwood box on the side table and prepared it, lighting it with a heavy onyx lighter. He sat back in the comfortable leather lounge chair and savored the rich aroma of the cigar.

Marangol watched him, smiling gently. "For someone embroiled in such a proposed campaign you appear extremely relaxed, Kadir."

"We have set things in motion," he said. "At this juncture we cannot reverse that, so why not take a moment to indulge ourselves."

"From the day we embarked on this, we accepted the possibility of problems," Kaplan said. "All we can do now is go forward."

Marangol waited until the fresh coffee arrived, took a cup and said, "I have heard from three of my people. Military units under their command will be moved into place as soon as I send each of them a coded message."

"Good," Kaplan said.

Polat glanced at Marangol. "What about the fourth?"

"I was coming to that. Major Uzun is wavering. The man cannot make a decision."

"His area of responsibility would be quite crucial," Kaplan said. "His missile group will be extremely important in case we need backup."

"You do not have to remind me," Marangol returned as he sat upright. "We agreed at the start that any military involvement must be absolute. It would be counter-productive if we had a breakdown in the structure."

Polat said, "Is it not possible to have Uzun replaced? Even at this late stage. Have someone on our side who could take command of the missile group?"

Marangol considered this. "There is another officer. Major Ahmet Yilmaz. Younger than Uzun but extremely radical. He doesn't like the involvement of the Americans in Turkish military affairs. I have been observing him for some time and I am certain he would step into the position if it was offered."

"Then offer it," Polat said.

Marangol inclined his head. "And Uzun? If he is suddenly removed from his responsibilities, he would suspect something was wrong. He would speak up."

Kaplan said, "Make his removal a permanent one. Accidents happen all the time."

Marangol smiled. "I'm sure we could arrange something."

"Can something be done quickly?"

"Leave that with me," Marangol said.

From the attaché case sitting on the thick carpet at his side he took out a cell phone. It was unused, still in a plastic wrapper. Marangol removed the wrapping and powered up the phone.

"Is that safe?" Polat said.

The general nodded. "What they call a burn phone," he advised. "Unregistered and untraceable." He tapped in a number, waited, and then spoke when his call was answered. "The matter we discussed yesterday. It appears our concerns were correct. It has been decided his usefulness has come to an end…Exactly. An unfortunate accident that will not arouse any suspicions…No, if you succeed I will know…Good."

Marangol ended the call. He opened the back of the phone, removed the SIM card and snapped it between strong fingers. The others watched as he stood, crossed to one of the windows, slid it open and tossed the broken card into the choppy water. Marangol closed the window and shook off the drops of spray from his sleeve. He poured himself a fresh cup of coffee and sat again.

"What call?" he said with a faint smile on his lips.

THEY HAD ALTERED COURSE, deciding to return to the jetty where Polat and Kaplan were left alone in the cabin, Marangol having departed to return to his military duties. Polat sensed his friend was troubled and as they had always been able to do many times before, he asked Kaplan what was wrong.

"Binice and Terzel—the two I had backed," Kaplan said. "I found out they have been stealing from us. From Özgürlük. Large amounts, as it turned out."

Polat looked shocked. "I thought they were truly with us."

"They had us all fooled. They were nothing more than a pair of conmen. The worst thing is they conned me. I have always believed I was smart enough to see through something like that. The harder part to accept was the fact they had an accomplice. It was Aziz Makar. He was in league with them. They managed to divert large amounts of cash and place it in secret accounts."

Polat paced the cabin. "Why would they do such a thing?"

"Because they were not truly part of Özgürlük," Kaplan said. "They were nothing but petty thieves who joined with a separate agenda."

"This cannot be allowed to go unpunished. An example must be made to show others what will happen if they betray us."

"It has already been done," Kaplan said. "It was my mistake, so I have corrected it, Kadir. The matter is settled. By trusting them I allowed Özgürlük to be damaged…"

Polat said, "I wont hear anything like that, Hakan. Your loyalty to Özgürlük and to me is never in question. Now, tell me how you repaid these traitors."

Kaplan explained what had happened to Binice and Terzel. As he explained he saw Polat give a ghost of a smile, the first since the death of Amal.

"Quite inspired," he said. "Considering our nuclear plan, a nice touch. Let others hear about this and it will dissuade any other incidents."

"Exactly what I thought."

"Are they dead?"

"Yes. Given a merciful bullet by Kumad. I let them suffer first."

"Nothing can be sweeter than revenge against transgressors. The old ways still have their uses," Polat said. "And our disloyal banker?"

"A bullet to the head."

"What he deserved for breaking our trust."

"Unfortunately there is a negative side to all this. Kumad was intercepted in Makar's office and killed."

"Do we know by whom?"

"I suspect by someone we have already been made aware of."

"The Americans again?"

"Our information from London suggests that."

"Three dead and a possible connection to us. Not the best result we could have expected."

"From what I have been told, the Americans were sent to London to look into our presence there."

"And they walked right into our business. Unfortunate how an incident so far away could come back to us."

"I had instructed Kumad to collect Makar's laptop and return it," Kaplan said. "With his death, that has not happened."

"Damn," Polat said. "He kept his accounts and contact details on that machine. If it has fallen into the hands of those Americans, or the British police, we could have further problems." He considered the implications. "Nothing we can do about it now. We must move ahead. Refuse to allow these matters to put us off track, Hakan. What is done is done."

CHAPTER FIFTEEN

Major Raf Uzun left his apartment in Istanbul as he always did at 8:00 a.m., climbed into his waiting army 4x4 and sat back in the rear seat. His driver moved quickly into traffic and picked up the road that would take them out of the city toward the military base where Uzun commanded the missile unit. Uzun took out a file of unit paperwork and immersed himself in the standing orders he was handling.

He lost interest in the documents after a few minutes, his mind wandering as he recalled his meeting two days earlier with General Marangol. As much as he admired the high-ranking superior, Uzun was unable to rid himself of the uneasy feeling that meeting had left him with. Marangol had been pressuring Uzun to consider a proposal that would have a far-reaching effect on Turkey's future. Uzun felt he was being primed for something that would go way above his normal duty.

Marangol, in his way, had been trying to get Uzun into his camp, and even though he did not say it in so many words, the implication was there: if the Turkish government refused to stand up for itself instead of leaning toward the Americans' lead, something might have to be done to force that eventuality. Marangol had gone on about returning Turkey to its own destiny and not being dependent on the whims of America and NATO. Somewhere during the discussion, Marangol had made reference to the presence of the Americans at Incirlik, the massive base that made Turkey vulnerable. While America sat safe behind its own borders, the Incirlik base offered itself as a prime target if hostilities broke out. Marangol's last words had left Uzun puzzled a little when the general hinted that the U.S. might find itself not as safe as it believed.

Out of respect for Marangol, Uzun had listened and absorbed what the general was saying. He found himself torn between his loyalty to the military and his love of country. Careful not to out and out reject Marangol's offer for Uzun to join him, Uzun had eventually made his excuses and left, leaving Marangol in silence. He suspected the general had not taken his reluctance well, and on his return home Uzun had gone over the conversation again and again. In the end he had decided that General Marangol had been suggesting some kind of scheme to overthrow the Turkish government. He racked his brain for the correct term and suddenly the phrase was there— a coup d'état. General Marangol intended to defy his military orders and attempt to remove the government.

When Uzun tried to call Marangol the following day he found he was unable to contact the general, and Marangol did not return his calls.

Uzun found that odd and somewhat disturbing. He had always gotten on with Marangol. The general was old-school. A dedicated man. Military to the tips of his polished shoes. As hard and authoritative as he was, Marangol always treated his junior officers with respect. He was courteous to a fault and maintained a thoroughly professional command. His troops were as faithful as any Uzun had known, and he considered himself one of Marangol's chosen officers. Which made it all the more curious that the general seemed to be bypassing him.

The only reason why this was happening, Uzun reasoned, was that he had not immediately allowed himself to be drawn into Marangol's proposed scheme. Uzun had balked at the broad hints the general had been proposing; as much as he was allied to Marangol, he could not envisage any situation where he could agree to what the man was suggesting. It went against everything Uzun believed in. He served his country because he loved it. Turkey was his homeland and he had sworn to protect it. To go against that was something Uzun could not consider.

Marangol had not pressed the point at their last meeting. There had been a trace of disappointment in his tone when he had spoken to Uzun, but they had parted company on a reasonable level. Which had made it all the more confusing when Uzun found himself shunted aside when he tried to contact Marangol later.

The call of duty had concentrated Uzun's thoughts and he found he was focusing on what he had to do once he reached the missile base.

Glancing out the side window, Uzun saw they were out of the city and taking the narrow road that wound through the wooded countryside. The road led high into the surrounding landscape, with steep, timbered slopes on one side and a steep, rocky drop on the other. There was only a wooden fence on the open side of the road. Uzun had traveled this route many times and never once considered it to be anything more than an isolated area, ideal for the location of the missile base deep within the forested hills. Today Uzun felt uneasy. He couldn't work out why, but he wanted the drive to be over quickly so he could be on the base, surrounded by the perimeter fence and in the company of his command.

"Sir," his driver said.

"What is it?"

"There is a vehicle behind us. Moving very fast."

Uzun took a look out of the rear window and saw the large, high-wheeled truck bearing down on them. It was painted in a dull ochre color, the paintwork marked and dirty. It had to have weighed many tons. Heavy-duty metal, with a powerful diesel engine. He could see the smoke belching from the exhaust stack mounted behind the cab. Even as the bulk of the truck appeared in Uzun's field of vision, it accelerated and came up behind them.

"Perhaps he wants to pass," Uzun said and knew the moment he spoke that was not the case.

"Not on this road," his driver said.

Neither man was given the chance to say any more as the solid front of the truck slammed into the SUV. Metal squealed as it buckled. The rear window shattered and showered Uzun with fragments of glass. He felt the rear of the SUV lift off the road. The driver wrestled with the wheel as the SUV swerved to one side. The truck dropped back a little, then surged forward again as the power was poured on. This time when it collided with the SUV the impact buckled the body so much that Uzun felt his seat twist out of shape and he was thrown forward. His upper body slammed into the back of the driver's seat, his face impacting against the headrest. Uzun felt a burst of dull pain as his nose was cracked under the impact. Blood gushed from his nostrils and spilled down over the front of his uniform.

With the brute power of the truck behind it, the SUV was driven against the wood fence edging the road. Such was the force that the fence broke, sending splintered timber spinning down the steep slope. The truck had angled its forward thrust and pushed the SUV to the edge of the road, through the broken fencing, and kept nudging it until the wheels dropped over the edge. The weight of the SUV did the rest as it canted to the side, toppled and went over the edge.

The driver let out a terrified scream as he felt the SUV drop into space. Uzun, still dazed from his contact with the front seat, found himself being thrown around the passenger compartment. The initial fall lasted for some twenty feet before the SUV slammed into the slope. More metal buckled. Window glass shattered. The stricken vehicle began a series of somersaults as it bounced and crashed its way down the long slope. Each time it hit, the damage increased. A wheel broke free and bounced down the slope ahead of the vehicle. Metal debris detached. Halfway down the slope the driver's shattered body was flung from the wreck when the door was torn free. He cartwheeled in a succession of bloody bounces, dead long before he came to a sudden stop against a large, solid chunk of rock.

Major Uzun remained inside the ever more compressed SUV, no longer aware of what was happening. In the descent, his body had been flung against the open section of the torn roof panel and the jagged edge of metal had sliced through his flesh, decapitating him. When the crumpled wreck of the vehicle came to its final rest, the major's body was still trapped inside while his head had come to a rest many yards back up the slope.

The truck responsible for the accident was not found. The moment the SUV went off the road it continued on its way and cut off along a narrow side road. No one had seen the incident, and it was hours before Major Uzun was posted as missing. The wrecked SUV was not located until the following day.

When General Marangol was informed, he expressed his sympathy for the loss of a good officer, then contacted the missile base and informed Major Ahmet

Yilmaz that he was to be promoted to base commander as a replacement for the late Major Uzun.

Later that day Marangol notified Kadir Polat of the unfortunate demise of Uzun. He also informed him that Uzun's military funeral would take place in two days and that they should attend as a mark of respect.

"Kadir, I will join you later and we will discuss things."

A visit to Polat's cruiser would be a welcome change from the daily grind of military affairs, Marangol decided.

CHAPTER SIXTEEN

Polat, Kaplan and Marangol were sitting on the open deck of Polat's vessel. Heat waves shimmered over the restless water of the Sea of Marmara. It offered a peaceful scene far removed from the thoughts of the two men. They had important matters to resolve. On top of the Özgürlük agenda there was now the problem of the Americans.

The timing could not have been worse. Arrangements were under way to transport and place the devices crucial to the operation. Until they were in place, the next stage could not go ahead. Nearly six months of preparation had gone into it. To say nothing of the effort and expense.

"These Americans are proving to be harder to eliminate than I expected," Polat muttered. "What do we do?"

"What we have tried and failed to do. Remove them. It has to be done. Kadir, my friend, I am not denying the situation. But we must try and maintain our cover. If we attack this matter without covering ourselves we might lose everything."

"We seem to be facing a number of problems," Polat said. "All happening one after the other."

"Battles are fought on a number of fronts," Marangol told him. "Units on both sides move forward and back. It is the nature of war."

"I never thought of what we are doing as war," Polat said.

"My dear Kadir, of course we are in a war. A war to save Turkey and force the Americans to retreat."

Polat had to give that one to Marangol. He had not even considered it himself, but now the general had raised the point he could see the parallels.

"We have people who will do this work willingly," Kaplan noted. "We can use the ones who disposed of those agents who were discovered working undercover. I'm sure they would do the same again if we show them enough money."

"True," Polat said. "Those men will do anything for the right price."

"I will contact them. Now, your appointment with Minister Shukla?"

"In a few hours," Polat answered.

"Do you believe he is still with us?" Marangol said. "After his performance on the jetty I am concerned."

Polat smiled; his expression held doubt, and Kaplan, the only one to notice, knew Minister Shukla was wavering.

"He understands our plight, but as always he holds back," Polat admitted. "Shukla has never been one who could commit without a great deal of hesitation."

"What he knows could cause us even more problems. If he decides to speak to the wrong people…"

"He was fine when he was first approached, but he started to question things when he realized the lengths we need to go."

"Then he needs to be made to realize how far we will go."

"If he panics he could go rushing to his friends and give away everything."

Kaplan stood and made his way to the trolley that held an assortment of drinks. He chose one and filled his glass, returning to stand in front of Polat.

"When we decided to make our demands noticed we all committed fully. Kadir, this is not the time to allow one weak link to break the chain."

Polat understood exactly what his friend was hinting at. He knew Kaplan was right. All it took was for one person to speak out. If that happened, they would all be arrested and the long months of effort would be lost.

"What can we do?"

Kaplan took a drink. "Why don't you let me take care of it? Have your meeting. Sound him out. If you are convinced he is still a risk, call me. I'll be waiting. If I hear nothing I will assume you have brought him back into the fold. If you call…finish your meeting and go home." Kaplan drained his glass. "Be prepared to shed a tear when you hear about a popular figure in the government having an accident."

Polat stared out across the water for a while, then said, "I think I need a drink myself."

MINISTER DARSHAN SHUKLA was in his midforties. The short, stocky man with receding and graying hair descended the stone steps outside Kadir Polat's business headquarters. The massive building, in Istanbul's commercial center, was an obvious showpiece for the man's business empire. Polat was wealthy and powerful, and his word carried great weight in Turkey.

It was midafternoon and Shukla had just finished his meeting with Polat. He paused on the last step, adjusting his jacket; he was a fussy man where his clothes were concerned, and he always checked to see he was maintaining his appearance.

He was feeling uncomfortable following the meeting with Polat. There was something about the man that made him nervous. On the surface, Polat was always polite; he never raised his voice, even during an impassioned confrontation, and the meeting today had been confrontational. Polat had once again expressed his views on the need to determine the country's independence from American influence. He wanted the U.S. out of Turkey. He'd stressed the need to display some actual resistance. He'd been clever with his words, but Shukla had read the meaning behind the man's moderate views. If the government refused to listen, then it was down to those with the belief to express their feeling by initiating strong action.

Shukla had eventually backed away from what Polat had inferred. In a moment of stubborn agitation, he had shaken his head and told Polat openly how he felt and that he would never agree. He'd spoken strongly, telling Polat he had been wrong to ever consider the plan. He would not remain within Polat's group.

For his part, Polat had merely nodded in agreement, telling Shukla he was free to withdraw his support. His polite acceptance of Shukla's standing down had almost made Shukla embarrassed, but he had made his decision and would not change his stance. At the end of the meeting, Polat had stood and shaken Shukla's hand as he left.

The harsh words that had followed the previous meeting on Polat's cruiser seemed to have been forgotten. The man had not mentioned the incident and had wished Shukla well at the conclusion to their meeting.

The minister was still troubled, and though the matter appeared closed, he was unable to forget what had been said.

THE MOMENT THE office door closed behind Shukla, Polat picked up his cell and contacted Kaplan, giving him the news.

"What do you think he will do?"

Polat said, "He will sleep on it. Then he will drive to his office in the morning and start to make calls."

"Why not tonight?"

"Shukla does everything by the book. He follows procedure, and procedure will force him to wait until the people he needs to speak to are behind their desks."

"If you are wrong, he could be calling them anytime soon."

"Trust me," Polat said. "Shukla is a creature of habit."

"If he does start to talk, we will really be in trouble."

Polat realized Kaplan was not going to back down on this. "We have to detain him. Preferably while he is still at home and before he talks to anyone."

"I will send in a team to keep him out of the way. Put him out of your mind. When our people have him, he will tell them if he has warned anyone."

CHAPTER SEVENTEEN

"Do you believe Darshan Shukla will speak to us?" Kartal asked.

"I'll answer that when we ask," McCarter said. "It's worth a try. We sound him out. Take it from there."

"He live on his own?" Encizo queried.

"Yes," Kartal said. "He's not married—except, as you would say, to his work."

"I know how that feels," Encizo said.

James nudged the Cuban. "Man, you said that with a straight face."

"Are they always like this?" Kartal commented.

"Unfortunately yes," McCarter said. "It's like being a teacher taking kids on a field trip."

"For a guy who lives on his own, he's got some early visitors," James said. "Two vehicles kind of hidden around the side."

As they drove by a curve that hid them from the house, Kartal eased the SUV to the side of the road and cut the engine. She watched as the Phoenix Force trio checked their weapons. They did this quietly, with no overt show of anything but professionalism. Almost as an afterthought she did the same with her own handgun, then returned it to the holster.

"It's quiet," Encizo observed, and those few words put them all on alert.

"Can it not be quiet without it meaning something may be wrong?" Kartal said.

"In our line of work, usually no," Encizo said.

James opened his door and stepped out, scanning the area.

The rest followed and stood in a loose formation.

"Just stay on top of it," James said. "Watch each other's backs."

"Check com sets," McCarter said.

The compact communication equipment was set and activated.

McCarter and Kartal split from the others at the Briton's signal. They moved into the stand of trees that bordered the property. Encizo and James cut off in the opposite direction, moving up to cover the far perimeter of Shukla's house. When they were in position they would be covering both front and rear of the house.

McCarter led Kartal through the trees. They didn't speak and they moved with caution. When McCarter raised a hand, Kartal froze.

Through the close trunks, McCarter had seen a lone figure standing watch. The guy held a squat SMG in his hands. He moved his head back and forth as he scanned the area around the house. The man hung his weapon from his shoulder, produced a handset from the pocket of his coat and raised it and spoke. There was a slight delay before he received an answer. The guy spoke again, clicked off the handset and dropped it back into his pocket.

Kartal leaned close to McCarter and spoke in a whisper.

"He asked if Shukla has talked yet. He was told no."

McCarter nodded. He put away his Browning and motioned for Kartal to stay. The Briton eased his tall figure through the trees, moving with a quiet grace that brought him up behind the standing sentry. Stretching to his full height, McCarter made his move with a suddenness that startled Kartal.

McCarter's left arm went around the sentry's neck, pulling him close, his right hand flat against the guy's skull. Applying pressure, McCarter shut off the man's air supply and hauled the struggling man back into the trees, keeping up the encircling noose formed by his arm. The sentry struggled, but all that did was use up the little air he had left. McCarter lowered the unconscious man to the ground.

"Berna," McCarter directed, "keep watch."

He stripped away the sentry's SMG and searched the guy's pockets. He located an extra magazine for the SMG. From one of his pockets, McCarter produced plastic ties, which he used to secure his wrists and ankles. Using his lock knife, McCarter cut off a wide strip from the unconscious sentry's shirt and gagged him.

All this was done quickly and smoothly, convincing Kartal that the Americans were more than skilled at what they were doing.

McCarter moved to her side.

"He won't be the only one," he said. "So we stay sharp."

McCarter took out his com set and keyed the alert key. It would activate a vibrating function on the other team's sets.

Encizo answered with a brief, "Hear you."

"One sentry down," McCarter said. "Any contact your end?"

"Only one? We have two down and sleeping."

"I hate a bloody smart arse," McCarter said.

"You'll get over it."

McCarter grinned. "Listen, hotshot, our guy was

speaking to his pals inside the house. It sounds as if they have Shukla and they're not playing nice."

"Understood. We good to go?"

"Let's do it."

McCarter led the way across the short lawn that gave way to a half-circular stone-slabbed frontage. There were three vehicles in sight and they were able to use them as cover, reaching the house without any challenge. There were two large windows on either side of a wooden front door. The door was open a few inches, and as McCarter reached it he heard a voice from inside. Deep and heavy, someone speaking Turkish. The door was jerked open and a heavy guy, suited and armed, appeared.

Brief seconds passed as the guy and McCarter registered each other.

The Briton responded quickly, reversing the Browning and slamming it butt first into the man's forehead. The blow was delivered with all of McCarter's strength and the guy went over backward, blood starting to pour from the deep gash the blow had opened. McCarter followed him down, striking a couple more times, and when the man hit the floor he was unconscious. Plastic ties were quickly placed around his wrists and ankles.

Kartal moved in behind McCarter and fanned out across the hallway.

From behind a partly open door to their left came angry voices.

A man cried out in pain.

"Go," McCarter said.

Striding ahead, he raised his right foot and kicked the door wide, sending it back on its hinges.

Three men were standing over a fourth. The fourth

man, elderly and gray-haired, was tethered to a straight-backed wooden chair. He was stripped to the waist.

The trio, in shirtsleeves, startled by the door crashing open, spun around. The one in the center had a bloody knife in his right hand. He stared at McCarter and company, yelling something in Turkish. He made a threatening gesture with the knife as he stepped forward, and McCarter put a 9 mm slug into him, knocking the man to his knees. The guy dropped the knife and toppled over, blood welling from the ragged throat wound the slug had made.

The reaction was instant and deliberate as the other two men moved to the side, reaching to pull out auto-pistols. The room echoed with the sound of heavy fire from the Phoenix Force commander and Kartal. The Turkish shooters were hit by a solid burst, bodies going into spasms as the combined onslaught of slugs struck home.

Beyond the room, from somewhere at the rear of the house, came the muffled sound of more shots.

McCarter clicked his com set.

"Talk to me."

"Clear," Encizo said. "Coming in."

McCarter saw that Kartal was bending over the bound man.

"Shukla?" he asked.

She nodded. "I must call for medical help. He is badly hurt."

"Go ahead."

Kartal took out her cell and tapped in a number. The call was answered by Cem Asker.

"We have located Shukla at his house outside the city. He has been tortured but he is still alive...Yes, there was opposition. We need medical aid quickly...Yes, sir."

Kartal held out the phone for McCarter. "Agent Asker for you."

McCarter took the cell. "Coyle."

"Are you all safe?"

"Thanks for asking. My people are unhurt. Can't say the same for the ones who had Shukla. They cut him up pretty badly."

"Will he be able to talk to us?" Asker queried.

"Let's hope so, Agent Asker."

Asker sighed in frustration. "Has Kartal spoken to him yet?"

"She'll get her chance," McCarter said.

The Turkish agent muttered something in his own language that McCarter couldn't understand. The tone of Asker's voice suggested he was not happy with the situation. McCarter imagined the agent was frustrated.

"I will send assistance," Asker said finally. "I would like to speak with Agent Kartal again."

McCarter passed the phone back to Kartal. She spoke with Asker and it appeared she was not happy with the way the conversation was going. When she ended the call she snapped the phone shut and thrust it back into her pocket.

"Problems?" McCarter said.

Kartal's face was set. Whatever Asker had said did not sit well. She looked away from McCarter and stared at Shukla as Encizo and James entered the room. James, having opened his med kit, was doing what he could for the man; trying to stop the blood leaking from the knife cuts.

"He wants me to question Shukla and hinted that any extreme force, if needed, should be used."

McCarter could see Kartal was uncomfortable with that. The Phoenix Force warriors, in a combat situation, were as direct and ruthless as any. Torture used on a defenseless prisoner, however, did not come under their brief. The very thought was repugnant to the Briton. He reached out and rested a big hand on Kartal's shoulder.

"Right now you're under my command," he said. "And that sort of thing doesn't happen while I'm in charge. Just forget what Asker said. I'll take any flak when we get back. Okay?"

Kartal nodded. "Thank you."

"Constantine, go and bring our wheels back here. Take Berna with you as backup."

Encizo nodded at McCarter's use of his cover name. He and Berna made their way out of the house.

"What was that all about?" James asked.

"Berna got rattled at her boss telling her to get rough with our prisoner. She didn't like that."

"So you sent her away with Constantine so she could clear her head. Nice one, boss. Can I have some words of comfort next time I get stressed?"

"No, but I can plant my boot on your arse if you don't pull your weight."

James grinned. "See, I'm feeling better already."

"Let's check these blokes. See if they have anything on them that could give us any information."

THEY HAD FOUND a cell phone on one of the men.

As Kartal scrolled through it, she shrugged at most of the messages. Until she came across one that made her pause and read it through a second time.

"That look tells me you might have something," Mc-Carter said.

"Perhaps."

"I'm waiting."

"These are instructions from Hakan Kaplan. If Shukla

doesn't tell them anything helpful, he is to be taken to the island and questioned further."

"That island again. Okay. I think it's time we paid it that visit we were considering. Berna, we're going to need another boat."

CHAPTER EIGHTEEN

"We confiscated this some months ago," Kartal said. "It belonged to a gang of smugglers dealing in narcotics."

"Looks like a dirty fishing boat to me," Encizo quipped.

Kartal smiled. "Exactly what it was," she said. "The gang thought they were being extremely clever. The drugs were dropped by the delivery vessel in plastic containers placed in lobster pots, with a floating marker so the smugglers could see them. They would sail out in the early morning and pick them up."

"Not the most original idea," McCarter said. "Been used before."

"The smugglers were quite successful for a few months, but they didn't count on an undercover agent infiltrating the supply gang. He managed to plant a direction locator in one consignment. We picked up the signal and caught the smugglers in the act. Result—one narcotic gang arrested and drugs recovered. And we inherited one old fishing boat."

"At least it can earn its mooring fees," Hawkins said.

Tied up at the quayside, the boat was no showpiece. The paintwork was bleached and peeling, the smokestack soot-streaked and rusty. A couple of windows in the wheelhouse were missing, while others were cracked and grubby. A pile of mildewed fishing nets lay on the aft deck and it was possible to smell the lingering odor of dead fish.

"Does it run?" Encizo said.

"Yes. It may look to be in a bad way but the engine is in excellent condition."

"Load up, gang, we're going on a sea voyage," McCarter said.

"No need to make it sound like it might be fun," James said. "This could turn out to be a disaster."

It was just getting light. A faint breeze ruffled the water beyond the shoreline.

Kartal smiled. "It will be a smooth crossing," she said. "No rough water today. And why would anyone be concerned about an innocent fishing boat going about its business?"

"It's not the crossing I'm worried about," James said. "It's the reception."

McCarter ignored him as he helped Encizo load their gear onto the boat. They had all dressed in black combat suits and boots for the insertion with a traditional Turkish fishing smock over their clothing. Each of them wore a handgun and had a knife sheathed on their belt. The carryalls they placed on the deck held subguns and ammunition supplied by Kartal from the NIO armory.

Encizo took charge of the engine, going through the startup procedure. When the diesel power plant burst into life, it quickly settled into a throaty, steady pulse.

"Sounds good," Encizo said, taking his place behind the wheel.

Kartal released the mooring lines and as Encizo boosted the power, the fishing boat pulled away from the quay and out into the open water.

Spreading out a navigation chart, Kartal indicated their destination. McCarter studied it with her and noted the navigation coordinates she had penciled in.

He crossed the deck and set the compass mounted on the instrument panel.

"Keep us on that heading," he said to Encizo. "You can stop when we hit land."

"I hope that was metaphorical land," James said.

McCarter shrugged.

"The island is thirty miles north to south," Kartal said. "East to west at its widest point is twelve miles. From where we land, the Polat house is roughly three miles inland. Due west from the coastline."

"Nice distances for a walk," McCarter said.

"Your men, Rankin and Allen, will be leaving London now?" Kartal asked, referring to Manning and Hawkins.

"Any time now," McCarter said.

McCarter had spoken to Stony Man the previous evening, establishing that Manning and Hawkins were departing the UK for a touchdown at Incirlik. Decisions as to their next moves would be made later. McCarter had chosen to go ahead with the infiltration of the island, aware that delay was not something they could safely allow. The time scale relating to the nuclear device was still an unknown and McCarter didn't want to waste it unnecessarily.

The situation they were in presented Phoenix Force with unknowns.

The locations of the nuclear device here in Turkey and on the U.S. mainland.

And the countdown threat.

Was it days away?

Hours?

Even now counting down to zero?

McCarter kept his frustration under wraps. He refused to allow his composure to break and be allowed to show. James, Encizo and Kartal would harbor their own thoughts on the situation. They would be feeling the same: aware of what might be about happen, yet unable to do a thing about it while the scenario unfolded around them. They were putting in their best efforts, hoping to make a breakthrough that might point them in the right direction, and until that happened all they could do was push forward and hope to make that breakthrough.

Their way led them beyond Istanbul, the Sea of Marmara and the Dardanelles Straits, taking them clear of the last piece of land. They were in the Aegean Sea now, on the empty water, with a heat haze misting the air. Out here it was quiet, with only the throb of the boat's engine and the slap of the water against the hull. If it hadn't been for the urgency of their mission they might have been on a pleasure cruise, not heading toward Polat's island and something far removed from anything peaceful.

McCarter sensed someone standing close. It was Kartal.

"I have remembered," she said. "The dead man at the ambush."

"You know who he was?"

"Unfortunately yes. Amal Polat."

"A relative of Kadir's?"

"His younger brother. Around twenty-four if I recall."

"That's not going to make Polat a happy man."

"No. Polat has looked after him since their parents died when both boys were young. Amal grew up in his brother's shadow. He was the wild one of the two. Always getting into trouble. Spending the family money. Girls and cars. Polat tried to calm him down, but nothing really worked."

"If this Amal was the family joker, why did he get involved with Özgürlük? Doesn't seem to fit his profile."

"My guess is he did it to impress his big brother. Amal wanted to be like Kadir. To prove himself. If he could have succeeded, his standing would have grown."

McCarter sighed. "He made a mess of that, didn't he? He should have stayed with the cars and the girls."

"I suppose it's the same for everyone," Kartal intoned. "Life. About making choices. If you don't make them, nothing will ever change."

"Very deep, Agent Kartal," McCarter said, his eyes on the sea ahead as Encizo brought the fishing boat in line with the extreme tip of the eastern coastline.

Kartal had told them the trip would take around two and a half hours. Her calculation was close. She had also advised that Polat's property was on the western side of the island.

As they approached the island from the east, Encizo aimed for a curved stretch of sandy beach protected by a stand of trees in the background. He guided the boat into a wide inlet, taking it as close as he could to the sandy strip. Coming to a stop as the bow pushed into the soft seabed, Encizo cut the engine.

"End of the line," he said.

The Turkish fishing smocks were discarded. SMGs were picked from the carryalls. Magazines checked and loaded. Harness rigs carried additional magazines and sat phones.

Encizo was the first over the side, dragging a mooring line with him. The water barely reached his knees as he moved to the beach. He looped the mooring line around the trunk of a tree close to the water and secured it.

"You want me to put my finger on the bow so you can

tie off tightly?" James quipped as he followed the Cuban to shore.

"Ever thought of becoming a stand-up comedian?" Encizo said.

"Not really."

"Hold that thought."

McCarter and Kartal waded up through the ripple of water. The Briton checked his sat phone display.

"Eyes and ears open," he said. "We don't know what kind of security Özgürlük has here. They might keep watch around their base and figure that's all they need. On the other hand there might be roving patrols. Let's play it cautious until we work it out."

"We're going to look foolish if this turns out to be a holiday camp," James said.

McCarter took the lead, Kartal close on his heels. James came next and Encizo chose to take up the tail end where he could observe their six.

They moved steadily. Not rushing, observing their surroundings. From the beach they walked into untended terrain: trees and thick undergrowth. No defined path. At times they pushed through heavy foliage that hampered their passage, yet the day maintained a constant temperature that was comfortable for walking.

The close-standing trees and rich undergrowth reduced their ability to see too far ahead. No one spoke unless it was necessary; sound would travel in the close confines of the forest.

And sound was what alerted Phoenix Force. The overlapping exchange of voices.

James clicked his fingers to attract McCarter's attention. The Briton halted, turning to acknowledge the signal.

Kartal reached out and touched his arm, pointing.

Through the trees they saw moving figures, the light catching gunmetal.

And then someone opened fire.

Slugs lashed through the undergrowth. Snapped and tore at tree trunks. Slivers of bark were ripped free, showing pale wood. The cathedral silence was shattered by the volleys. Slugs thudded into the timber, the harsh crackle of the autofire sending birds winging into the sky.

Phoenix Force went to ground. McCarter felt Kartal land beside him, her military training having kicked in. An instilled sense of preservation.

Chunks of chipped tree bark fell on them.

"This wasn't advertised in the Come to Turkey holiday brochure," McCarter said.

Kartal managed a weak smile.

"Let's move," McCarter said. "Sooner or later one of those cowboys is going to get lucky."

They stayed low, crawling forward, eyes and ears tuned to any sound or movement.

The initial heavy fire had subsided. It hadn't ended, but the shooters were holding back for want of targets.

Ahead of McCarter a shadowed figure became visible. An armed man moving in a search pattern, his subgun pushing and probing the foliage.

"All right, sunshine," McCarter said.

He rose on his elbows, settled his SMG and fired as the man turned in his direction. The short burst hit the guy in the chest. He fell away with a short grunt of pain and didn't move again.

Behind McCarter's position James opened fire. Someone gave a cry. Return fire went high over Phoenix Force's heads.

"With me," McCarter said.

He pushed to his feet, Kartal on his heels.

James and Encizo were not far behind, each loosing covering fire to the right and left as they raced through the forest.

Shots followed them. Whoever was firing, using automatic weapons, made a lot of noise and expended a great deal of ammunition. Slugs that whipped through the foliage did little except shred leaves and chew at tree bark.

Not, McCarter thought, your trained soldier. More likely Özgürlük's volunteer warriors.

The shooters wasted shots without achieving much damage. The Phoenix Force leader was thankful for the lack of controlled fire.

He could hear the pounding of boots behind him and Kartal.

James and Encizo stayed on the same heading.

The copse of trees abruptly thinned out and they found themselves in a wide clearing with a long ridge that dropped away only feet ahead.

"Bugger," McCarter said.

Kartal was beside him. As James and Encizo cleared the trees, McCarter waved them to one side so they were not bunched together.

Crashing sounds came from the undergrowth behind them. Armed figures emerged from the timber.

James dropped the first man as he raced into view. The man went down in a tangle of arms and legs. The shooter behind him almost tripped over his fallen comrade. If he had, Kartal's burst from her subgun might have missed him. Instead the stream of 9 mm slugs burned into his chest, knocking him off his feet.

The engagement was short and effective from Phoenix Force's perspective. The attacking group came on with little organization and ran into the directed fire from the Americans and Berna Kartal.

Then McCarter spotted a guy with an RPG-7 over his shoulder as he emerged from the trees. The launcher was aimed in Phoenix Force's direction.

Where the hell did that come from? the Briton wondered. He didn't waste too much time on the answer because the way the man was holding the launcher told him it was about to be fired.

An extreme move but one that might have a serious outcome.

"Incoming," McCarter said above the firing.

James and Encizo followed his jerking hand motion and spotted the shooter. They immediately fell back as the man took a final step forward, misstepping as he triggered the Russian-made missile.

Kartal had barely had a chance to register the launch when McCarter reached out and grabbed her around the shoulders, jerking her aside as the rocket burst from the tube, sizzling in their direction. Due to the shooter stumbling, the rocket flew in a downward curve, hitting the ground and burying itself in the soil.

There was no time for any kind of finesse. McCarter put everything he had into hauling the young woman out of the path of the missile. When it detonated, most of the blast was muffled by the earth, yet there was enough force from the explosion to physically hurl McCarter and Kartal over the edge of the drop-off. As they bounced and slithered, unable to check themselves, McCarter and Kartal tumbled blindly down the steep slope, tearing through tangled undergrowth and thick grasses.

McCarter registered the din of the explosion behind him and felt some of the heat wash.

He had no more time to worry about that. He was

making a grab for Kartal to halt her downward plunge. He caught hold of her shirt and tried to pull her close as they tumbled. The fall seemed to go on for a long time.

It ended abruptly when McCarter and Kartal were brought to a sudden, jarring stop as they reached the bottom.

CHAPTER NINETEEN

Everything moved so fast. James and Encizo saw the guy wielding the RPG-7. They realized it was turned to McCarter and Kartal and knew they were too late to stop the guy firing it off. The misdirected rocket swept across the area and detonated in the earth close to where McCarter and Kartal had been standing. The burst of fire and smoke blocked the view of McCarter and Kartal.

The RPG-7 shooter dropped the launcher and was shouting to his companions to join him. He dragged a handgun out and turned toward James and Encizo.

Down on one knee, ignoring the buzz of distortion in his ears from the blast, James tracked his subgun to the guy, delivering 9 mm slugs that put him down.

Encizo had seen the two figures coming up behind and backed James with his own weapon. The subgun in the Cuban's hands crackled sharply, laying down a stream of slugs that dropped the pair in a moment. The Cuban laid down another long burst that raked the foliage and held back any further rush.

"Let's get the hell away from here," James said, and he and Encizo turned and cleared the area.

"You see them go over?" Encizo said. "The blast pushed them off the ridge. They're down there. We need to find them."

James realized McCarter and Kartal were somewhere below, hopefully unhurt, but on their own for the time being until James and Encizo could work their way around to the base of the steep drop.

"First we need to lose these assholes," he said. "Let's move out."

In the distance they could hear voices. The sounds of pursuit. They knew Özgürlük would follow them and their only hope was to pull them away from McCarter and Kartal. The Phoenix Force warriors were new to the island—it was home ground for the opposition—and it left them at a disadvantage for the moment. That would not stop them searching for McCarter and Kartal. Phoenix Force would not abandon two of their own.

"ARE YOU HURT?" Berna Kartal asked as she pushed to her feet.

She felt no damage to herself, just aches from her descent.

Somewhere beyond the rim of the slope she heard shots, the crackle of autofire.

McCarter stood, checking himself out. He was bruised and had the odd scratch on his face. Apart from that he seemed to be in one piece.

"I'm okay. How about you?"

Kartal brushed at the dirt clinging to her clothes and pushed her tangled hair back from her face.

McCarter saw that she had a bleeding gash on her right cheek.

"Nothing to worry about," she said. "I expect I will have plenty of bruises to show. But thank you for what you did."

"I think we need to move. Clear the area before our Turkish chums decide to look for us."

"Do you think Constantine and Landis will be all right?"

"They'll head for cover and come looking for us when they get the chance." McCarter, knowing she was referring to his partners by their cover names, scanned the surrounding area. "I'm guessing they'll head across that way. Look for us in that direction."

He pulled out his sat phone. The moment he looked at it, McCarter saw that the screen had been cracked badly during his fall.

"Bloody hell," he said.

Kartal watched as he worked the keys, muttering to himself.

"It is not working?"

McCarter shook his head. "I'll keep trying," he said. "Right now we'll have to play it smart and walk our way out of trouble until we can catch up with them."

They had both lost their SMGs in the fall. The weapons were somewhere in the thick tangle of undergrowth, but they couldn't afford to spend time searching. McCarter took out his Browning and checked it over. Beside him Kartal did the same with her Glock. They each had full magazines in their pistols and carried a couple of reloads.

"Berna, you enjoy hiking through the countryside?"

"It's not something I have given much thought to."

"Well, now's the time."

They moved off, cutting through the foliage and into the trees covering this section of the island. The thickness of the heavy growth slowed them occasionally and they were forced to detour until they could pick their path again.

McCarter called stops every so often, checking noises that didn't sound natural. He was convinced he and Kartal were not alone. He had to depend on sounds. The light penetrating the upper branches of the trees, filtering down in hazy shafts that merged with the shadows, was diffusing shapes.

Kartal maintained a check on their back trail. She had slipped into this role without being asked, falling back on the training that had been given during her military service. Knowing his six was being covered allowed McCarter to scan the way ahead and to the sides.

"Will your friends find us?" she said.

"They'll give it a good try. We just need to keep moving until we can pinpoint each other."

"Özgürlük will not give up," Kartal said.

McCarter turned to stare at her. The look in his eyes told her neither would he.

"Let 'em bring it on," he said. "Those buggers opened a can of worms when they threatened us with those nukes."

Kartal could sympathize with his feelings. Any form of violent threat was bad enough, but Özgürlük was playing with so many lives by their actions. A nuclear explosion would kill so many and put future lives at risk. There was little redemption for anyone willing to participate in such a thing.

THEY TRAMPED THROUGH the forest, time slipping by unheeded. Trapped warmth made the air musty and they sweated heavily, their clothing clinging to them.

Kartal used her sleeve to wipe away the moisture from her forehead. As she blinked to clear her eyes, she saw movement to her right, a figure emerging from the trees, the weapon in his hand turning in McCarter's direction.

She snapped the Glock up, aimed and fired with barely a moment of hesitation. The 9 mm slug caught the shooter in the upper chest, knocking him back before he went down.

"Your left," Kartal said, voice taut. As she spoke she angled the pistol and triggered a pair of shots at the man appearing behind the shooter she had just put down.

McCarter had turned himself, the Browning finding his target, and he let go a triple burst that ripped into the upper legs of the moving shooter. The guy uttered a hoarse scream as the 9 mm burst split flesh and chewed bone. His legs gave way beneath him and he pitched forward on the ground, his SMG spilling from his fingers. McCarter put a follow-up shot into the exposed skull and the guy jerked, then lay still.

"Let's keep moving," McCarter said, bending to snatch up the fallen subgun. He passed it to Kartal.

They angled across a slope, making for the denser cover provided by the canopy higher up. They crashed through the outer thicket, ignoring the pull and scrape of the vegetation. Any minor injury was ignored in their flight; a few scratches from the undergrowth were preferable to the damage from a burst of autofire.

The chatter from the opposition's SMGs followed their headlong dash. Slugs hammered and chewed at the foliage. Other shots sent slugs into the trees, scarring the trunks and ripping bark off in chunks.

"Any suggestions?" Kartal said as they moved.

McCarter caught her arm and pulled her off track, taking them deeper into the timber. The autofire died momentarily as their pursuers briefly lost contact. McCarter knew that wouldn't last for very long.

He hauled Kartal to a dead stop, pushing her to a crouch in the shadow cast by the undergrowth. She stared up at him, her face streaked with sweat and a few bleeding scratches.

McCarter didn't speak. He touched his fingers to her lips to warn her to silence.

In the distance, but coming in their direction, McCarter could hear multiple approaches. The tread of boots on the forest floor. The soft rustle of clothing. These people were not experienced combat veterans; they were armed aggressors but not seasoned warriors. McCarter even heard voices as the stalkers approached. They were forgoing one of the basic rules of combat—the one that said no talking while the enemy was around. Giving away your position was not good practice.

He held his pistol in position, ready to engage. These Turkish thugs were going to regret the day they signed on with Özgürlük.

He almost missed the moving figure as the guy burst from the overlapping foliage. He broke cover, pulling the subgun he was carrying up from his hip and made to target McCarter.

It was a slip that cost him. McCarter launched a sweeping kick that connected with the SMG, taking it out of the man's hands. Following through, McCarter resisted taking a shot that could attract anyone close by. Using the pistol in his hand, he slammed it against the guy's face. The solid bulk of the Browning struck the man over his eye, tearing flesh. Blood ran down the guy's cheek, yet he stayed upright, his right hand dropping to his side and reappearing holding a knife.

He slashed at McCarter, the ill-timed move allowing the Briton to lean back. As the blade swept by, he struck out with his left fist, catching the man across his lower jaw, rocking his head back. McCarter realized his opponent could take the blows and still keep coming. He jammed the Browning into its holster to free both hands.

Spitting blood from his mouth McCarter's adversary came at him again, leaning forward from the waist as he swept the knife in a right-left slash. He was trying for a body cut. McCarter let the blade cut to the right, then moved in quickly. He timed his move well, turning in toward his attacker's own body, his left hand reaching to lock on to the guy's knife wrist, fingers clamping down hard.

McCarter held the thick wrist and dragged the man in close, slamming his right shoulder into the guy's chest. The man grunted under the impact as McCarter's body slam took breath from his lungs; the move had caught him unprepared, not expecting such a response. With the thrust of the blade having been diverted away from his body, McCarter concentrated on bringing the attacker down.

With his left hand still hanging on to the knife arm, McCarter swept his right arm around his adversary's neck, fingers curling around the collar of the man's shirt. McCarter's hip thrust in hard and he hauled the man up off his feet, swiveling him in a continuous motion that dragged the guy over McCarter's body and launched him in a body slam. McCarter heard the guy grunt with surprise as he hit the ground on his back.

McCarter kept a grip on the knife wrist, spreading his feet apart to secure his balance. The guy was struggling to suck air back into his lungs, eyes bulging. The Briton drove a heel into the guy's chest, pushing what air he had left out of his lungs. McCarter moved in relentlessly. He swung his right foot around in a devastating arc that terminated against the guy's throat. The man gave a hoarse gasp—the last sound he ever made as his throat was crushed by the blow. As he began to struggle in his attempt to breathe, McCarter drew his foot back again, then slammed it down against the guy's knife arm with enough force to snap the bone between elbow and wrist. The knife dropped from suddenly lifeless fingers.

He moved quickly to where Kartal stood, still reacting to the speed of the confrontation. She made a defensive move when she felt McCarter's presence.

"Ease off, love," the Briton said, keeping his voice low. "I'm Coyle. Friend. Remember?"

Kartal raised her head and stared at him until recognition kicked in.

"Sorry. It's getting hard remembering us from them," she said.

Looking beyond McCarter, she saw the man he had just faced. He had stopped moving now, his body stretched out.

"Bugger was determined to stick this in me," he said, holding up his attacker's knife.

Kartal said, "I'm glad he didn't."

"You and me both. Just tell me not all Turkish blokes are as bloody-minded as the ones we seem to be coming up against."

"No, they are not. The majority are peaceful and very friendly." Her bruised and dusty face showed a warm smile. "I have the feeling you bring out the worst in them." She reached out to touch McCarter's cheek. "Don't let it disappoint you."

Close by, they both picked up raised voices moving in their direction.

"Something tells me Özgürlük isn't going away anytime soon. And it sounds like they're coming in bunches," McCarter replied.

Kartal checked their position. "I think we need to go in this direction," she said.

The young woman was proving herself to be more than just a liaison. She had turned out to be one hell of an asset in the struggle against Özgürlük.

As he moved to follow her, McCarter stuck the knife he was holding behind his belt and snatched up the subgun the attacker had dropped. At least the recent encounters had enabled them to increase their ordnance.

As they reached midway along the track, McCarter heard more voices. Closer this time. He risked a quick glance over his shoulder and spotted movement in the direction from which they had come. His brief check picked out at least four men scrambling up the track. The noise they were making would never allow them to qualify as scouts. They were announcing their presence too well.

Kartal pushed on ahead of McCarter. She didn't waste any time or effort talking, satisfied the Briton would keep up with her. Her silence continued until she came to a level section of the track and paused.

They halted and watched their pursuers through the foliage. The group stood around, discussing their next move and seeming to be at odds with each other. Finally one of them made a command decision and the men trooped after him in loose file.

Their pursuers had decided to move off in the opposite direction, giving McCarter and Kartal momentary relief. They stayed in cover as the others passed by. McCarter saw the expression on Kartal's face when she recognized the man at the head of the line.

"I know that one. The one giving the orders. Riz Yannis," she said quietly. "A man who trades information. He has sold it to the NIO. I have seen him in our department many times. At least we know about one who has betrayed us to Özgürlük."

"You can call him names later," McCarter grumbled. "Right now we need to get ourselves into the clear."

McCarter urged her to keep moving and, despite her anger, she maintained her pace, keeping her eye on their rear. They moved in a wide circle that took them farther away from their pursuers.

McCarter tried the sat phone again and this time he got a shaky signal. He punched a speed-dial number and waited while the signal traversed the various satellite setups before securely reaching the Farm.

Barbara Price answered. The connection was not that clear, but McCarter was glad at that moment to have some contact.

"Am I glad you got through," Price said. "What's going on?"

"Not exactly fun and games," McCarter said.

He gave her a brief update on what had happened since Phoenix Force had breached the island and clashed with Özgürlük.

"The rest of the team has been trying to contact you but told us your sat phone was offline."

"It took a bloody beating during a fall. To be honest I don't know how long it's going to stay operational. Pass it along to the others that Kartal and I are still on the east side of the island. To be honest, love, we could do with some backup."

"Are you injured?"

"No, but we have an unfriendly bunch tracking us and limited ammo. If it comes to it, we'll have to throw rocks at the Özgürlük monkeys if they surround us."

"You—" Price began.

The sat phone went dead in McCarter's hand. He tried to make another call, checked it as best he could, but nothing made any difference. McCarter realized there was nothing he could do short of taking the phone apart or banging it on a rock.

"Stopped working?" Kartal asked.

McCarter held up the lifeless piece of hardware.

"We want to send any messages it'll have to be by smoke signals."

"My cell will not pick up anything out here." Kartal sleeved her face, but all that did was move the dirt across her cheeks.

"If I look as bad as I feel," she said, "I am in a bad way."

"Looking good to me," McCarter told her. "Berna, love, a little bit of dirt on your face isn't you. It's what goes on inside that matters. And you are not missing a stroke there."

She gave a little laugh, more to comfort herself than anything. Berna Kartal was a field agent with a few years' experience behind her. But she would have been the first to admit that what she had been through recently went far beyond anything she had faced before. Her only consolation at that moment was the presence of the man she knew as Jack Coyle.

She knew it wasn't his real name, which was something she most probably never would know. His sometimes cavalier attitude to the dangers they had faced might have marked him as not entirely trustworthy. In reality he had turned out to be the kind of partner anyone could trust with their life. Which she had been doing and which looked to be the case for the foreseeable future.

They saw the dense spread of the forest thinning out ahead, exposing a wide area of flatland that stretched in both directions.

And a lone armed man was standing between them and the space they needed to cross to continue their way. While he wasn't exactly moving around, the guy had restless feet, plainly tired of having to wait around.

They stood in the shadows of the tree line, aware that Yannis and his crew might decide to return in their direction.

"Can't shoot him. Too noisy," McCarter said. "He'll see us once we step out. So, Agent Kartal, how do we get out of this bloody mess? I'm at a loss."

Kartal didn't believe for a moment that he was at a loss. He was simply bringing her into the decision making to keep her in the game. Coyle would continue to pull them through with all the tenacious attitude he had been showing since they'd arrived. He was a dangerous man, and despite being unable to use his firearms, she realized he was far from helpless.

"Can you throw a knife?" she said.

McCarter handed her the subgun and slid out the knife sheathed on his belt. He freed the knife he'd picked up and juggled the pair of weapons, weighing their balance and judging distance. He was only going to get one chance. If he screwed it up they might lose the chance of staying ahead of the opposition.

"Bloody hell, girl, you must like to gamble. If I miss, you shoot that bloke and get ready to run like crazy."

He felt Kartal close by him and glanced at her. She inclined her dark head, reaching out to touch his hand.

McCarter sheathed his own knife. The one he had acquired felt right in his hand. It had more of a balanced formation than the Cold Steel Tanto.

"Do it," she said. "I know you can."

"You've obviously never seen me play darts. Watching me trying to get a double top has made grown men cry."

The slight frown on her face told him she didn't quite

make the connection. McCarter didn't have the time to explain the rules of playing the game in a noisy East End pub.

"When we get out of this I'll explain."

"I like the fact you said *when* we get out, not *if* we get out."

"That goes without saying."

McCarter moved so he was positioned without anything close that might obstruct his arm leverage. The slightest touch of an errant piece of the undergrowth could easily send the knife off at an angle. He watched the pacing figure, wanting the guy to stand still long enough for him to make his throw.

Come on, you son of a bitch. Take five. Just long enough for me to sling this bloody shiv and stick it in your scrawny neck.

The man positioned himself in one spot. Turned side-on to present himself as a target McCarter couldn't have set better himself. McCarter balanced the knife by its tip, drew back his arm and launched it. Light caught the metal blade as it covered the distance to target in a couple of seconds.

And hit the guy in the neck.

"Yes," Kartal said very softly.

McCarter could see where the blade had penetrated the man's flesh, the forward velocity sinking it to half its length. The guy responded by throwing up his left hand to clutch at the rigid object in his neck. Almost immediately his fingers were glistening red with the blood pumping from the wound, and McCarter realized he had severed a main artery. The wounded man yanked the knife free. With the knife removed, the blood started to jet from the gash, soaking his shirt as it erupted.

"Let's move," the Phoenix Force leader said, breaking cover.

Kartal was on his heels as they covered the distance, McCarter reaching the man first. Without a pause he snatched the MP5 from the guy's right hand. There was no resistance as the man sank to his knees. As McCarter lifted the SMG he saw that a second magazine was taped to one already in place, offering fast reloading.

Kartal stepped around the guy as he slumped facedown on the ground, clutching at his side to pull the autopistol holstered on his right hip. It was a 9 mm Glock with a 17-round magazine. A similar model to the one she was carrying. With cool efficiency she plucked two extra magazines from the leather pouch attached to the guy's belt.

"I feel better having this in my hand," she said, indicating the Glock. "Now we have more weapons. I just wish your phone had stayed on line long enough so your people could have fixed our position."

McCarter was in full agreement on that.

"WE GOT THEM," Calvin James said. "Barb got a fix before David's phone went dead. Give me a girl who can multitask any day."

"Zero?" Encizo said.

James nodded. "As soon as David came on line she initiated a search through the Zero platform. It had a hit in thirty seconds."

He showed his sat phone to Encizo. The display screen showed a small signal-lock image. James traced the spot back to his current position. At the bottom of the screen a text line gave distance and location.

"Let's do this," James said. "I'm starting to miss David's ugly mug—but don't ever tell him that."

McCarter and Kartal, having crossed the exposed stretch, had headed farther into the forest. They were still not out of danger. The forest at least offered them a degree of cover.

"When your old mate Yannis finds that sentry, he'll know we headed this way," McCarter said.

They came across a stream flowing through the undergrowth and decided to take a fast break to refresh themselves. Kartal scooped up water to splash on her face before taking a drink. She knelt back, studying the flow of water.

"We are still moving in the right direction," she said. She indicated the flow of the stream. "That way will take us back toward the coast. And maybe your friends."

McCarter grinned. "It's like being with Tonto."

"Who?"

"The Lone Ranger's Indian tracker friend. Old black-and-white American TV show. Tonto could tell you anything from a mark in the dust or a bent twig. Knew all the signs. Never got lost."

Kartal smiled. "Yes, I remember. A masked man. He rode a white horse. He fired his gun many times but never seemed to hit anyone. Why was that?"

McCarter shrugged. He'd never worked that one out himself.

They moved on again.

Saw movement ahead of them.

Figures in the dense foliage.

McCarter immediately thought of Yannis and his crew. He dismissed the thought. They could not have gotten so far ahead without...

He picked up a low sound.

A voice.

Not Turkish.

Or any foreign tongue.

It was familiar.

McCarter raised the subgun as a precaution and gestured for Kartal to drop to a crouch. They remained motionless, waiting for the newcomers to show themselves.

When they did, a feeling of relief washed over McCarter.

CHAPTER TWENTY

"Better late than never, ladies," McCarter said as a familiar face appeared through the foliage.

"Son of a…" Calvin James swore.

He emerged from the greenery, Encizo on his six, and walked forward to confront McCarter.

"You guys okay?"

"A little bruised and battered," McCarter said, "but still on our feet."

"Hell of a way to get down a hill," Encizo said, referring to McCarter and Kartal's fall.

"Not by choice," Kartal said.

"He been looking after you?" James said to her.

The young woman nodded. "Like a big brother," she said.

Encizo nudged McCarter in the ribs. "Hear that? Like a brother."

McCarter ignored the gibe.

"How did you locate us?"

"That last call you made. Home base managed to get a lock on your phone. Passed the GPS coordinates to mine."

"Technology is sometimes a very useful thing," Kartal said.

"You heard anything from Allen or Rankin?" McCarter asked.

"Last we heard, they were being airlifted out of the

UK on a direct flight to Incirlik," James advised. He turned to McCarter.

"Check with home," McCarter said. "See if you can get an update."

James pulled out his phone and tapped the speed-dial number that connected to Stony Man. He spoke to Price when she came on.

"Not a happy face," McCarter said when James finished the call.

"Our people picked up an intercept. A text message to a party on the Özgürlük list. About two Americans flying into Incirlik."

"Make sure our guys know," McCarter said. "I don't want them heading into trouble."

James put a secure call through to Manning.

"Rankin," he said when Manning answered, "have you touched down yet? Looks as if Özgürlük has been tipped off about you coming in. We don't have any details, but there could be a reception party waiting for you to leave Incirlik."

"Understood," Manning said. "How are you guys holding up?"

"Let's say this island won't be getting a mention at Club Med. Neighbors are decidedly unfriendly."

"Watch your backs," Manning quipped.

James handed the sat phone to McCarter.

"You blokes okay?"

"Why wouldn't we be?"

"Just curious."

"We heard the NIO has a suspect in custody," Manning said. "We should go talk to him. See if we can pry any useful information out of him."

"You okay to do that?" McCarter said.

"Can't be any more crazy than London."

"Just watch your backs. Work on the 'do not trust any-one' principle. Even old ladies and children."

McCarter passed the phone to Kartal so she could give Manning the name of the hospital. From the address they would be able to pick up GPS directions. She handed the sat phone back.

"Keep in touch," McCarter said and signed off.

"We heard shooting a while ago," James said to him. "You had problems?"

"Nothing me and my mate couldn't handle. Berna made one of the Özgürlük guys. Name of Yannis. She told me he was a snitch. Giving information to the NIO. And to Özgürlük, by the sound of it."

"Bunch like Özgürlük has to have fingers in a lot of pies," James said.

"Time we got back to why we're here on *Fantasy Island*," McCarter said.

Encizo held up his own phone.

"Hey, we got a location from our eye in the sky." He showed McCarter the on-screen data. "Polat's old family homestead. They can't run—they can't hide. We have them."

"Why don't we go pay Özgürlük a home visit?" McCarter said. "Go see what we might be up against."

CHAPTER TWENTY-ONE

The AMC aircraft had been diverted to Ataturk airport near Istanbul. Manning and Hawkins were told the plane would sit on the tarmac and wait for them. A rented SUV had been made ready, courtesy of Senior Agent Cem Asker, and the Phoenix pair immediately drove off. Hawkins fed the GPS location for the hospital into the sat nav and Manning, behind the wheel, quickly located the direction they needed to take.

The Canadian's mind was still alive with questions, all relating to the nuclear device matter.

Where would it be located?

When would Özgürlük demand the matter be resolved?

Was there still the possibility they would detonate the bomb?

More questions than answers.

Unless they could learn what they needed to know ahead of time, there was little to give them physical assistance, while the perpetrator only had to work through a plan of action known to himself, and as long as he kept his plan secret he was at an advantage.

Özgürlük had an extra advantage. The nuclear device they had obtained could be detonated outside the Incirlik base, the detonation causing structural and human damage, while the spread of radiation from the burst could still inflict longer-term suffering.

They were on an empty stretch of road when Hawkins said, "Company. Behind and coming up fast."

Manning checked the mirror, nodding as he picked up the image of the dark-colored car traveling at high speed. It was closing the distance very fast.

"He's in a hurry," Manning said.

"Hell of a hurry. That boy is way too eager."

Manning swung their rental to the side of the road to see if the vehicle wanted to pass. From the driver's reaction it was obvious he had no intention of doing that. The car, now identifiable as an early-model Lancia, raced up behind the Phoenix Force SUV, then swung out, tires squealing as it moved to run alongside.

"These guys have been watching too many old gangster movies," Hawkins said as he pulled himself over his seat into the rear and hit the power button to lower the window.

The Lancia drew level and a guy leaned forward, pushing the barrel of a shotgun into view.

"Gas," Hawkins said, and felt the SUV surge forward.

At the same time, Manning swung the wheel and brought the big 4x4 up close to the Lancia. The car's driver didn't have nerve enough to challenge the larger SUV and turned aside. The car swayed as the guy tried to bring it back on line. The sudden swerve forced the shotgunner to lose balance and he slipped back inside the vehicle.

Given that opening, Hawkins let go a trio of shots from his Beretta, driving 9 mm slugs into the front passenger door. The glass shattered and Hawkins saw the driver jerk aside, but he wasn't sure whether he had hit the man.

Seizing the opportunity, Manning turned the SUV in again, this time going for actual contact. The front corner of the heavy 4x4 crunched against the passenger side of the Lancia, just ahead of the road wheel. The SUV shuddered but maintained its line of travel. The Lancia began to spin, the front pointing in the direction of the opposite side of the road. As it slid away, the shotgunner dragged himself to the open window again, one hand gripping the frame as he pushed the shotgun forward. Hawkins caught a glimpse of the guy's pale face. He turned the Beretta and triggered a pair of shots that hit the would-be shooter in the face and neck. Hawkins caught a blur of red as the guy fell back inside the car, the shotgun falling out the window.

Manning kept the SUV on an even keel as he witnessed the Lancia rock to a stop. Any thoughts he and Hawkins were in the clear vanished when his partner yelled a warning.

"Second wave! Dead ahead!"

Manning saw the oncoming vehicle as it slid into sight from a bend ahead. He spotted the figure leaning from the passenger window, weapon coming on track.

"No way," the Canadian said.

Instead of slowing, he put his foot down, the powerful SUV responding with a breathtaking surge. In the rear, Hawkins was pushed against the seat back. He spread his left arm to keep himself upright as Manning rocked the vehicle across the road to directly face the opposition. It was a new BMW SUV—a large, solid-looking monster.

"You up for this?" Manning said.

"Do I have a choice? Be honest, partner, I was never very taken by playing chicken."

Manning gripped the steering wheel, hoping the other driver had the same feelings. He tensed, ready to haul the SUV aside if the other driver stayed on course. He heard Hawkins's hiss of breath.

At the last moment the BMW swerved aside, tires smoking. The vehicle missed the SUV by a fraction, flashing past in a blur.

"Whoa, boss, that was too close," Hawkins said.

Behind them there was a heavy sound as the BMW slammed into the side of the stalled Lancia. The impact pushed the smaller car along the road.

Manning brought the SUV to a skidding stop and he and Hawkins bailed quickly. They turned and closed in on the BMW as doors were flung open and armed figures scrambled out, showing the weapons they carried. One of them had a bleeding gash on the left side of his face. He could have still been dazed from the impact, as he triggered his SMG before he had it fully raised. The burst punctured holes in the road, raising dust. Hawkins double-fisted his Beretta and put two 9 mm slugs into the guy's chest, dropping him instantly.

Seeing the other men separating, Gary Manning swiveled at the hip and fired at the closer of the two. Manning had a reputation of being an excellent shot and proved it by putting the guy down with a single 9 mm slug above the target's left eye. The Özgürlük soldier kept moving for a few seconds, his momentum keeping him upright. Before the guy dropped Manning had turned his Beretta on the third man, firing fast and laying a double burst in the man's chest.

A burst of flame showed from the crushed Lancia, flames licking up the side of the body. Manning and Hawkins backed off.

"They really didn't want us around," Hawkins said. "These Özgürlük jokers don't give up gracefully."

"You think?"

"Time we moved out," Hawkins said. "We need to get back to the others."

Hawkins nodded. "I'll feel safer with a whole bunch of people around me."

Manning took out his sat phone and called Agent Asker. He gave him a rundown on what had just happened.

"I am glad you survived the attack," Asker said. "Under the circumstances it would have been safer if you had not made the trip."

Manning wasn't sure he liked the sound of that.

"What are you saying, Asker?"

"I was about to call you. I received the news a short time ago that Darshan Shukla passed away in his bed at the hospital. So your journey would have been wasted."

"They give you a reason why he died?"

"A massive heart attack," Asker said. "We must remember Shukla was not a young man. I was told the treatment he received during his captivity had put too much of a strain on him. The doctors tried to revive him but failed."

"Lucky for Özgürlük. They're racking up quite a body count," Manning said. "Okay, we'll pick up our flight back to Incirlik. I think it's time we rejoined our team."

"Whatever you wish," Asker said, his tone a little strained.

Manning put his phone away.

"Something bugging you?" Hawkins asked.

"T.J., my man, there's a little voice inside my head whispering something I don't like. Let me think on it and I'll tell you when it's clear."

They returned to the SUV.

Manning felt certain their encounter with Özgürlük would not be the last.

"Sooner we're back with the guys, the safer I'm going

to feel," Hawkins said as Manning swung the vehicle around and headed back toward the Ataturk airport.

"You and me both," the Canadian said.

"Son of a bitch," Hawkins said slowly. "I figure we've been set up like turkeys at a shoot. If I was the suspicious type, I'd be looking at someone in the NIO."

"Hell, T.J., you are a suspicious guy."

"You figure we might be on to something? Hell, Gary, that's what you were hinting at back there."

"Only thinking out loud here, T.J., but Asker has tabs on us. Way this business is going down most anyone we meet could be with Özgürlük. This kind of thing runs deep. Özgürlük isn't going to have its members wear buttons telling the world they're part of an extremist group ready to attack an American base. So Agent Asker could be involved. Doesn't it strike you how easy it would have been for Asker to have fingered us? We head for the hospital after he tells us where the wounded guy is and we get picked up by those guys. Some coincidence, T.J."

"You mean the way the guys were hit not long after they first arrived in Turkey? Right after they left the NIO. So how do we handle this?"

"We get out of Dodge. Get the guys at Incirlik to chopper us out to that island and join up with the team."

Manning took out his sat phone.

BROGNOLA LISTENED TO Manning's report.

"I'll get Aaron to fish around Asker's background. If we find anything, I'll give you a heads-up. If he's mixed up with Özgürlük it gives him a hell of an advantage. He's a higher-up in the NIO. Gives him full access to data. We'll have to tread carefully on this."

"What he doesn't have is access to Stony Man," Manning said. "Hal, we're heading back to Incirlik. Time we joined the rest of the team. T.J. and I need assistance getting to that island and we need to take in some equipment."

Brognola sighed. "Get your butts back to Incirlik. I'll have Barb fix a ride for you to the island."

WHEN THE AMC plane touched down at Incirlik, it was obvious the base was on full alert. Humvees were in evidence. Displaying .50-caliber machine guns, the vehicles patrolled the base, riding the perimeter and moving around the buildings and hangars. There were also armed personnel on foot patrols.

As the Phoenix Force pair exited the aircraft, observing the activity, Hawkins paused to stare.

"I know they have to put on a show," he said, "but is any of this going to prevent anything?"

Manning understood his partner's point of view. The prevention of any deliberate act of terror was a difficult exercise to mount successfully. A determined perpetrator had all the cards in his hands, while those charged with preventing any strike were often forced to work with little or no advantage. They might know an attempt was due to take place—but there was more than that they would need.

Whatever Brognola and Price had done, it had been fast. Manning and Hawkins were immediately directed to a meet with an Air Force liaison. Major Lee Jellicoe, midthirties, was a no-nonsense individual who could have been a recruitment model for the service. His uniform didn't have a crease on it and his shoes had that shine that made even Manning slightly embarrassed that his own were less than perfect.

"Rankin? Allen? Follow me, gentlemen," Jellicoe said. "We're all set up for you."

"Nice to know the right people," Hawkins said.

Jellicoe managed a taut smile. "My orders are to set you up with equipment and a ride." He didn't elaborate or question as he led the Phoenix pair into a side building. "We can outfit you with whatever you need. Your ride is being prepped as we speak. We've been provided with coordinates, so no problem there."

The building was light and airy, lined with shelving racks packed with equipment. An Air Force senior master sergeant was waiting for them.

"Master Sergeant Walker here will gather whatever you need. I was told to cater for six people?"

Manning nodded. "Yes, Major. Some of our team are already in place. We need to reinforce them with equipment."

Walker, a broad six-footer with a blond buzz cut, said, "Just call out what you need, sir."

He had a pair of large black nylon carry bags spread out on the trestle table in front of him. As Manning told him what they needed, Walker moved along the racks, picking up the items and packing them. It took no longer than ten minutes to fill Manning's requirements.

The first thing Manning and Hawkins did was change into combat clothing and boots. Wearing the black gear made them feel a little more at home.

A uniformed airman appeared, carrying a thermos jug, mugs and foil-wrapped sandwiches. He placed them on the table.

"I imagine you haven't had much time for anything," Jellicoe said. "Just help yourselves."

The Phoenix Force pair did just that, realizing how ready they were for the refreshments. The hot, black coffee was welcome. So were the ham sandwiches.

"Ordnance?" Jellicoe said. "We were told you'd need weapons."

"Handguns are covered," Manning said. "We need SMGs and 9 mm ammunition."

"You about to start a war?" Master Sergeant Walker returned.

"Hoping to avoid one," Hawkins said. "Kind of preventative action."

"MP5s?" Jellicoe asked. "We can provide those."

"Good," Manning said. "My preference."

"Anything else?"

"No, we'll keep the gear to basics, Major," Manning said.

"A Stateside flight would be nice," Hawkins interjected.

"Only if we can come with you," Walker said.

"Master Sergeant, get what these men want. I'll handle the paperwork."

Jellicoe signaled for Manning to join him some distance across the hut.

"My orders came from high up in the chain. I was told this was a need-to-know situation, Rankin. I'll follow my orders, but being curious is one of my failings. Is there anything you can say?"

Manning could understand the man's interest. He hated having to maintain silence. Matters of security necessitated keeping people out of the loop. The Air Force was there to help protect America and its friends. If danger threatened—and in this instance it threatened the whole of the Incirlik base—Manning did not like having to remain silent. It went against his whole being. But he had his orders and, whether he liked it or not, there was nothing he could say to advise Jellicoe.

The man must have read Manning's dilemma.

"I'm putting you under pressure, sir. I apologize for that. There are times when I think only the Air Force has to maintain a tight-lipped posture."

"If it was up to me," Manning said, "I'd give you chapter and verse."

"In place of giving you a hard time, the Air Force will give you our best help. Whatever your mission, I hope it works out."

"We've got no problem with agreeing on that."

Walker had disappeared into the back of the hut. When he came back he was carrying the requested weapons. He laid them out on the trestle table and then went to collect the ammunition.

"Mags for the MP5s are already loaded," he said. "There're a couple hundred extra rounds in these boxes. Be enough?"

"If it's not," Hawkins said, "we are going to be in trouble."

A cell rang and Jellicoe took it from his pocket.

"Thank you, Peters." He looked in Manning's direction. "Your ride is waiting."

Manning and Hawkins finished their coffee and sandwiches.

Master Sergeant Walker had packed the weapons and ammunition in the second of the nylon bags. He hefted it across his shoulder.

"Walk you out, gentlemen."

Hawkins picked up the other bag and the four of them stepped outside and headed in the direction Jellicoe indicated.

"A night insertion would have been preferable," he said, "but it appears you're on a tight schedule. We'll bring you in from the coast and take a wide sweep across the water. Drop you down at the extreme north end of the island, well up-country. You can utilize the GPS reader on your sat phones to link up with your people…"

"And then it's down to us," Manning said.

The U.S. Air Force UH-60 Black Hawk helicopter was painted a drab gray and had no official markings.

"There are times when we have to make need-to-know flights," Jellicoe said. "Luckily the gray lady is on stand-down right now, so be our guest."

Walker slid the ordnance bag in through the open hatch. Hawkins did the same with his bag.

"Whatever it is you have to do, good luck," Jellicoe said.

"Thanks," Manning said. He shook hands with Jellicoe and Walker. "Been a pleasure, gentlemen."

Manning and Hawkins climbed into the chopper, feeling the aircraft power up as they closed the hatch. Manning made his way forward to speak to the flight crew, leaving Hawkins to make himself as comfortable as he could on one of the basic seats.

"Should take us a couple of hours to reach the island," the helmeted pilot said through his headset. "We have to go the long way round."

Manning had donned a headset himself so he could communicate over the noise of the engine.

"In your hands," Manning said, dropping a hand on the pilot's shoulder.

"You should go and relax," the copilot said. "Sorry, but no movie on these flights. Or complimentary drinks."

"Last time I fly AF economy," Manning joked.

He returned to the main cabin and plugged his headset into one of the jacks fitted to the side of the fuselage. He took a seat across from Hawkins. It looked as if the Phoenix Force commando had decided to take time out.

Manning couldn't argue with that. He folded his arms over his broad chest and did the same.

"Two minutes," the pilot finally said through the headset. "You guys getting out here?"

"We only bought one-way tickets," Manning said.

"Coming around to the north end of the island. Looks like a mess of trees. I'll find the clearest spot and put you down."

"Okay." Manning leaned over and patted Hawkins's knee. "Come on, Texas, looks like our ride is over."

Hawkins was upright in seconds.

"Knew it was too good to last."

"Coming in now," the pilot said in Manning's headset.

Through the side window Manning and Hawkins could see they were over land, a rough patch of ground covered in clumped grass and rocks. The pilot brought the chopper to within a couple of feet. Staying airborne meant he would not have to take off from a standing start—simply power up again and quickly gain height.

"Good luck, guys," he said.

Manning acknowledged before removing the headset, "Thanks for the ride, Air Force. Have a safe trip home."

Hawkins had slung the ordnance bag over one shoulder. Manning picked up the second bag and opened the side hatch. Chill wind gusted in through the opening. The gently swaying chopper was hovering no more than two feet above the ground. The Phoenix pair dropped to the surface. Between them they slid the hatch shut. Manning banged his hand on the fuselage, then turned and followed Hawkins clear of the powerful rotor wash. The UH-60 rose smoothly, gained height and made a 360-degree turn before picking up speed and streaking away.

"Can't change our minds now," Hawkins said.

"And miss all the excitement? Wouldn't think of it."

Manning took out his sat phone. The connection with McCarter was faster than he expected, and clear.

"Hi, honey, we're home," Manning said when McCarter came on.

"We spotted your ride. Could be the opposition did, as well. Stay put and we'll link up."

LOCATING THE RENDEZVOUS was made simple by the use of James's sat phone, which was fully equipped with a GPS locator. He'd synced it with the one Manning was carrying and the signal allowed the meet to be made with little problem.

An hour later the team was at full strength again.

"Miss us?" Hawkins said as he and Manning joined them.

"No," McCarter said. "But we heard you pair managed to create a fuss in London."

"Good to see you, too," Manning muttered.

"Do they always act like this?" Kartal asked.

"This is nothing," Encizo said. "You should be there when they really get going."

"I think you are all a little crazy," Kartal said.

"At last," Encizo said, "she's figured us out."

CHAPTER TWENTY-TWO

They stretched out in the shadows thrown by the undergrowth and studied the layout of the run-down house and outbuildings.

"We got this right," McCarter said. "They've got quite a setup here. Bloody hell, they've even got a mobile radar unit."

The radar unit, a twenty-foot box mounted on a four-wheel chassis and powered by a separate generator, carried a scanner dish on its roof. The unit was painted in military livery. The scanner was not moving, so McCarter decided it was not in operation at the present. Working or not, the unit existed and proved to the Briton that Özgürlük was serious.

"It looks as if General Marangol has been providing some military backing," Kartal said. "Look over there."

McCarter followed her guiding finger and saw a couple of armed figures standing in front of the configuration of a helicopter draped in a camouflage net at the side of the house.

Encizo said, "This is getting worse all the time."

"Military involvement makes it really heavy," James noted.

"If that bomb goes off, Polat will have a lot of reaction on his hands," Manning said. "Military intervention might be needed to keep calm."

"If Marangol can muster enough backup…" James let his thought trail off.

"These people have to be stopped before they decide to use that nuclear device," Kartal declared.

"No argument from me," McCarter said. "A mushroom cloud over Turkey is not a good idea. Threatened or not."

"So what do we do to stop it?"

"*We* carry on handling it. Calling in the military, or the cops, isn't an option because we don't know how deep this goes. We'll look like idiots if the bloke we call up is one of them."

"Talking about contacting help if we hadn't showed up," James said, "how *would* you have called anyone?"

"Bit below the belt," McCarter said. "Hit a bloke when he's down."

"Oh, that's right," Kartal said, grinning. "You broke your phone."

"Hey, don't rub it in, Agent Kartal."

Kartal nudged him, rolling her eyes when McCarter turned to her. "Oops," she said.

"Berna, you're starting to sound just like me, and that's worrying."

"Bad influence," Manning said.

They spent some time assessing the layout. The once prestigious house belonging to the Polat family was in a sad state. Overgrown with weeds and vines covering large sections of the wall, it was in need of extensive repair. Where there had once been wide lawns was now a mass of untended grass. There was a collection of old garden machinery, rusted and obviously abandoned. To one side of the house stood a barnlike structure. It, too, was long neglected; the roof had fallen in and the doors sagged on rusted hinges. The whole place looked ready to be pulled down.

"Doesn't look like the Polat mansion is the upmarket property it once was," James said.

"Might just be handy for hiding things Polat doesn't want anyone knowing about," McCarter mused.

"I wonder what that could be," Encizo grumbled.

"A couple of backpack nukes. They could have brought them in by sea, transferred them to a small boat and landed it here. Pretty remote. Make a late-night rendezvous. More I think about it," McCarter said, "I reckon that's what happened. From here to the mainland by a similar setup. Quiet section of shoreline. Offload into a vehicle and drive to location X. Berna, how tight is security along the coast?"

"There is security but never enough to cover every inch of the coast. Smugglers have thrived for years on the same basis. Plus, there are always a few officials who can be bought. Turn their backs at a given time."

"Especially if they're part of Özgürlük."

"Anything for the cause," McCarter said. "They wouldn't even know just what was being brought in."

"We need to find out if that's what's happened," McCarter said. "Is the device here, or has it already been shipped on?"

"Hey, three o'clock," James warned.

A couple of armed men slouched into view, wandering across the area fronting the house. After a couple of minutes they vanished inside the house.

"Marangol must love these guys," Encizo said. "He seems to have plenty of them. Not exactly soldiers of the month, are they?"

"Polat gets his people from the rallies," Kartal said. "They come for the promised offers. For them it's a call to fight for their country, though I'm doubtful Polat has given them the truth about the organization's agenda.

He gives them his rallying speeches, feeds them, and if they sign up they get weapons."

"Pretty cynical way to recruit your cannon fodder," James said. "Poor guys have no idea what they're getting into."

"If some knew the reality, they would still hang on," McCarter said. "Okay, enough idle gossip. Let's complete our recon before we go storming in and upset the locals."

They remained where they were for as long as it took them to get a feel for the opposition's numbers. It seemed that the island's defenders had decided to fall back to the house to make a stand. That didn't worry McCarter. Having the enemy all in one place kept things contained. He didn't discount the possibility there might be Özgürlük personnel still out in the field, so there would be no relaxing their watch.

McCarter made a final weapons check. He looked around at his team, including Kartal. No words right now. No last-minute wisecracks. They each knew what was waiting for them and accepted the possibility that one or more of them might be injured, even killed, during the upcoming clash. This was the time when plans could be lost and fate stepped in to deliver a backhanded twist. They were all aware of the stakes. It was the one chance they were getting to prevent the possible strike Özgürlük was threatening to make. If the opposition won this round, a great many people were going to die, and others might suffer from the fallout. The Incirlik base would be destroyed, on top of significant human causalities.

And there was the added threat of possible destruction from a similar device being detonated in America. On U.S. soil. A cold and deliberate threat to add to the problem.

Two threads that added up to a terrifying conclusion to Özgürlük's manifesto.

Phoenix Force had been sent to Turkey to unearth and put a stop to whatever Özgürlük was planning. To this point they had discovered the plan existed. Here, now, their mission brief had reached crisis point. There was no going back. This was where it would have to end if they located the nuclear device.

It was still an unknown as to where the B-54 backpack nukes might be located. Phoenix Force was dealing in vagaries with their search. Which was all they had. No matter what they might, or might not, find inside the house, it was something that had to be done. It was their overriding objective at the moment.

Move in, assess the situation and follow through.

"Allen, Constantine and Rankin, you work your way around to the back of the house. Make your assault from there. Can you be in position in fifteen minutes?"

"Watch and learn," Manning said. "I'll contact via my sat phone once we're in position."

Manning, Hawkins and Encizo eased away and started their move to cover the rear of the house.

"We move once the time is up," McCarter said, glancing at Kartal. "Sure you're ready?"

"Yes. It's very comforting that you keep worrying about me," she said. "You don't need to. As your friend said, watch and learn. I *have* been watching and learning."

"Has it helped?" James said.

"Only to make me realize I am safer to have you on my side, rather than against me."

"No sweat, then?" James said.

"Only from the heat," Kartal said as she performed

a final weapons check and made sure her extra ammunition was handy.

"It would be an added bonus to find Polat or Kaplan here," she said. "Even General Marangol."

"The big guns tend to watch from a distance," McCarter said. "They'll want to be where they can make any announcements in safety."

"And with a waiting car if things don't go to plan," James said.

"I find you are very cynical," Kartal observed. "Do you always see things so bleakly?"

"It can be a dark world, love," McCarter said. "In our line of work we don't see many soft and fluffy rabbits."

Kartal smiled, a soft laugh following. "I do not believe you are as bad as you pretend to be. Tell me what you do when you are not pursuing bad people."

"As little as possible," James said. "Lie in the sun. Watch the scenery."

"I do not see you doing anything like that."

"He does," McCarter said. "The man is a lazy bugger with no redeeming qualities."

"Listen to the man," James said. "He knows me. Too damn well sometimes."

Their talk drifted away as the minutes slipped by. McCarter checked his watch. Two minutes to the stated time.

"Let's get ready to move out, people. Only one rule here. Anyone not part of the team you can shoot. Don't give these buggers an inch. We already know what these blokes are like. They won't give us any leeway, so treat them the same. Hit them hard. Any way you can. It's going to be them or us. Just remember what they're threatening to do. If they succeed, a lot of people are going to get hurt. I don't want that to happen."

He glanced at Kartal. "Have to ask this, Berna. Do you have any concerns about what we're going to be doing?"

"If you mean because those people are Turkish?"

"Yes."

"As far as I can see, Özgürlük has made its position clear. If their own countrymen are hurt because of their policy, they won't care. That makes them enemy combatants. I'll have no problem dealing with them, Mr. Coyle. Trust me on that."

"We don't know what we'll find when we get inside. And it's no certainty we'll find a nuclear device. But we might get a lead on where it's being stored."

"Let's hope they're not dumb enough to keep it lying around," James said.

"One of the reasons why we're here," McCarter said. He looked around. "If you manage to grab one of these buggers, do it. But not if it means risking any of your lives. I want that understood."

"You know," James said, "we could spend the day talking about this. Or go ahead and do it, boss."

McCarter held up his hand. "Okay, children, let's move."

He led the way in toward the house, the group spreading out as they approached. The scattering of old and rusted machinery provided a degree of cover that allowed them to reach within twenty-five feet of the main building.

James threw up a warning hand and they ceased their forward movement, taking immediate cover. McCarter joined him and followed his pointing finger. He saw the lone guy on watch, an assault rifle slung from his left shoulder.

"I don't see any others," James said, voice low.

"Don't bet on that too much," McCarter said.

They spent a couple of minutes watching, checking the area, until they were as confident as they could be that there was only one man on watch. Which did not eliminate the possibility of others in the area.

"Him first, then," McCarter said. "We need to get inside."

James nodded, understanding, and broke away, staying in cover as he worked his way as close as he could to the sentry. From one of his pockets, James took out a Gemtech Tundra suppressor, supplied by Kissinger, the Stony Man armorer. Phoenix Force had fire tested the suppressor back at the firing range and accepted Kissinger's recommendation. There wasn't a man on the Stony Man teams who took the stand that suppressors eliminated the sound of a firing pistol completely. They did, however, have the belief the attachments significantly lowered the harsh crack of a 9 mm round to a reduced capacity and under certain criteria served their purpose.

James screwed the suppressor onto the threaded barrel end of the Beretta. The Phoenix Force pro held the pistol two-handed, sighting in on the slow-moving sentry. His finger eased back on the trigger and he let the man walk into his field of fire. The pistol held and steadied, James pulled the trigger and sent a 9 mm Parabellum slug from the barrel.

Kartal, who had fixed her gaze on the sentry, saw his head snap back as the slug hit him above the left eye. It was a through-and-through, the slug emerging in a blossom of red flecked with darker debris. The sentry went down without a sound, crumpling against the outer wall of the warehouse. He curled up at the base of the wall, his body shuddering in a few moments of final reaction to the effects of the slug.

The falling brass shell casing made a sharp sound as

it hit the concrete at James's feet. He unscrewed the suppressor and slipped it back into his pocket, holstering the Beretta and bringing his subgun into play.

McCarter raised his hand and made a signal. The three of them broke cover and advanced on the building, moving quickly now, their concentration focused on their target. Kartal stayed close to McCarter, following his lead as he took long strides toward the front entrance. The NIO agent pushed ahead, eager to move the attack forward.

They had almost made it when the front door swung open and a figure stepped through. The man had a rifle slung over one shoulder and a steaming mug in his right hand. He took a step clear of the door and then spotted the armed figures coming at him. The mug dropped from his hand, shattering when it hit the ground, and the guy snatched for the shouldered rifle.

Berna Kartal was closest to him. McCarter was to her left, a few steps away. Kartal didn't hesitate or break her stride as she swept her subgun in a powerful arc, the body of the weapon thudding into the guy's face. The guy fell back, blood streaming from his crushed nose. Kartal followed through and slammed the SMG into the guy's throat, hard. It was a brutal blow and collapsed the man's throat. The guy went down on his knees, already beginning to choke.

With everyone clustered at the door, McCarter gave the nod and they slipped through and into the building.

The wide entrance hall had a tiled floor littered with trash, debris and dried leaves that had blown inside.

A wide archway to their right gave access to the room beyond. They could hear murmuring voices coming from the room. McCarter led them to the archway.

The large room extended across from them, furniture

piled up against the walls in dusty rows. A group of men
was standing around what had once been a large dining
table. They were bent over as they debated the paperwork laid out on the table…

MANNING, ENCIZO AND HAWKINS skirted the barn and used
its bulk to conceal them as they moved toward the rear
of the house. The camouflaged chopper helped to keep
them partially concealed.

Two armed sentries came into view. Moving back
and forth, the pair was not doing all that thorough a job
of guarding their section. There was a slackness in their
attitude and it showed again that the bulk of Özgürlük
recruits was little more than drafted civilians given guns
and tasked with protecting the island headquarters.

An organization such as Özgürlük would pull in men
wanting to fight for its cause. There were always those
willing to join a group proclaiming to fight for the country; to free Turkey from the grip of American control
of its defense. Impassioned speeches and heady rallies
would draw the impressionable in droves; the need to
belong, to join a struggle, appealed to many and the
promise of arms and the opportunity to fight Turkey's
enemy would be eagerly taken up. It had happened before and would again. Concentrating on the easily influ-
enced would attract the men Özgürlük needed, and when
the time came for decisive action, there would be a rush
of individuals ready to defend what Özgürlük stood for.

That was the easy part. Add to it money and weapons and Özgürlük had an army of sorts. They saw the
excitement, the intoxication of being handed a weapon
and thrust into the front line to defend Turkey's freedom.

Freedom.

Özgürlük.

It was a simple word that could stir strong feelings in those caught in the fervor of rallies and speeches. In the heat of excitement, no one would have pointed out the other half of the picture. The cold shock when faced with hostile guns in the hands of whoever was termed the enemy. The moment when the surge of patriotism was blown away, to be replaced by the sight of spilled blood and torn flesh, reducing euphoria to suffering. Any call to arms veered toward the glory and the excitement; it seldom mentioned the darker side.

Özgürlük might not have covered that during its rallies. Might have forgotten to tell its recruits that intended victory was a two-way street. Suffering and death was kept in the background. Recruits were wanted to carry out the frontline tasks; they wanted the thrill and the buzz of something dangerous.

Özgürlük wanted confrontation.

Phoenix Force would oblige.

Aware there might be others covering the rear of the house, Phoenix Force had to take down these sentries as quietly as possible. Gary Manning handed his subgun to Hawkins and attached his own suppressor to the muzzle of his Beretta.

In the cover provided by the camouflaged helicopter, the Canadian leveled his autopistol and targeted the first man. The range was short, no more than twenty feet. The Beretta spit a single 9 mm slug that cored in through the side of the man's skull. It lodged in the brain mass and the guy dropped without a sound. Manning immediately sighted in on the other man as he registered his partner going down. He fumbled with his SMG, head swiveling as he attempted to spot the shooter. Manning put a shot into his forehead. The slug went all the way through and blew out the back of his skull in a spurt of red.

Manning regained his subgun and the Phoenix Force threesome moved along the side of the house to the rear corner.

The untended foliage around the property allowed Manning, Encizo and Hawkins to reach their objective unseen and unheard. They were far from being novices, and concealment was an integral part of their skill set. Using the tangled undergrowth for cover, they achieved their objective with a couple of minutes to spare.

The rear of the old house showed signs of once having been a tended garden, with the remains of outhouses and even a long-abandoned tennis court, all of which had all but vanished beneath the shrouding greenery. Closer to the house was a wide paved patio section. The gaps between the stone slabs were filled by weeds, and many of the slabs themselves were cracked and uneven. The stone walls of the building were partly overgrown with vines that reached to the roofline three stories high. The exterior stonework of the house was grimed with dirt, streaked and discolored from exposure to the weather.

The Phoenix Force trio crouched in the undergrowth a few yards from the back of the house. They had easily picked out the two sentries who had been assigned to that section of the building. None of the perimeter guards seemed to be carrying communication equipment. Dressed in civilian clothing, they were all armed with SMGs and holstered handguns.

The patrollers moved aimlessly back and forth across the rear of the house, with no regular pattern to their moves. The only drawback was the fact they stayed in sight of each other at all times.

Unaware of any danger, the Turkish extremists walked toward each other. Their murmured conversation carried to Manning as he waited patiently for his best chance.

One of the men reached inside his jacket and produced a pack of cigarettes. He offered the pack to his partner and they stood face-to-face as they paused to light the cigarettes.

It was Manning's moment. Time to employ his suppressed pistol. He leaned forward, the pistol rising smoothly. He didn't waste time on the action. His first shot took the target through the back of his skull, the 9 mm slug erupting from his left eye in a spurt of blood that spattered the face of the other man. Before the man could react, Manning altered his aim and placed his second shot in the guy's forehead, directly between the eyes. The man's head snapped back under the impact, cigarettes flying from hands as both men dropped to the ground.

Hawkins and Encizo joined him as the Canadian unscrewed the suppressor and pocketed it. He took out his phone and made quick contact with James.

"Set to go," Manning stated.

"Go," McCarter said as he made his presence known to the group around the table.

RIZ YANNIS HEARD a sound and looked up from the table. He saw three armed figures moving in through the archway, weapons up and searching for targets.

"Look out!" he shouted, snatching up the pistol he had placed on the table close by.

The three newcomers had separated, moving across the breadth of the room.

The four men with Yannis turned on his warning, grabbing at their own weapons.

Yannis began to gather the documents; he did not want them to fall into the wrong hands. These people were not friends of Özgürlük. And when he saw Berna Kartal with them he felt a chill course through him.

He heard the crackle of distant autofire and knew the situation could quickly become out of control.

The snap of gunfire increased as his people and the intruders exchanged shots.

One of his men, Imir, stumbled back as he was hit. He fell against the table and, as his body turned, Yannis saw the ugly wounds in his torso and the blood bubble from his mouth. Imir's eyes were wide with shock.

The increase in gunfire startled Yannis as he attempted to thrust the gathered documents inside his coat. He had never heard so much weaponry being fired. Though they were willing, Yannis's men were not as skilled when it came to sudden, violent combat situations.

Yannis saw two more fall, bodies jerking under the heavy return fire.

Then there was only Kazim, who clutched a powerful AK-47 in his hands, the rifle set to fire on full-auto. He ran forward, yelling loudly as he confronted the enemy. The muzzle of the Kalashnikov spit flame as it expended a stream of 7.62 mm rounds.

On full-auto the sheer power of the discharge affected the stability of the weapon, which needed a steady hand to keep it on target. Kazim's inexperience firing the auto rifle left him without that control. The burst climbed and flew over the heads of the invading group. Kazim's lack of control led to his death as more than one of the opposing weapons tracked in on him, firing with accuracy. Kazim was thrown back by the impact of concentrated fire, his body punctured in a number of places. He fell, too shocked to even cry out, and hit the floor slack and lifeless.

From the rear of the house the crackle of more auto-fire reached them.

Yannis caught one of their attackers nodding to the other and watched as the tall black warrior moved out of the room and into the hallway.

FRENCH DOORS LED into the house. Beyond lay a wide, spacious room with only a smattering of furniture, some of it covered by dust sheets. Scattered trash littered the floor. On areas of the bare walls, someone had painted the word *Özgürlük* in large, uneven letters.

Hawkins, stepping forward, raised a booted foot and shattered the wood around the lock. He pushed the doors open, ignoring the slivers of glass falling from the frames. The Phoenix Force team pushed inside, scanned the empty room and moved quickly to the door on the far side.

They were midway across the room when the far door crashed open and an armed man positioned himself in the opening, subgun sweeping the room as he checked it. His eyes widened as he saw the three Phoenix Force warriors and the muzzle of the weapon turned in toward them.

Encizo was faster, dropping to a crouch and triggering his subgun. He placed a burst into the guy's body that slapped him to the floor.

"No more easy options," Manning said.

He moved to the door, his partners close.

Out of sight they picked up scuffles of sound, the low but urgent voices. A rush of movement as someone ran the length of the corridor, coming into view, subgun angled at the opening. Manning pushed the others back as the figure appeared, an object clutched in one hand.

A grenade.

The guy, small and wiry, tossed the grenade toward the door. It landed just inside the room, bounced and rolled. Hawkins reacted with a speed that surprised even Manning and Encizo. His foot shot out and trapped the spherical object. Without a break in his move Hawkins bent, scooped up the grenade and tossed it back out the door at an angle that took it to one side.

All three Phoenix Force veterans pulled away from the door frame.

They heard someone yell.

The grenade detonated and the magnified sound hammered at their eardrums. A cloud of smoke filled the corridor, debris rattling from the walls and ceiling.

"Let's do it," Manning said.

He stepped out through the door, his subgun tracking ahead of him as turned to the right, Encizo close behind. Hawkins angled left to cover that area.

Dazed figures were attempting to gather themselves in the aftermath of the explosion. They stood little chance as Phoenix Force engaged.

Autofire echoed along the corridor as Manning and Encizo opened fire. The staccato rattle of their weapons added to the confusion.

Two figures went down, bodies riddled and bloody as the 9 mm slugs tore into them. A third man at the far end of the corridor managed to fire off a burst that scarred the already damaged wall. Encizo concentrated his fire on that shooter and planted a tight group of shots into the guy's chest. He went down in a loose sprawl.

At their backs, Hawkins had seen the hunched body of the man who had thrown the grenade. He had been caught in the full blast of the projectile. He lay facedown, his back and upper legs turned into a mass of lacerated flesh and bone, blood glistening in the open wounds.

The three Stony Man warriors moved to the end of the corridor and paused at the door leading through to the main house. Pushing it open, they checked the long hall that led toward what they assumed would be the front of the house.

Hawkins took up the tail end of the trio, watching the opposite end of the passage. There were no second chances in operations like this. Three men with their backs to the seemingly clear area presented an opportune target for any Özgürlük who might show himself.

With Manning and Encizo taking the lead, they moved quickly along the passage. A wide staircase angled away from them, reaching to the upper floor

They were able to see the wide archway the rest of the team had breached when autofire sounded.

"I think our friends have made their entrance," Encizo said.

"With their usual stealthy approach," Manning said.

As they neared the archway, Calvin James appeared.

AS THE GUNFIRE CEASED, Yannis realized he was on his own, faced by the armed intruders, and that his own life would be forfeit if he offered any kind of resistance. The bodies of his comrades lay around him.

As much as he was totally committed to Özgürlük, that commitment did not extend to throwing his life away on a whim. He was enough of a realist to understand that if he died here and now, very little would change. The only fact would be his death, and Yannis wanted very much to stay alive. Staying alive meant he would still be able to offer himself to the cause; he understood that being taken prisoner would reduce his contribution in the short term. What happened in the future had yet to be determined.

"I surrender," he said. "No more shooting."

Berna Kartal reached him first and disarmed him. Yannis had almost forgotten he was holding the weapon.

"The first time I have seen sense from a member of Özgürlük," she said. "Put down your hands. Behind your back."

Yannis did as he was instructed and felt the bite of plastic cuffs encircling his wrists. Kartal reached inside his jacket and pulled out the documents Yannis had been attempting to conceal. She smoothed them out, scanning the printed text.

A tall black man appeared, three other arms-bearing commandos trailing behind him. Two of the men stayed outside in the hall.

Yannis was moved away from the table as one of the men gathered up the discarded weapons and put them aside.

In English, Kartal said, "I understand why he didn't want us to see these. You'll be interested in what we have here."

The tall, lean-faced man who appeared to be in charge of the group moved to her side.

"LET'S HOPE IT'S not just a recipe for *kuzu tandir*," McCarter said.

"Much more interesting," Kartal said. She glanced at McCarter. "You like *kuzu tandir*?"

McCarter grinned at her. "You kidding?" he said. "Roasted lamb. Spices. Lemon. Bloody fantastic."

Manning said, "Hey, don't distract him, Berna. He'll talk about food all night if you let him. Just tell us what's in the documents."

Kartal turned her attention back to the paperwork.

She laid the sheets on the table and smoothed her hand across them.

"This is the Özgürlük statement of intent. Written down for distribution at a time of their choosing. It tells why and how they will do what they say," she said. She read some more, shaking her head in disbelief. "They really intend to do this if their demands are not met. Here on Turkish soil…"

She straightened and turned to face Riz Yannis. Her face was dark with anger as she spoke to him in a low voice, using her own language. He stared back at her, attempting to remain indifferent, but even McCarter could see the indecision in his eyes. Kartal ended her speech with an angry yell, and before anyone could step in, she launched a full-on, open-handed slap that echoed loudly. The force was enough to rock his head, and the imprint of her hand showed red and angry on his flesh. The man might have stumbled if James had not caught hold of him.

Kartal leaned over the table, supporting herself on her hands, breathing fast through her nose.

"I am sorry," she said. "That was wrong. I apologize."

"From what you told us about their plans," Manning said, "I'm surprised you didn't shoot him."

Kartal took a couple of deep breaths. "I will need to read those documents thoroughly. But from what I already saw I believe Özgürlük really does plan to detonate one of their devices at Incirlik. At the air base. If their demands are rejected and Incirlik not shut down, they will destroy it. And a second device in America to show their strength."

"Just what we'd figured," McCarter said. "The bloody idiots are determined to make their voice heard, at the cost of killing hundreds, maybe thousands."

HAWKINS AND ENCIZO prowled the wide hallway, weapons up and ready as they neared the stairs leading to the upper floors.

It was Hawkins who held up a warning hand to his partner. Encizo stepped closer.

"I have a feeling we still have rats around the place," the Texan said, his voice low. "Staying out of sight until we get careless."

They concentrated on the upper landing and picked up a whisper of sound.

Encizo backtracked and leaned inside the main room, gesturing to attract McCarter's attention.

"We still have some house clearing to do," he said softly. "Somebody playing it cautious."

McCarter nodded and Encizo returned to where Hawkins was still observing.

They moved away from the foot of the stairs and positioned themselves at the side, crouching in the shadow of the main riser.

A few minutes passed. From where they waited, Hawkins and Encizo remained patient. Until the unseen men made a move, there was little they could do. Trying to mount the stairs would only expose the Phoenix Force warriors to deadly fire. They were not about to offer themselves to that kind of situation.

Encizo raised his head as he picked up the faint creak of a board at the top of the stairs. He eased his head up and peered between the railings, straining his eyes to focus on the top of the stairs.

He made out feet and lower legs. Moving his head slightly, Encizo saw the dark outline of an SMG clutched in the man's hands. Movement to one side caught Encizo's attention and he saw a second man to the left.

He held up two fingers.

Hawkins acknowledged.

Above their heads the stairs creaked again briefly as the first man moved down.

Hawkins nodded a go.

Encizo pushed upright and stepped around to the foot of the stairs, bringing his subgun on track.

The stocky, bearded guy partway down the stairs yanked his weapon into position. Encizo was way ahead of him, his SMG already on line. He triggered a burst that slammed the guy back flat against the stairs.

Hawkins snapped his subgun into position as he rose from concealment and raked the upper landing balustrade and the shooter behind it. The 9 mm slugs shredded the wood staves, filling the air with raw splinters and catching the shooter in the torso. The guy fell back, his subgun firing, tearing ragged holes in the ceiling above him.

James appeared behind them.

"Up there," Hawkins said and led the way up the staircase at a run, stepping over the man Encizo had put down.

They pounded up to the landing, weapons arcing back and forth to counter any further moves. They reached the head of the stairs. A corridor stretched away right and left.

A scuffle of noise reached them, coming from the left.

Encizo and James moved to watch the corridor while Hawkins checked the right side.

Down below, McCarter ordered Manning and Kartal to cover the lower floor. He ran from the main room and mounted the stairs. On the landing he saw Hawkins kicking open the two doors along the right side of the landing. Both rooms were empty, unmarked dust on the floors.

"Clear," he said and moved up behind the Briton.

Encizo indicated the first door they reached. They heard a brief scuffle of sound and positioned themselves to either side of the door, staying clear of the main panel.

It proved to be a wise move.

Autofire came from beyond the door and the wood panel was riddled, sending wood splinters across the corridor. The slugs embedded themselves in the opposite wall. The firing stopped for a moment, then started again, the slugs passing through the door's already damaged panels.

McCarter stood to the side and leveled his subgun, pulling and holding back the trigger. The long burst reduced the door's central panel to ragged strips. From the other side of the door, Encizo fired off his own weapon, repeating McCarter's move, their combined fire sending a double stream of 9 mm slugs into the room. While Encizo fired, McCarter ejected his used magazine and snapped in a fresh one. The moment the Cuban emptied his subgun, McCarter lunged forward, booting the door open and bursting into the room, with James right behind him, Hawkins a close third, covering from the rear. Encizo held back long enough to reload.

As McCarter went into the room, he broke to the right. James went left. Hawkins was close on their heels.

Sunlight created dusty beams where it shone through the slats partly covering the room's big window. There was a scattering of furniture, a number of camp beds and a wooden table holding a radio and other electrical equipment. Discarded drink cans and wine bottles lay strewed across the floor.

There were two men on the floor. One still had an AK-47 clutched in his hands. He had been hit by a large number of shots and his front was bloody and ragged. He was not moving. The second guy had caught slugs in his right arm and was hugging his wounds. Blood was pulsing from between his fingers.

"Check him out," McCarter told James, indicating the wounded man. "Send Berna up here and stay with Gary," he said to Hawkins.

James crouched beside the wounded Turk. He sliced open the man's sleeve and inspected the bleeding wounds. He pulled his emergency first-aid kit from his backpack. On this trip, James was carrying only a basic med kit, but he used what he had to help the wounded man. As Phoenix Force's medic, it was his job to tend to the injured, friend and foe alike. He eased the man's bloody hand from his arm as the man kept clutching at the raw wound, his manner and gestures convincing the Turk that he intended no further harm.

Kartal came into the room and McCarter pointed to the casualty.

The wounded guy was staring at Kartal, seeing she was Turkish, and began to speak. She stood over him, answering him when he directed his words at her. Her reply was short and sharp, accompanied by severe gestures with her hands.

"She has a sharp tongue," Encizo said. "A fiery young woman."

"I thought you liked your women with spirit," McCarter said, moving across the room to inspect the equipment on the table. There was a radio communication setup. Next to it was the unit that would be used in conjunction with the mobile radar scanner they had seen outside.

Encizo prowled the room. It was plain to see it had been occupied for some time. As well as the unmade camp beds, there were scattered items of clothing. Magazines and packs of cigarettes. Empty field rations. A few packs of canned beer were stacked against one wall.

Encizo also saw weapons leaning against the wall. The ubiquitous AK-47 rifles. Grenades. RPG-7 launchers and rockets. Handguns. Stacks of the familiar curved magazines for the Russian weapons. A brief thought flashed through the Cuban's mind about the number of Kalashnikovs that had been manufactured over the years since its introduction. He couldn't remember the figure, but he did know it ran into the millions. Maybe even more when the variants and copies were added. A Russian weapon that had spread across the globe and was still being used in a large number of countries.

Kartal stood at McCarter's side, looking over the electronic equipment. She pointed to the markings on the radio.

"Turkish military," she said. "I remember the designations from when I was in the army."

"The more I hear about you," McCarter said, "the more I'm impressed."

"You prefer your women in uniform, then?"

McCarter grinned. "You are pushing it, young lady."

"Marangol. General Marangol," Kartal said. She had moved to check out the radar unit. "Military grade again. It would be so easy for someone like Marangol to divert equipment for Özgürlük's use."

"Suggesting he is well involved with the group," McCarter said.

"He is known for his obsessive views on the country being removed from American influence. Marangol comes from a long line of Turkish military people. All high-ranking and extremely nationalistic. And as I said before, he is known to associate with Kadir Polat. Taken on its own, that doesn't mean a great deal, but when you add in their extreme politics and now this military-designated equipment…"

"As they say in crime books, the plot thickens."

"That one I can understand," Kartal said.

"What was our wounded friend saying to you?" Encizo asked as he joined them. "Apart from the rude words."

"You understand my language?" Kartal said.

Encizo shook his head. "Some of the inflections in his speech told me he wasn't being very polite."

"He had some interesting suggestions about my personal history and sexual preferences. But he is young and he was trying to impress on me how tough he is. He was being very childish. When I was in the army I heard much worse. From what he was saying there are no more hostiles in the house."

"Anything else?" McCarter queried.

"Only one thing. He did say we were wasting our time here. That this is only a backup unit. I believe he was impressing on me that what we are actually looking for is not here."

"You believe him?" Encizo asked her.

"I do not believe the nuclear devices are here," Kartal conceded. "They may have been, when they were first delivered. I think they have already been moved."

"I was wondering about that," McCarter said. "This place, as isolated as it is, wasn't all that well defended. If there were nuclear weapons here, I would have expected stronger resistance. This place is just a backstop now. The main event will be staged somewhere else."

"Closer to Incirlik, maybe?" Encizo suggested.

"But that could mean time is running out for us," Kartal said.

"Time is always running out on operations like this," McCarter said. "Constantine, Landis, go check out the rest of the house."

IT DIDN'T TAKE LONG for Encizo and James to complete their inspection. They were back in a few minutes.

"More ordnance," Encizo said.

"We found weapons. Grenades. Explosive packs."

"No nuke?"

James shook his head.

McCarter concluded, "So Özgürlük has it stashed somewhere else. And the first one to say 'time's running out' gets my boot up his arse."

Kartal offered a quiet laugh. "If nothing else, I am getting a crash course in alternative English."

"That's nothing," James said. "Wait until he gets really wound up."

"Berna, you willing to go have another chat with Yannis? See if you can dig out any more information," McCarter said.

"Of course."

"So where do we go from here?" Manning said. "This looks like a dead end, David. If the bombs have been moved, where have they gone? And, risking getting my butt hammered—how long do we have left?"

"Tough question of the day," McCarter said. He glanced around the room. "I don't like leaving all this ordnance unattended." He looked across at Manning. "Your department. Less there is for Özgürlük to play with, the happier I'll be."

"Helicopter, as well?" Manning said.

"Don't leave anything they can use."

"You get to the boat. I'll join you."

"Let's move out, people," McCarter said. "Back to the Jolly Roger while Rankin sets up the firework display."

IT WAS DUSK by the time they were back on the fishing boat. Yannis and the wounded man were secured on the deck, being watched by Phoenix Force.

Kartal continued her questioning of the prisoners.

Twenty minutes later, Manning appeared and climbed on board. Encizo powered the engine and reversed away from the shore. He swung the boat around.

Manning glanced at his watch.

"Any time now," he said.

The darkening sky was lit up by the explosions, followed by the sound that echoed across the island.

"No more cozy family breaks for Polat," James said. "Place needed a makeover."

"Someone is going to be royally pissed off," Hawkins said.

Kartal said, "Very much so."

McCarter contacted Stony Man and was put through to Brognola.

"Situation is the island has been cleared of the Özgürlük force. We came across weapons and explosives, which, by the way, we used to great effect. But no bomb."

"We're pushing Özgürlük to react," Brognola said. "Maybe too fast."

"Not much else to do," McCarter told him. "Minute we set foot on that island they went for us. Look, I understand we're on a deadline. Those crazies could set their bomb off in the next ten seconds. So worrying about upsetting them is futile. Ten minutes. Ten bloody days, it's all the same."

CHAPTER TWENTY-THREE

"There has been a report of an explosion," Cem Asker said. "From the island. We have lost all contact."

Wild, raging words would have been easier to handle than the protracted silence that followed. Asker's hand gripping the phone became moist. In his mind he could see Kadir Polat's face. Unsmiling. His eyes staring. Mouth in a taut line.

"Did—" he said.

"I heard what you said, Asker."

Not *Cem*.

No familiarity this time.

"In the morning, send a helicopter to investigate what happened."

"That could be difficult," Asker said. "By then there will be others looking at—"

"But you are the NIO, are you not? A legitimate agency with as much authority to look over the incident. Why would your presence cause any problems?"

"You are correct, sir. I will arrange it."

"See that you do." Another lengthy pause. "Let us not fool ourselves. It is obvious who is responsible for this. That damned team of Americans under the instructions of our misguided president. He has given them a free hand to interfere with our operation."

"Dealing with them has proved difficult," Asker admitted. "If we make too much of a move against them…"

"Yes. Proof if proof was needed for the president. Let them continue to chase their tails. Put obstacles in their way. False information fed to your female agent working with them. Keep them busy while we move ahead."

"I will see to it," Asker promised.

"No more disappointments, Asker. We had everything worked out before these damned Americans came onto the scene. They are a burden we must deal with. Just like Incirlik. An American thorn in our side. Something to be eradicated. Removed from Turkish soil. One way or the other. They will be given the opportunity to withdraw—if they choose to stand fast, then we will use our final solution and burn them to the ground. Either way, we must stand firm. You do understand, Cem?" Now the friendly epithet. "Tell me you understand."

"Of course… I…yes…"

Asker failed to hold back the uncertainty in his reply.

"I hope so."

The cell phone fell silent in Asker's hand. He sat motionless, thoughts whirling in his head. And the growing realization that Polat's threat was becoming less of a dream and more of a reality.

He will do it.

Polat will set off his bomb at Incirlik.

His determination had not lessened.

Kadir Polat would turn the American base to radioactive ash. Blow away the base and incinerate every man, woman and child on it. Allow Turkey to become a victim of nuclear destruction.

Asker had always considered himself a patriot. His country first, his needs following. But this ultimate act of sheer horror had suddenly become more than a wild scheme intended to push the Americans from Turkish soil. The most drastic solution to what Polat considered a Turkish abomination.

He had devised the ultimate solution.

The double threat: one bomb in Turkey, one in America.

Madness, of course.

And he was part of it.

Cem Asker, senior agent of the NIO. He had fallen under Özgürlük's spell. The excitement of Polat and Marangol's outlandish scheme. They had drawn him in, filled his mind with the fullness of the plan to drive out the Americans. To weaken their dominance and allow Turkey to become self-aware once again. It had appealed to Asker's pride and he had allowed himself to be swept along by Polat's exuberance. His powerful words and vision.

In the cold light of realization, Asker understood Polat's decision. His supposedly clear and logical way of removing America from Turkey.

Asker suddenly felt cold. The walls of his office seemed to pull in on him. Crowd him behind his desk. The cell slipped from his hand and dropped to the floor. He sat and stared across his office, the knowledge of what he had committed himself to eating away at his conscience.

Realization became a heavy weight on his chest. Too much responsibility. His participation in Polat's scheme had been a reckless decision. He saw that now. Reviewing what he had involved himself in, Cem Asker saw little ahead for him. He was in too deep and had allowed his head to be filled with the excitement and thrill of Polat's vision. That vision was clouded now. Tinged with the stark horror of what would happen if Polat actually went ahead and detonated his bombs.

Through the glass partition separating him from the main office, Asker could see the agents going about their business. Daily tasks were performed with no knowledge of what their senior agent was involved in. That he was ready to place their lives at risk. They were going to be damaged by Özgürlük's operation. And he was part of the conspiracy.

Something else pushed its way into his thoughts.

Kadir Polat.

The man was misguided, yes, but he was no fool.

He was also aware that Polat would be having doubts over Asker and his solidarity. Their last conversation had not ended well.

Asker could remember the tone of Polat's voice. Less than friendly. A cold edge to his words. Asker's moment of hesitation would not have gone unnoticed. Polat was a perceptive man. Once he had ended the call, Polat would have started to consider Asker's situation.

"THAT CONVERSATION DIDN'T go too well," Kaplan said.

He crossed the room and faced Polat across his desk. He didn't need telling when something was wrong. Just seeing the expression on Polat's face was enough to set off alarms.

"Asker," Polat said.

"You know I…"

Polat wagged an admonishing finger at his friend.

"I understand you have never had much faith in the man," he said. "Hakan, I know what you feel about Asker. But his position in the NIO has been of great help to us. Through him we have been able to stay ahead of things in the past."

"Yes, in the past. But we are not in the past. Right now I see Asker as more of a hindrance. A liability. He's weak. And since he has been pushed into placing one of his agents to assist this American team, his reliability is in question. He can't serve both masters without compromising himself."

"I agree. And that conversation with him has convinced me his usefulness may be coming to an end." Polat spread his hands. "Now that things are becoming critical, Asker is wavering. I could tell. Perhaps he has fully realized what we intend to do and he doesn't like it."

"Then we handle him. Just like we handled Shukla, and Marangol removed Uzun. Kadir, in war there are always going to be casualties. It is inevitable. The nature of conflict demands them."

"Like Amal? Like my brother?"

It was the first time Polat had brought up Amal's name. The tone of his voice told Kaplan there was still a great deal Polat needed to deal with. The sudden death of his younger brother had affected him more than he might openly admit. He had pushed it all to the back of his mind, but he would never deny what had happened. It would remain with him for a long time. It was something Polat would never relinquish.

Kaplan had been Polat's friend for many years. They were as close as friends could be.

But friendship would never defeat family ties.

"Kadir, nothing can take away what Amal did. It was a sacrifice he made because he believed in you. Believed in what you are doing for Turkey. Remember that as something good."

Polat reached out and took his friend's hand. Gripped it for a moment.

"Then let us do what we have to. Asker represents yet another risk. He has too much knowledge about our plans. Names and places. If he is starting to crumble, who knows what he might do. We have to cover ourselves."

Kaplan said, "Yes. As soon as possible. Watch him. If he makes any suspicious moves, follow him until he can be dealt with."

He turned to leave the office. At the door, he looked back at Polat's motionless figure. Polat raised his head.

"I will be fine," he said. "Go and arrange things, Hakan."

KAPLAN PICKED UP his cell and listened. The expression on his face hardened as he was told about Asker's intercepted call to Agent Berna Kartal. It was plain that Asker was becoming a risk. The man had a lot to tell if given the chance. He told his informant to maintain his watch. It had been a wise move to have a second string to his NIO bow; the ranks of Özgürlük were well served by those who followed its policy, even in the security world. Cem Asker may have been in a position of authority, but he was not the only Özgürlük recruit.

General Marangol listened when Kaplan told him about Asker's call to Kartal.

"The man is going to give us up," Marangol said. "To be honest, I am not surprised. The man has no character."

"Maybe," Kaplan said, "but that isn't important. If he is going to meet Kartal we have to prevent it."

Marangol sighed. "Then I will handle it. Show you how a professional works."

CHAPTER TWENTY-FOUR

"I can't believe the call I've just had," Kartal said.

"Go ahead, surprise us," Encizo said.

"Agent Cem Asker."

McCarter, who had been standing at the window of his hotel room, turned quickly.

"Doesn't sound like an office call, by your tone."

"He isn't at the NIO. He has asked to meet me. Away from the city. Alone. Said there are things he needs to tell me. That both you and I need to hear."

Manning said, "He didn't say what things?"

"No. But he sounded strange. Not his usual brisk self."

"Could be those thoughts you had are closer to the bone," Hawkins said to his Canadian partner.

"What thoughts?" McCarter asked.

"After the attempted hit after we left Ataturk—on our way to check Darshan Shukla. Allen had a suspicion."

"About Asker?" McCarter said.

Manning nodded. "It occurred to me he could be a leak from the NIO. Seemed odd that the minute we arrived back in Turkey, mentioned to Asker that we were going to see Minister Shukla, we picked up a tail and someone tries to off us. Just like the way you were followed the day we first arrived at the NIO."

McCarter caught the expression on Kartal's face. She had been harboring suspicions of her own, unable to take it too far because of her position. He could sympathize—caught between helping Phoenix Force and her loyalty toward Asker and the NIO. Berna Kartal was an intelligent young woman. If she felt Asker might have been working against her and feeding information to Özgürlük, she was going to be angry. And letting her emotions take control could land her in more trouble than she might be able to handle.

"Have you set up a meet?" McCarter said.

"Yes. In four hours he wants me to drive out of the city and meet him…" She rounded on the Brit. "I have to go alone. No backup. If he sees anyone he'll walk away. If that happens we lose any chance of getting information."

Encizo asked, "How do we know this is genuine? He could be setting you up. Just getting you on your own."

"Perhaps he just wants to declare his undying love for me," Kartal said. She delivered the statement with deadpan seriousness on her face.

"I thought you made all the jokes, boss," Hawkins quipped.

"Hard to top that one," McCarter said. "Berna, look, we don't want anything to happen to you. This sounds like a risky play."

"After what we've been through the past couple of days," she said, "I don't imagine Asker being too tough to handle."

"Don't get too confident."

"I didn't mean it to sound that way. Do you think I want to do this? It scares me. But it's my job."

"If I tell you no?" McCarter asked.

Kartal's smile was too quick. "I still have to go."

"Okay," McCarter said. "Let's see what we can do to help the lady. No arguments, Agent Kartal. You can have your face-to-face with Asker, but you'll do it with our backup. Out of sight but bloody close."

KARTAL RECOGNIZED CEM ASKER'S vehicle as she turned off the main road and rolled along the rough track. She could hear wind buffeting her own NIO vehicle. A hundred yards on her left the water of the Sea of Marmara rolled in to the shore. The terrain lay open around her. The only sign of habitation was a small farmhouse a half mile farther along. The only living creatures, a crowd of goats cropping at the short grass. Asker had chosen his meeting spot well. There was no cover for yards. Just open countryside.

"Remember to keep that sat phone switched on," a voice said in her ear.

She wore an earbud wirelessly connected to the compact transceiver in her back pocket. The sat phone was in the NIO uniform jacket she wore over her holstered Glock.

"Understand?" the voice said again. Gentle but firm.

"Yes," she said.

Her contact with Phoenix Force was the man she knew as Constantine—Rafael Encizo.

"When I meet Asker I will have to speak in our own language," she said. "If I start using English he may become suspicious."

"Okay," Encizo said. "Just talk slowly so I can use my pocket language dictionary to translate."

"Funny," she said. "Now no more talk. I am almost at his car."

Kartal rolled her SUV to within a few yards of Asker's. She cut the engine and climbed out. Saw Asker do the same and walk toward her.

Kartal met him halfway between the two vehicles.

She received a shock at his appearance. The senior agent she knew had vanished. In his place was a visibly shaken individual. Dark shadows beneath his eyes. He was unshaved, his hair uncombed. He was not in a suit. Just a shirt and pants, his loose jacket flaring open in the breeze.

"Agent Kartal," he said. "Thank you for coming."

"I believe we can drop the pretense of rank," she said. "Right now office protocol seems useless."

"You are probably right," Asker said. "We should make this quick. In case I was followed."

"Who by? Your friends from Özgürlük?"

Asker stared as if her knowing was such a revelation. "I…"

"Cem, let us not waste time pretending. I know and you know who you are working with."

Asker seemed to shrink as she spoke. His shoulders dropped.

"Then I can tell you I have broken from them. Berna, they *will* set off that nuclear weapon. They will soon issue their mandate, and if it is not met they will detonate that device. I believe it now. If the demands they have made are turned down they intend to see this through. It is madness. I cannot let this happen."

"Your change of heart has come too late for the American agents working with us."

"I regret that. As I regret what I have done. It's too late for me, but perhaps you can do something to stop this from happening."

He was standing close to Kartal, his body shielding hers.

Asker reached into his pocket and pulled out a compact voice recorder. He handed it to Kartal and she slipped it into a pocket. He stepped back, nervously staring around.

"This may help," he said. "I hope not too—"

His chest burst open as a slug hit between his shoulders and cored through his body. The distorted slug brushed Kartal's right sleeve as it went by her. The distant crack of the shot reached Kartal as she dropped to the ground, rolling frantically. Asker's blood was on her face.

"Shot fired," she said. "Asker is down."

Encizo's voice came through her earbud. "You hurt?"

"Not yet," she said, clawing her Glock free.

Dust blew in the air as another shot struck close by and dirt peppered her cheek.

"On our way."

The distant shooter dropped two more shots at her. Each one came closer, kicking up grit and dust. Kartal wriggled backward until she could slide under her SUV. The distant shooter put more shots in her direction. They slammed into the ground inches away. Kartal heard one strike the front of the vehicle. Her line of vision was restricted lying beneath the SUV. It wouldn't have made a great deal of difference if she could have seen the shooter. He was well out of range of her Glock.

"Stay where you are," Encizo said. "Sixty seconds."

An eternity in Kartal's world as more shots hammered the SUV. The shooter had his range now and he was seeking to put his slugs beneath the vehicle. Confirmation came when a slug powered into the ground below the SUV's body. It blew dirt into Kartal's face. Stinging grit peppered her cheeks. It would take only a shot landing inches closer to find her flesh.

She pulled herself backward. Gasped as she brushed

against the still-hot exhaust. Kartal used language she hadn't expressed for a long time as a couple more shots hit the ground. Too close. She felt something slice her cheek and blood stream down her face. Then a stray slug hit the transmission housing. Distorted and striking the SUV's fuel tank, it opened a ragged tear that started to leak gasoline. Kartal felt it splash on her boot.

"No way," she said and began to roll out from under the SUV, the strong smell of gasoline in her nostrils.

She understood the volatility of gasoline. All it would take was a spark hitting the fumes and...

She rolled to her feet, ready to move around the SUV and take herself out of the shooter's field of fire.

Seconds were all she needed.

A thin window to allow her to reach better cover.

Kartal didn't hear the shot that hit her.

She just felt the powerful impact as the slug struck in the middle of her chest. She lost the power to breathe or to control her body as she was thrown back by the kinetic energy of the bullet. Her feet left the ground as she dropped.

She couldn't even drag a breath into her lungs. The day went dark around her...

CALVIN JAMES SWUNG the SUV around and brought it to a sliding halt across the fronts of the two parked vehicles. It had not fully become stationary when Encizo pushed open his passenger door and jumped out, rushing around to where Kartal lay on her back beside her bullet-riddled vehicle.

A volley of shots slammed slugs into the side of the Phoenix Force SUV. Window glass shattered. A tire flattened with a soft bang as a slug tore through it.

Kartal was on her back, arms and legs thrown wide, motionless.

"Over here," he said as James appeared.

The team medic knelt beside Kartal, dragging open her coat and shirt. The Phoenix Force pair looked at the black body armor she was wearing, the protective vest covering her from waist to neck.

Directly between her breasts they could see the deep indentation in the vest where the sniper's slug had hit. The gleam of metal showed at the base of the hole.

"She going to be okay?" Encizo asked James.

Kartal gave a gasping cough, sucking air into her lungs as she reacted to the trauma. She clutched at her chest, hugging her aching body.

"She'll survive," James said, checking her pulse. "Bruised but fine."

"I might never be fine again," Kartal said, her voice harsh and ragged. "How can it hurt so much and I can still be alive?"

"I'll leave you to work that out for yourself," James said.

They were too involved with checking out Kartal to take any notice of the second SUV, holding the rest of Phoenix Force, as it sped by, heading for the shooter's position.

James checked out Asker. It wasn't a long examination. The slug had flattened as it passed through his slim body, tearing and splintering as it did.

"His friends wanted to make certain he couldn't talk," James said. "Bastards are running scared."

Kartal, on her feet and leaning against the side of her SUV, held up the voice recorder Asker had given her.

"They didn't stop him doing that," she said. "He gave me this before he was shot."

Their other SUV rolled back and pulled to a stop. McCarter was the first out, checking Kartal, relief on his face when he saw she was upright.

"And I thought I was the impulsive one," he said. "You sure you're okay?"

"Shaken but not stirred," Kartal said with a hint of a smile on her lips.

"Bloody hell," McCarter said. "Another joker in the pack."

"And one with a gift," Encizo said.

Kartal showed the voice recorder. "Asker left us this," she said. "It may give us some guidance."

"What about our shooter?" Encizo said.

"Gone by the time we found his spot—" Manning held up a cartridge casing "—7.62 mm NATO loads. They were on the ground where he'd fired from. I collected a few and dropped them in a plastic bag. He didn't have time to collect them when we showed up. We can have the NIO check them for fingerprints. Might give us a connection. Worth a try."

"Berna, you should call this in. Have your people deal with it."

Kartal took out her cell and called the NIO office.

"They will send out a team and inform the local police. We will need to wait until someone shows up."

"You go sit in one of the cars," McCarter said. "Take it easy while we wait. Listen to Asker's recording and see if it's going to help. As soon as we can, you're going to be checked out."

Encizo stayed at her side as Kartal slowly moved off. She was still hurting from the impact of the sniper's bullet. The physical trauma of the hit would remain for some time. McCarter knew the young woman wouldn't allow it to hold her back, but he wanted her to be watched until he was sure she was back in form.

"That is one hell of a lady," Hawkins admitted. "Knock her down and she just naturally bounces back up again."

CHAPTER TWENTY-FIVE

"The situation is becoming difficult," Kaplan told Polat. "We will have to change our plans."

"Postpone what we were going to do? Delay? Perhaps we should surrender."

The last sentence was delivered with a trace of sarcasm.

Kaplan could recognize the tone. Polat's voice became higher, almost shrill, when he felt under pressure. And he was under pressure now. Recent events had rolled over them during the past few days. Their carefully orchestrated plans had slowly unraveled around them. At any other time, Kadir Polat would have shouldered his responsibilities calmly. Attended to each mishap with his usual quiet resolve. Now, with each break in the natural order of things, Polat was finding it difficult to keep on top.

It was not difficult to work out the reason. Despite his attempt to keep the death of his younger brother under control, Polat was not succeeding. Kaplan wished there was something he could do that would ease the loss. He realized there was nothing he could do. Except attempt to keep things moving as smoothly as possible.

He admitted, to himself, that the recent incidents had damaged Özgürlük. They had lost men when attempts had been made to deter the team of Americans brought in by the Turkish president.

Regardless of his feelings toward them, he could not deny their ability to face up to whatever was sent their way. They took on the undisciplined Özgürlük loyalists and handled them as only professionals could. The eager Özgürlük recruits, flocking to Polat's meetings and drinking in his persuasive words, were loyal to his aims. When the call went out for volunteers to become the Özgürlük army of defense the numbers had swelled.

Weapons had been handed out discreetly. The men had been given instruction by those who'd had previous training, but it took more than a few lessons and encouraging words to turn them into skilled fighting men. Kaplan knew that many of the volunteers were there for the chance to use violence for its own sake. The food and drink passed out so freely, along with the weapons, was not enough to give Polat the force he needed.

Not all of the men who joined Özgürlük were untrained. Polat had brought in specialists to handle the nuclear devices once they had been smuggled into the country. On his isolated island they had worked to prepare the weapons so that when placed at the chosen locations it would only require a simple sequence to finally arm them, set the timers and walk away.

All so simple in Polat's way of thinking.

Up to a point everything seemed to be working to plan.

The death of Polat's brother had been a blow that was still unresolved. Polat had repressed his feelings, but Kaplan saw signs that he was far from over what had happened. The foolishness of the attack on the American team only a short time after they had arrived had been a reckless move. Amal had engineered the attack in a bid to assert himself in his elder brother's eyes. The attack had failed. Amal had died and the Americans had showed themselves to be a competent force. With one of their men in hospital, possibly able to talk, the rapid decision had been made to silence him. This time Özgürlük had succeeded. The hit had worked and the team had escaped from the hospital.

With the reluctance of Darshan Shukla to join Özgürlük and one of General Marangol's military connections showing hesitation, the need for decisive action had become imperative.

Major Uzun had been removed in an unfortunate accident and had been replaced by an officer sympathetic to Marangol's connection to Özgürlük.

Shukla, in Özgürlük's hands, had been rescued by the Americans in an action that had cost a number of the group's members. Although they'd had the man hospitalized he had eventually died from his wounds.

Matters failed to improve for Özgürlük.

The Americans, who seemed to possess charmed lives, resisted all attempts to eliminate them. They had staged a strike against Polat's island stronghold that reduced the property to ashes and destroyed the weapons and equipment General Marangol had diverted there.

The need to regroup became imperative.

When Cem Asker allowed his weaker side to push him away from the overall plan Özgürlük had devised, Kaplan took the decision to have him removed. Asker held background information on Özgürlük and in his condition might have exposed too much. Unbeknown to Asker, his cell phone had been monitored by an Özgürlük operative within the NIO. The man's task had been to keep track of NIO business, and he had overheard Asker's call to Agent Kartal arranging a covert meeting away from the city.

Kaplan had spoken to Marangol. The general had

agreed that allowing Asker to speak to Kartal was a risk too far. They'd known the location of the isolated meet, so Marangol had arranged for one of his military snipers to be dropped by helicopter near the spot, with orders to take out Asker.

The general had been a little reluctant to involve one of his elite soldiers; Marangol had tried to keep his people in the background during this stage of the operations. Involvement of the military might alert interest he'd wanted to avoid. He'd known of the scarcity of professional operatives within Polat's ranks of volunteers. He also realized that if Asker had had a change of heart, the information he carried would carry a big risk—a threat to them all. So he had volunteered his help, choosing one of own people.

The sniper was one of Marangol's operatives who belonged to the general's select group. He'd asked no questions, simply collected his weapon and taken an unmarked helicopter to the prearranged meeting place, concealing himself at a safe distance, where he'd waited for Asker and Berna Kartal to make their rendezvous.

The sniper had explicit orders. Both Asker and Kartal were to be eliminated. At least Kartal would be in the right place when Asker was killed. Her association with the Americans implied she would be in the know about everything that had happened. If Asker had requested the meet it was obvious he was ready to talk.

The first part of the operation went well. The sniper put his first shot into the NIO man. It was a killing shot. No question. The military sniper had been trained not to miss. He saw Asker fall as the 7.62 mm slug ripped through him, bursting clear as it exited.

The sniper had turned his rifle on the woman. She had reacted far quicker than he had expected, dropping to the ground and working her way beneath her SUV. The sniper had taken up the challenge, calmly targeting the underside of the vehicle with spaced shots. He had a 10-shot magazine in the BORA JNG-90 sniper rifle, with a second one at his side ready for reload if needed. The shots had driven Kartal out from under the SUV and that was when the sniper had put one in her chest. He'd not been able to confirm his kill.

At that moment her backup vehicles had appeared and Marangol's sniper had been forced to withdraw. He'd called in his helicopter after the backup's SUV turned around and left, and had been flown back to his base, where he'd reported to the general.

"I WILL FIND OUT if we have two dead, or just one," Marangol said.

"Does your man believe Asker was able to tell Kartal anything?" Kaplan said.

"From his report only a few seconds passed before he fired and put Asker down. There would have been little opportunity for Asker to have said anything of significance."

"Perhaps Asker passed her some information," Polat suggested. It was the first time he had said anything since Marangol had boarded the cruiser.

"Something to consider," Marangol conceded.

Polat had made a useful observation. Marangol had never had much time for Asker. He had found the man self-important, a little too overbearing. When the pressure built, the man backed down. Unable to stay the course. And that had made him unreliable.

It had not caused Marangol any trouble sleeping after he had made his decision to remove Asker. One man against what Özgürlük had planned.

"Let our people check on Kartal. See if she is actually dead and whether that coward Asker actually offered her information," Kaplan said.

"It is a good thing we moved the device," Polat said. "If Asker was able to pass details to Kartal, even if she is dead, those damned Americans could have found it. Asker presented too much risk, problems we can do without, at the moment."

"Good thinking," Marangol said.

"Hakan, we will need to make sure everything is safe. Arrange things for a transfer."

CHAPTER TWENTY-SIX

It was late when Hal Brognola returned to Stony Man. Rain was sheeting down across the Shenandoah Valley when his car came to a stop. The big Fed grabbed his briefcase, got out and wrapped his topcoat around him. He said good-night to his driver and made a dash for the entrance. The on-duty blacksuit hauled the door open as he hurried inside.

"Hell of a night, sir," the blacksuit said.

"And it's not over yet," Brognola said. He shook the rain off his topcoat.

He made his way to his office and hung up his damp coat, dropping his briefcase on the floor beside his desk. He had barely had time to sit when Barbara Price appeared at his door.

"How did it go with the President?" she asked.

"That all depends on your definition of 'how did it go.'"

Price leaned against the door frame. "How about you tell me when you have a steaming mug of coffee in your hand?"

"Best thing I've heard all damn night."

"You take a breather and I'll be back."

Brognola slumped back in his office seat, enjoying the moment of relaxation. His head had been swimming after the session with the President, and a call from his wife had only added to his discomfort. She'd been her usual forgiving and consoling self when he'd told her not to expect him before dawn. Brognola blessed the fates that had given him such a woman. In all their years of marriage, and especially since his becoming the man in charge of Stony Man, she had never once complained at his unsociable hours or his habit of disappearing from the family home at a moment's notice.

He glanced up as the odor of coffee drifted across the office.

Price placed the mug on his desk and waited as he took his first taste. "Better?"

Brognola nodded. "Better. Update me."

Price sat across from him and gave him a full briefing of the events that had occurred while he had been away.

Brognola, absorbing the information, asked, "So we still have nukes on the move but we have no idea where they are?"

"I guess the President isn't too happy about that."

"Not exactly doing handstands across the White House lawn. He's contacted the Turkish president and they both agree this situation has to be handled ASAP. If there are any nuclear detonations, in either country, we are all going to be in a no-win situation. He's under a lot of pressure here. The Turkish problem aside, if there's a nuclear explosion inside our own shores he's going to have to face a great deal of criticism."

"Hal, you have Able Team on that. They won't let you down."

"I have to believe that," Brognola said.

"Aaron and the team are working flat out, trying to get a lead on where these devices might have originated. The consensus is they must have been purchased from an outside source. Stealing nukes from inside Turkey would be next to impossible. But any device detonated inside the country would not go down too well with the general public. Turkey is a valuable member of NATO, so her credibility would take a big hit if that happened."

"Özgürlük wants Turkey free of American influence," Brognola said. "It wants us gone from Turkey. Out of NATO. But what do they gain by detonating a nuke on Turkish soil? I can accept they have an agenda, but does irradiating a large piece of their own country achieve that?"

"There are people willing to go to extremes to get what they want," Price said. "Fanatics have a habit of not looking at the consequences of their actions."

Brognola swallowed more coffee. "That's part of the problem," he said. "There *are* those kinds of individuals."

"But you don't go along with that, Hal. So what are you thinking?"

"That right now this is all giving me a damned headache. And there's a piece of the puzzle I still can't see."

"About?"

"I'll accept we're dealing with extremists," the big Fed acknowledged. "But these are people who want their country free from foreign involvement. American involvement. They have a passion for Turkey. But I don't see that poisoning a chunk of it is going to give them what they want. Blowing up a nuke just doesn't fit… Maybe it is all just a big bluff."

"And when we call that bluff?"

"Someone decides to say, 'to hell with this,' and does it anyway." Brognola drank from his cup. "Özgürlük knows if it wants to make its point, something big has to happen. If they chicken out from detonating a bomb on Turkish soil, they might not back down from doing it here."

"If they did, it would make us take notice. But we would still be a presence in Turkey. A big presence."

"That might not be strictly true," someone said.

AKIRA TOKAIDO HAD spun his chair around and raised his hand to attract Kurtzman's attention. The young cyber wizard, clad in jeans, his hair in a ponytail, permanent headphones in place, might not have looked the part, but when it came to manipulating the internet and all things out there, the Japanese American had few equals.

Kurtzman wheeled over to his protégé.

"You got something, or were you waving because you got lonely?" Kurtzman said.

"Would I waste your time, boss?" Tokaido pointed at his monitor. "I think we have a lead on who was working that nuke deal."

Kurtzman read the name on-screen. "Gennadi Antonov. Have anything new on him? Tell me you pulled finance details."

"First thing I did. He covers his banking deals pretty close but not close enough. I found out where he does his financial deals. A bank in Germany. I was able to get into his account there."

"You realize that is extremely unlawful," Kurtzman said. "Now you'll tell me I was the one who showed you how to do that."

Tokaido grinned. "Yes, boss. I printed off Antonov's statements for the past year. Incoming and outgoing. A few months back he received one extremely large deposit from an account in London. Incidentally the source came from an account in the name of the late Aziz Makar. Mr. Makar was Turkish. Our guy who ran a finance business in London and seems to have had very few clients. One of which is Özgürlük. Makar was the collector of donations for the group, which you already know. Moving on, Antonov paid most of the Özgürlük money to a Russian bank in Moscow. It was moved on to another deposit in Vladivostok."

"Anything significant there?"

"The account belongs to a Boris Yenkanov," Tokaido said. "Hunt is running a wide sweep for information on him now."

Huntington Wethers, another of Kurtzman's team, put his findings up on another plasma screen. There was also a grainy photograph of a balding middle-aged man.

"Tell me if I'm wrong," Kurtzman said, "but that looks like a military ID to me."

"Not wrong," Wethers said. "Yenkanov has a Russian army background. Rank of major. And his last two years have been spent overseeing nuclear storage sites."

"That sounds ominous," Kurtzman said. "Army major doesn't pull in all that from his paycheck. He hit the Moscow lottery win list?"

"Do they run the lottery in Russia?" Tokaido said.

"Exactly my point."

"For your interest," Wethers said, "I pulled up an item. Two, actually. Yenkanov was reported missing from his unit three days ago. Around the same time two B-54 backpack nuclear devices went AWOL from one of the storage units he was responsible for—"

"How the hell did you find that out?" Kurtzman said.

Wethers offered a faint smile. "We all have our ways. It's why cultivating foreign contacts is a worthwhile consideration."

"The Russians are not going to be happy about losing those nukes," Kurtzman noted. "Even more when they won't be able to trace them. They'll be long gone from Russia by now."

"We need to update the teams," Wethers said. "Let them know exactly what they're dealing with."

"Yeah, I'll go talk to Hal and Barb," Kurtzman said, wheeling himself over to the coffeemaker. "By the way, fellas, great work. Help yourselves to a mug of my coffee. You earned it," he said as he poured himself a large mug.

"Thanks," Tokaido said. He stared at Wethers, his expression betraying his thoughts on Kurtzman's offer.

As Kurtzman exited the room, he was grinning from ear to ear. He knew exactly what Tokaido and Wethers would be thinking about his offer. He was still smiling when he reached Brognola's office.

BROGNOLA AND PRICE turned to see Aaron Kurtzman in the open doorway to the big Fed's office. The silent running of his wheelchair had allowed him to come up behind them.

"I don't like pronouncements like that," Brognola said.

"Has an ominous ring to it," Price admitted.

"That's because it could be—ominous," Kurtzman said as he rolled himself farther into the room.

"And I was hoping today couldn't get any worse," Brognola sighed. "Go ahead. Spit it out."

"This detonating a bomb on Turkish soil had me concerned, as well," Kurtzman said. "So I had the team run down anything and everything that might be linked to the premise. They came up with so much stuff it even made my head spin. We were drowning in theories and suppositions and downright rumor. We were discarding feedback as fast as it was coming in. And then Akira and Hunt found something that might be a link to what we've been searching for.

"Between them, they located massive deposits of cash wormed into a Russian army major's account," he continued, "and unearthed details of an inventory problem at an old Soviet Union nuclear storage facility. Apparently two B-45s, classed as SADMs—Special Atomic Demolition Munitions—have gone missing."

"The press calls them 'suitcase bombs,'" Price interjected, "because they are small and transportable by hand. But most of these reports were refuted as being dreamed up by journalists."

Kurtzman nodded. "The truth is that SADMs existed as portable devices but are not as miniature as portrayed. The B-54 was a Soviet copy of the American backpack nuke, built but never used back in the 1980s. Although a number were constructed, the U.S. let the concept lapse—but not before design plans were stolen and passed to the Russians, who built their own."

"The loss of the schematics was suppressed," Brognola conceded, "partly through a need-to-know basis and not a little embarrassment."

Kurtzman nodded and expanded on the history of the devices. "The compact units were housed in a steel drum about the size of a standard oil drum and strapped in a canvas cover. The intention was to parachute the packs into enemy territory, where a two-man team would place and activate them if and when needed. Actual use was never ordered, and as tensions around the Cold War receded, the backpack bombs were stored in numerous Russian enclaves, and in some cases forgotten about as years and policies changed.

"The B-54 held a half-kiloton nuclear charge and was considered a low-yield weapon. Not for ultimate destruction but more of a localized tactical weapon that could destroy an enemy installation and lay down some degree of radiation fallout that would be kept to a minimum. Its activation was by a basic mechanical device to be set into motion by the installation team. Detonation would be from a straightforward timer."

"This would work well for Özgürlük," Price said. "Small explosion and a minimum of fallout. It would effectively close down Incirlik and put the whole base off-line."

"Publicity you couldn't buy," Brognola said.

"Almost the best option," Kurtzman said. "Remove the main objective and prevent it being returned to action. Minimal fallout, always a risk because it's hard to control, but we have to accept that Özgürlük is in this for the long haul. These people are set for a long battle."

"And we don't forget they have a similar scenario for the U.S.," Price said. "They might not be so forgiving with anything they want to detonate here."

CHAPTER TWENTY-SEVEN

Carl Lyons read the text a second time. His partners saw the hard gleam in his eyes and knew without asking he was not seeing what he wanted. It wasn't telepathy, but close. Schwarz and Blancanales could read Lyons's expressions as clear as the written word.

"We're not going to like this?" Schwarz said.

Lyons shook his head.

"Stony Man had a call from Phoenix. They hit Polat's base off the Turkish coast. Some island. Took down the armed resistance and went into the house..."

"No nukes?" Schwarz said.

"Nothing. They found weapons. Communication setup, but no bombs. If the nukes had been there, they've been moved."

"Clock still ticking," Blancanales said.

Lyons stared at his phone, his fingers threatening to crush it. "We have no idea where the damn things are," he said. "Hal is having a close-up meeting with the President right now." He made a deep sound in his throat. "We need to go back and start over. Squeeze every damn contact we have until we get something."

He hit the Stony Man speed-dial button and waited until Price came on.

"Barb, tell Aaron he needs to go back through everything he has on this deal. We need something—anything. Right now we're facing a blank wall and we need a new direction. I don't care if those computer geeks have to stay up all day and night. Find me something."

"I'll convey your diplomatic request to Aaron and hope he sees it in the way you intended," Price said. "Call you back."

"I won't use Carl's exact words," Price said, "because I have a feeling they might upset you."

Kurtzman's chuckle reached her through the phone line.

"That man never understood the value of diplomacy," he said, "but given the situation, he's allowed a slip."

Price smiled. Kurtzman never ceased to surprise her. Cutting Lyons some slack told her the cyber chief understood the gravity of the problem.

"Able Team has exhausted every lead and right now they haven't anywhere to go. In other words, Aaron, they need…"

"Help," Kurtzman said. "They'll get it. Time to fill up my coffeepot again."

Kurtzman was as good as his word. He faced his team, and in a few words laid out the situation. Wethers, Tokaido and the third member of the team, Carmen Delahunt, listened in silence, understanding what this would mean for them and accepting the responsibility without question.

"Anything coming through, unless it's unavoidable, you push across to me. You three are on this situation full-stop. Give it your best. Find something we can send to Able. They're coming up empty and they need our help. I don't give a damn if you come up with something so thin it's transparent. Just find something for them to grab hold of."

He waited as his words reached his people. The team he considered the best in their field.

If there was any scrap of information out there, they would find it. Kurtzman had no doubt about that.

"We'll find you something," Delahunt said. "Just promise you won't force us to drink your coffee if we slip up."

"I HAVE A HIT," Tokaido said three hours later, instantly capturing Kurtzman's attention.

"This may be what we've been looking for," he continued. "The name of a small container ship that belongs to one of the Polat business consortiums. She's called the *Crystal Sea*. And she tied up at Baltimore docks two days ago. She left from Turkey and did a slow run, picking up and dropping off cargo on the way. Nothing in that, but why is she included in the data belonging to our Turkish organization?"

"Because she has something special on board?" Kurtzman suggested. "I'll pass that over to Able Team. They can check it out. It fits our timeline. Get as much detail as you can—and send it to me."

Kurtzman rolled his chair back to his desk and was smiling when Barbara Price joined him.

"Smiling during working hours?" she said. "That must mean you have some good news for Able Team."

Kurtzman showed the information to the Stony Man mission controller.

"Now, that is just what the guys want."

"I'll call Carl," Kurtzman said. "He'll be champing at the bit."

"And I'll call Hal with the update. He needs some good news," Price said, thinking of the big Fed.

HAL BROGNOLA WAS seated in the Oval Office, his gaze fixed on the scene beyond the window. Between Brognola and the window was the desk of the President of the United States. As he waited for the President he reflected on how many times he had visited this office, how many different Presidents he had served.

He heard the door open behind him and started to rise from his chair.

"As you were," the President said as he crossed to his desk. He sat behind it and stared at Brognola. "Hal, you look like hell."

"I've been considering asking for a raise in salary and a reduction in hours."

"I'll have to think about that," the President said lightly. "You had coffee?"

"No, sir. I was waiting for you."

"No need to stand on ceremony here. Go and pour us both a cup. I need one. Hal, there are times when this job seems wrapped up in nothing but petty details."

Brognola filled two cups and brought them back to the desk. They both took a moment to drink.

"I take it this visit is not to encourage happy thoughts."

"Sorry, sir, I wish it was."

Brognola gave the President chapter and verse. He left nothing out and the President allowed him to finish his report without interruption.

"So now we know exactly the type of weapons we're dealing with. But not where they are. Kind of leaves us dancing on the spot, Hal. I'll speak to the Turkish president shortly," he said. "He needs to know how things are playing out. I owe him that much. His country is at risk as much as we are."

"In view of our not yet having located the device, what can we do about our people at the Incirlik base?"

"I'm glad you managed to say *not yet*, Hal."

"Phoenix Force doesn't quit. The same goes for Able Team, sir. They'll keep looking."

"As to our people at Incirlik... I spoke to the base commander this morning and filled him in on the threat. He was adamant about remaining on station. There are over five thousand personnel at Incirlik. With families. Plus a contingent of UK and Turkish air force officers and men. I don't give a damn about equipment, but I do about people. It would take a long time to get everyone clear. Too long. And the moment we start evacuating, our Özgürlük friends, who will undoubtedly be watching, could detonate that device for maximum effect. As long as business goes on uninterrupted, Özgürlük will stay with their timetable. The longer they give us, the more chance Phoenix Force has of finding the damn bomb. And we can't ignore the presence of our own stored nuclear devices bunkered at Incirlik. Özgürlük's detonation could start a chain reaction. One small device could blow ours. Not a definite but a possibility."

"Hell of a gamble, sir," Brognola said.

"Don't remind me, Hal. What other way can we go? I could order the evacuation and sit by and watch Özgürlük set off that device regardless. Then they could be bluffing. There's no way of knowing. They have me over a barrel. Damned if I do, damned of I don't."

"And we have a copycat scenario here at home," Brognola noted.

"Hal, what would be your take on this?"

"Look at the cards in my hand and make my best guess, sir. Test Özgürlük's strength of purpose. See if they're willing to go that extra mile and hope our people can bust them before they decide to press the button.

Mr. President, I'm just glad I don't have that decision to make."

"Unfortunately, I don't have that option, Hal," the President said.

Brognola stood. "Time I was back at the SOG, sir."

"You can reach me anytime, Hal. Day and night. Don't hesitate if you need anything."

"How about an extended break in Hawaii? Starting ten minutes ago."

"When this is over, we'll both go."

"I might hold you to that, sir," Brognola said.

The President picked up his phone, presumably to connect with the Turkish president.

"I'll wait for your call," he said just before the big Fed shut the door to the Oval Office.

CHAPTER TWENTY-EIGHT

"Do we approach this as professionals, or simply as Iron-man followers?" Blancanales said as he rolled the SUV to a stop outside the fence at the Baltimore docks. He switched off the engine and glanced at Carl Lyons.

The blond Able Team leader pretended he couldn't hear what was being said. He was loading the Colt Python before returning it to his shoulder rig.

"Something tells me the guys on this ship aren't going to be receptive to anything we have to say," Schwarz said.

"Just how I like it," Lyons growled.

They climbed out of the SUV and gathered in a tight group. Beyond the docks a light mist was hanging over choppy water. Fine rain had drifted in, leaving a glistening sheen over the area.

Lyons had counted three freighters tied up at the dock. The one they were looking for was the middle vessel. They could see figures moving around on the open deck. By container ship standards the *Crystal Sea* was a small vessel, a regular workhorse of the trade lanes. They could see almost a hundred containers on deck.

"You figure they've brought the bomb in?" Blancanales said. "We are working on really thin evidence."

"Right now it's the only evidence we have," Lyons said.

"Dock would be a good target, though," Blancanales noted. "It would cause a great deal of disruption."

"Even a small device is going to cause a lot of damage," Schwarz said. "And the drifting radiation would have long-term effects across the area."

Blancanales said, "Then let's do something instead of talk about it. We need to pin this down in case that computer information turns out to be correct."

"Hey, we have visitors," Lyons warned.

A Baltimore PD cruiser had crept into view and was approaching. Their weapons were out of sight beneath Able Team's jackets; they had left the heavier arms inside the SUV. The patrol car rolled to a stop and the uniformed two-man team climbed out. They wore holstered automatic pistols and kept their gun hands close to the butts as they stepped clear of their car. They were both young, capable-looking.

"You fellows have business here?" the lead officer said as he reached Able Team.

Lyons already had his ID wallet in his hand and he held it discreetly so only the cops could see the Justice Department shield.

"I'm Matthews," he said. "These are Comer and Hartz. Right now we're close to bringing an operation down. Appreciate your cooperation, Sergeant Bellman."

Lyons had seen the stripes on the man's uniform shirt and read the name badge. The other cop was called Logan.

Bellman looked from man to man. His eyes flickered across the jackets Able Team wore, spotting the slight bulges that showed the three were armed.

"If you need confirmation," Lyons said, "I can put you through to our section commander. He can confirm our operation."

"So what's happening?"

"The middle ship behind you, the *Crystal Sea*, we believe has something on board we need to get to ASAP. We need to reach it before some trigger-happy guy decides to detonate it."

"Jesus," Logan said. "You serious? A bomb?"

Bellman studied Lyons's face and saw something there he didn't like. The cop was far from being a rookie and he suspected the worst.

"Not just a bomb, is it?" he said. "Something bigger than that."

Lyons simply nodded, the implication registering quickly.

"Fake checking us out in case we're being watched," Lyons said.

While Logan stood by with his hand resting on his gun, Bellman ran his hands over Able Team, checking pockets and turning the three around as he frisked them.

"Should we call the bomb squad?" Bellman asked.

"These perps see those vehicles roll up and sprout cops in protective gear they'll know we're on to them," Lyons said.

"You saying they might set it off if they figure we've made them?"

"They could do that," Lyons said. "Nothing to go on but my gut feeling. I'd rather not chance my luck."

Bellman stepped back and slipped his notebook from his pocket and began to take notes.

"Matthews, you talk just like a cop," he said.

"I was once LAPD."

"Then tell me what we do right now."

Lyons's mind had been working overtime as he'd submitted to the fake search. A random thought had occurred to him about the ship and the crew, plus any cargo it might be carrying apart from the containers. His instincts were very often correct. Lyons knew it was a long shot but worth investigating. It had been a casual glance along the quayside at the line of warehouses that had piqued his interest.

What he had seen confirmed a thought at the back of his mind.

The more he debated with himself, the more the thought took on solid form.

"Can you find out any details about that ship?"

"We can patch through to the dock central office," Logan said. "What are you looking for?"

"Everything you can find about it. They have security cameras dockside?"

"Yeah. Like everywhere these days."

"Ask if they have recordings of the *Crystal Sea* since she tied up."

Logan returned to the cruiser and leaned inside to pick up the radio handset.

"What's on your mind?" Schwarz said.

"Take a look at the warehouse fronts," Lyons said.

It only took a moment for Schwarz to make the connection as he registered what Lyons had seen.

"Son of a bitch," he said. "Same name."

When Blancanales checked, he saw it, too.

The Turkish Spice Company.

It was emblazoned on the identification board above the warehouse main doors.

The Turkish produce company they had visited earlier, where they had had the run-in with the men from the delivery truck.

"From seller to the buyer to Turkey. Put on board the container ship bound for Baltimore and docked right alongside the warehouse. Ship to shore. Sailed right inside under our noses. Ship unloads, sails away out of danger when she's ready," Lyons said. "Warehouse insiders set the countdown, lock the warehouse and get out of Dodge before the big bang."

"I'm not too happy with the big bang," Bellman said.

Logan came back after a couple of minutes.

"Security ran the recording. That ship unloaded a few containers," he said. "Took on a few more. They also unloaded a pallet of smaller goods that went into the warehouse, waiting for inspection. Manifest lists the load as goods for the Turkish Spice Company. Delivery comes in every few weeks. Nothing moves out of the warehouse until it has been Customs checked and passed. It stays there until cleared. Ship is due to sail later tonight. All being played by the book."

"Turkish Spice Company again," Schwarz said.

He had noticed the way Lyons was acting. The doubt on his face warned Schwarz he was working something out.

"What are you thinking?"

"The ship leaves later tonight," Lyons said. "Gives them time to get clear before anything is set with the bomb."

"You saying the crew has nothing to do with it?" Bellman asked.

"Ship is just a way of getting the package into the country. Once it's off-loaded, the ship is clear. These are no suicide terrorists. They deliver and go about their business. Sail away. No fuss. No alarm raised because they leave the package behind."

"Customs agents could show up anytime," Logan said. "They can carry out spot checks whenever they want."

"It's a gamble," Lyons said. "By the time the check is done, that package will have been substituted for an identical one holding real Turkish Spice Company goods. The device will be hidden somewhere in the warehouse, waiting for someone to press the switch that starts it ticking. Long enough countdown for our warehouse guys to get well clear."

"Plenty of question marks in there," Bellman said.

"I didn't say it was written in stone. Just offering a suggestion. This is all on the hoof."

"You think this could be happening?" Logan asked.

"I can see the sense in it," Bellman said. "It could happen that way. If you figured how much stuff comes into these docks every day, there has to be some that slips through. No use pretending it doesn't happen. Maybe these people figured the odds and took a gamble."

"They do it nice and quiet," Schwarz said. "Gives them time to set it up and let that ship leave. The bomb stays, ready for the final countdown after our Özgürlük locals have been long gone."

"Özgürlük?" Bellman said.

"They're Turkish extremists wanting to make a political statement," Blancanales told him. "They're pissed because we have our Air Force at Incirlik. They want us off Turkish soil."

"*Extremists?*" Bellman said. "Come on, Comer, don't you mean terrorists? Just another bunch of bastards who want to take shots at this country. One hell of a shot, the way you tell it. They going to fry Baltimore?"

"*Fry?* What are you...? Christ, are you guys talking about a nuke?" Logan said as the penny dropped.

"Hey, don't stand there with your eyes out on sticks," Bellman said. "Let's talk this through quietly."

"There a back way into that warehouse?" Lyons asked, counting on the local cops knowing their beat.

Bellman made a show of putting away his notebook and wagging a finger at Able Team as if he was having words with them.

"Back out the way you came in. You'll see the service road leading onto the delivery area. Loading dock and way in."

"Let us check this out."

"You want us to give a hand?"

Lyons nodded. "Cover the area out here. When we go in through the back, there might be breakout onto the dock. And you can keep an eye on the ship in case they have any kind of backup."

"You got it. These guys," Bellman said, nodding toward the ship, "they the kind who quit easy?"

"I'd say no," Blancanales said. "So do whatever you have to do to stay healthy."

Bellman nodded. He and Logan turned and went back to their cruiser.

Able Team climbed into their SUV, Blancanales behind the wheel. He fired up the engine and swung the vehicle back the way they had come, out of sight of anyone who might have been watching.

"Well, that was different," Schwarz said.

Lyons had recovered his shotgun. "Take us in," he said as the feeder road brought them around to the chainlink fence and the open gate giving access to the delivery area. There were only a couple of parked cars near the loading ramp under the sign for the Turkish distribution company. A lone figure sat on a plastic chair outside the entrance.

"Pull over and go tell him you're looking for a company you can't find," Lyons said to Schwarz. "And watch yourself. I'll bet my next paycheck he's carrying. He needs dealing with so his buddies inside can't hear."

Blancanales pulled the SUV to a stop as Schwarz made sure his jacket was secured over his Beretta. He stepped out of the vehicle and walked around to Blancanales's door.

"Give me something I can pretend to be checking," he said.

Blancanales took a folded map from the side pocket and handed it to his Able Team partner.

"This is where acting lessons would come in handy," Schwarz said.

He showed an amiable expression as he turned and crossed to the loading dock, gesturing to the guy watching him.

"Be easier to just shoot him," Lyons said.

"And warn the others inside? I thought we just covered that."

Lyons simply shrugged.

The Able Team pair watched Schwarz stroll to the dock, hands expressing his request as he spoke to the guy. The man stared at Schwarz, and only the odd word reached Lyons and Blancanales. Schwarz held up the map and pointed at something. Whatever it was brought the guy up off his seat. He stepped to the edge of the loading dock and part-crouched as Schwarz continued gesturing with the map. The guy, wide-shouldered and stocky, bent a little closer as Schwarz continued to talk.

And then Schwarz struck. Without warning and almost too fast for his partners to catch. His left hand shot out, fingers fastening on the man's loose shirt. He yanked the guy forward, right into his bunched right fist. Lyons and Blancanales heard the solid sound of the blow. The guy's head snapped back, blood trailing from split lips. Giving the guy no opportunity to fight back, Schwarz dragged him off the ramp and dropped him to the concrete. He flipped the dazed guy onto his back, hit him a couple more times, then snapped his neck with a swift movement. The guy jerked, then lay still. Schwarz removed an autopistol from the guy's belt and straightened, showing the gun to his partners.

Lyons and Blancanales exited the SUV and joined Schwarz on the loading ramp. Blancanales had brought Schwarz's MP5 along with his own, and Lyons was carrying his Franchi SPAS.

There was a single Judas door set in the main roll-up door to give access to the warehouse. Lyons peered in through the small access window set in the door. It allowed a view into the main warehouse, which was stacked with packaged goods around a central open section and a series of worktables.

A group of seven men was standing around one of the tables.

It took seconds for Lyons to recognize the configuration of the B-54 backpack device. The canvas outer cover had been pulled back to show the drum-shaped nuclear weapon. Two of the men grouped around the device were deep in conversation as they adjusted something on the bomb casing.

"We hit the jackpot?" Blancanales said. "Or are they just defrosting kebabs?"

"Only a half-kiloton one," Lyons said.

He tried the handle on the Judas door and felt it give.

"Take a look," he said, stepping aside so Schwarz and Blancanales could check out the layout.

"I see weapons," Blancanales said, noting an assortment of arms on one of the tables.

Lyons racked the shotgun.

"I'll take out the pair working on the device first," he said. "Get them out of the way."

"No shooting the nuke," Schwarz said. "I know a

bullet isn't supposed to set it off, but I don't want to test that theory."

"I'm with you on that one," Blancanales agreed.

"Quit being a pair of old ladies," Lyons said.

He eased the Judas door open and slipped inside, his partners crowding in behind. They separated as they moved across the smooth floor of the warehouse.

Lyons slung the SPAS around his neck by its carry sling and took out the Python; he needed controlled shots to remove the technicians working over the device, and a hit from the .357-caliber slugs would do that for him.

Blancanales and Schwarz, understanding that Lyons needed space, moved farther to the side.

Able Team was as close as fifteen feet before one of the watching men stepped back to give himself some space. He must have picked up movement in the periphery of his vision. His head came around and he saw Able Team moving in to intercept. He yelled a warning, snatching at the pistol pushed into his waistband.

Blancanales shot him, putting a triple burst into his body that dropped the guy without a murmur.

Lyons leaned forward, the Python rising in a two-handed grip. He triggered his first shot, then pulled the revolver toward the other target. His second shot hit a bare second after the first. The powerful .357 slugs blew apart the men's skulls, bloody flesh and bone fragments blowing out the exit holes, brain matter mingling with the debris. The spatter was blown across the nuclear device as the shot men dropped.

Reaction from the other four was rapid. They hauled out weapons and opened fire, sending slugs across the warehouse in a haphazard sequence. They found no targets because Able Team had moved again, keeping themselves mobile and creating fleeting images.

Schwarz saw one guy turn to the table supporting the device and reach for an open laptop. He angled the MP5 and sent a long burst that ripped into the hand closest to the computer. The 9 mm slugs took the guy's hand apart, shredding it to a mangled stump. The guy rolled away from the table, clutching at his ruined hand. Blood was pumping from the lacerated flesh and bone.

A couple more armed figures raced into view from the front of the warehouse, shouting and yelling as they came.

Blancanales fed them a ragged burst from his MP5, the 9 mm slugs finding soft flesh and harder bone. The pair tumbled to the concrete, upper thighs sprouting blood as they fell.

In those brief seconds Lyons returned his Python to leather and swept up the SPAS shotgun. He faced down one of the surviving three men and triggered a 12-gauge shell. The spread hit one guy in the lower body and left him down on the floor, clutching his blood-streaming stomach.

The remaining pair broke away from the table, making a run for the front of the warehouse.

Schwarz took one down with a triggered volley from his subgun. The guy stumbled and fell, his lower back glistening red from the multiple wounds.

The lone survivor reached the front of the warehouse and yanked open the Judas door, stumbling outside, where he ran into Sergeant Bellman.

The Baltimore cop was carrying a Remington pump-action shotgun. He faced the armed Özgürlük thug, quickly reversing the shotgun and slamming it butt-first into the Turkish extremist's face. The man fell back against the door, blood streaming down his face from his crushed nose and mouth. Bellman brought the barrel of the shotgun down on the man's gun hand, crushing fingers and knocking the Glock pistol from his broken fingers. The man dropped to his knees, head hanging, strings of blood trailing from his skewed jaw.

"You piece of dirt," Bellman said. He was ready to hit the whimpering man again until Logan blocked his arm and gently pushed it aside.

"He isn't worth it, sir. We've got the son of a bitch. It's enough."

Bellman took a breath. "You said it, son." He picked up the dropped Glock. "Just cuff him to something while I go check out our Justice agents."

He stepped inside the warehouse and surveyed the bloody scene. A number of bodies on the floor. One man hunched over, clutching at a mangled hand. The three agents were clustered around what he assumed was the nuclear device in question.

"Tell me you stopped it with three seconds to go."

"Sorry to disappoint you," Blancanales said. "I think they were still arming it."

Bellman shoved his cap to the back of his head. "Oh well, that's okay, then."

He came to stand in front of the B-54 unit, scanning it without knowing what he was actually looking at.

It was, he thought, an ugly piece of apparatus.

"That would have blown up a piece of the city?"

Schwarz nodded. "It would. Take my word for it."

"Baltimore owes you guys one hell of a debt."

"This won't get broadcast around," Schwarz said. "It'll be kept low profile as possible. Why scare folk if we don't need to?"

Logan appeared and walked to stare at the device.

"That is one ugly hunk of machinery," he said.

"I was just thinking the same," Bellman said.

"They're not built to win artistic awards. Just to kill a lot of people," Lyons said. He was putting his sat phone away. "NEST is on its way to deal with that thing."

"Can't happen quickly enough for me," Logan said.

"It's bound to get busy around here for a while," Blancanales said.

"What about the crew of the *Crystal Sea*?" Bellman asked. "Could be some of them were involved."

"That ship isn't going anywhere," Schwarz said. "I made a call. U.S. Customs is sending a couple of vessels to watch over her. And the Baltimore FBI office is already on its way. This area will be sealed off in the next thirty minutes. And there are ambulances rolling."

"Maybe we should get back out there and keep an eye out for anyone trying to jump ship," Bellman said. "See you guys later for a coffee?"

"Keep you to that," Schwarz said.

"ONE DOWN, ONE to go," Brognola said, the relief in his voice palpable. "You guys okay?"

"We were lucky this time. If something like this crops up again…" Lyons replied.

"I guess we should be thankful Özgürlük has turned out not to be as sophisticated as they figured."

"Problem there," Lyons said, "is it's sometimes the damned amateur who walks into something like this and pulls it off. We need to be sharp."

"We can talk this through when you get back. See if we can brainstorm some new ideas. Carl, you all cleared away there?"

"More or less. We located a laptop. I'll bring it in. May be some intel we can use. NEST is dealing with the device. Their lab rats will be drooling over it for weeks. I'm not so sure which is scarier. The loony who wants to set it off or the brainiac who wants to tinker around with it."

"Take it easy coming home."

"Before we leave, we promised to buy our Baltimore cop buddies a quick coffee."

"I'll have Jack fly to your position in a chopper. He can get you back here soon as."

"If you speak to Phoenix, tell David if they need any advice, the top team is available."

When he put the phone down, Brognola wished the solution was as simple as that. He glanced up as a shadow crossed his office door.

Barbara Price stood there with a look on her face that told him the situation in Turkey was far from settled…

CHAPTER TWENTY-NINE

"Here," Kartal said. She put a finger on the map. The inscriptions were all in Turkish, so she had to translate. "It is an old monastery. Long abandoned. On a hill where anyone approaching can be seen. Asker's information spoke of Polat using it as a place where Oz could fall back to if they needed."

"Do you have any coordinates?" McCarter asked. "Anything we could use to get a fix on the place?"

He was thinking about the eye in the sky. The Zero satellite platform. If they could send data to it, the sophisticated camera arrays on the satellite might be able to give them guidance.

"Let me work this out," Kartal said.

They were in the NIO communications room, surrounded by computers and cyber techs. Kartal called over one of the operators and explained what she needed. The young NIO tech responded and went to his computer, his fingers flying over the keyboard.

"At least he looks as if he knows what he's doing," James said. "Even if he does look like he should be in school."

"I can assure you he does," Kartal said. "Kristos could work that keyboard in his sleep. He is of the new generation. Computers are his blood."

Minutes later, Kristos brought Kartal a printout. She

took it and scanned the text, thanked the young man and handed the sheet of paper to McCarter.

"I asked Kristos to print it in English."

"What took him so long?" McCarter said.

Kartal simply smiled; she was becoming comfortable with the Briton's humor.

"Will that give your people what they need?"

"Yes," McCarter said.

He punched the speed-dial button on his phone for Stony Man and when Price answered he asked to be transferred to Kurtzman. The man's gruff voice came on quickly. He had been expecting the call and wasted no time copying the coordinates McCarter read out to him.

"We're ready to contact Zero. Buchanan is waiting for our call. Zero is already on line for the catch. I'll come back as soon as he locks in."

"Thanks, mate." McCarter shut down the call. "Now we wait."

"I do not suppose it is any use me asking how you will do this," Kartal said.

"More than my life is worth," McCarter said. "But you will be able to see the result." He indicated one of the plasma screens fixed to the wall above the computer stations.

"Then we have time for coffee," Kartal said.

"This is the sort of news I like," Hawkins said.

The call from Kurtzman came within the next thirty minutes. He told McCarter the Zero satellite had an image based on the supplied coordinates. Kartal had already given McCarter the NIO link and the Stony Man cyber unit made the transition smoothly. The plasma screen came to life and the image from Zero was suddenly there. Bright and detailed.

Kartal stepped forward, her eyes fixed on the picture she was seeing.

"It is so clear," she said. "I would like something like that in here."

"It would cost you a bit more than a cup of coffee," Encizo said.

The image of the old monastery was displayed in detail: the stone building and the rough terrain around it. They could see the vehicles parked at the front of the main building, inside a walled courtyard. A figure was moving back and forth. Other figures could be seen around the perimeter.

"Is this in real time?" Manning asked Kurtzman, who was still on the line.

"Two-minute delay," Kurtzman confirmed. "What next? Popcorn and a bottle of Classic Coke?"

"You know how to hurt," McCarter said, thinking he hadn't tasted a bottle of Coke for some while and right at that moment a chilled one would have been welcome.

"Ground around that place is pretty exposed," Encizo observed. "Going to be hard to sneak up without being noticed."

"Not impossible," Manning said. "If we go in before dawn, someone should be able to move up and run a check. Pass intel back."

"I can do that," Hawkins said.

"Ah, the young warrior speaks," James chided.

"Exactly what I was thinking," Hawkins said. "It's a young man's job. Crawling around in all that damp grass isn't for you older guys."

"He's got a point," Encizo said.

"Okay, volunteer, you're up," McCarter said. Over his sat phone he sent his thanks to Buchanan via Kurtzman.

"I'll hold the feed as long as the camera is in range,"

Kurtzman said. "We can record the image in case anything breaks and call you."

The plasma blanked.

"We'll gear up," McCarter said. "Get some rest before we head out."

"You should eat, too," Kartal said. "But no *kuzu tandir* on the menu," she added for McCarter's benefit.

"Just one more disappointment I'll have to bear," the Phoenix Force leader said.

HAWKINS MADE FINAL adjustments to his com set.

"You're coming through okay," Encizo said.

His face darkened with camo paint, Hawkins checked his Beretta 92FS and made sure his Cold Steel Tanto knife was secure. He had handed his subgun to one of the others, not wanting to have too much to carry. This trip was purely recon to assess what the opposition might be offering.

"You sure you want to do this?" McCarter said.

Hawkins grinned. "Do I look as if I do?"

McCarter slapped the younger man on the shoulder. "You just want to show us oldies up in front of the young lady," he quipped.

"You got me there, boss."

"Eyes and ears open," James said, "and keep your butt close to the ground."

"Don't rush it, cowboy," McCarter said. "Take your time."

Kartal leaned forward and placed a hand on Hawkins's cheek.

"Come back well," she said.

"Shucks, ma'am, I'm blushing under this paint."

Hawkins turned and slipped away from where Phoenix Force was concealed. His lean, dark-clad figure quickly merged with the shadows and he vanished.

"He will be safe?" Kartal asked.

"He can do this," Encizo said. "But there is always a risk."

There is always a risk.

The thought crossed all their minds.

Phoenix Force. Berna Kartal. They all understood the element of risk their work exposed them to. The very nature of what they did placed them in risky situations all the time.

As the old phrase had it—it came with the territory.

THERE IS ALWAYS the risk.

Thomas Jackson Hawkins was aware of that as much as anyone. He was a soldier. He'd faced his share of dangerous situations and he respected the need to stay mindful of what lay ahead of him.

His military experience gave Hawkins the skills he needed for his current assignment. His service as a Ranger, then with Delta Force, equipped him with recon abilities, and Hawkins was about to put that experience to good use.

In the cool of the predawn, Hawkins eased his way through the rough terrain. The hilly landscape allowed him to move forward and make the best use of the cover offered. The coarse, thick grasses and the undulating surface allowed him to close in on his target with comparative ease.

He kept up a steady flow of movement, aware that it would have been easy to move faster. He resisted that. His approach demanded caution. Until he was able to ascertain whether Özgürlük had any extended security, he couldn't take any chances. One slip and any gain would be lost.

Hawkins kept in mind that Phoenix Force's previous encounters with Özgürlük had showed them that the Turkish extremists seemed to lack followers with military experience. The soldiers they had come up against, though well equipped with weapons, lacked anything that might be classed as fighting skills. Which did not exclude them from being dangerous. A loaded gun could not be dismissed lightly; it was designed for killing, and modern weapons had excellent capabilities where that was concerned.

Hawkins picked up movement ahead of him. He froze, lowering himself to the ground and focusing in on the spot. He saw the dark outline off to his left. Twenty feet away, directly ahead of him.

Hawkins stayed belly down, watching his mark. As his eyes adjusted to the ambient light he could make out the subgun the man was carrying. A dull gleam reflected from the outline of the weapon.

The sentry took a long, slow turn around. His gaze would have passed over where Hawkins lay. The man made no indication he had seen anything, and after a time he turned in the opposite direction and moved off. Hawkins remained where he was, watching the guy. Saw him pace away, his steps taking him farther from Hawkins's position.

Hawkins moved himself, in a wide curve that would allow him to circle the sentry and extend the distance between them. He activated his com set and gave a whispered update.

"One armed sentry. Moving north away from my position. No more contact yet."

Through his earbud he received McCarter's response.

"Twenty minutes out. Good so far."

"Will call with more. Out."

Hawkins clicked off.

TEN MINUTES LATER he picked up vehicle headlights approaching the ancient monastery. They curved up from the narrow trail leading to the structure, coming to a stop with the beams playing on the main gate. The gates opened after a couple of minutes and the vehicle moved slowly inside. Hawkins watched the gates swing shut.

The young Texan saw the distant sentry walk toward the gates and let himself inside through a smaller gate set in the wall. Whoever the newcomers were, they were attracting attention. Hawkins clicked on the com set and reported the new information.

"Visitors this early?" McCarter said.

"Something about to happen?" Hawkins asked.

"Never can tell, Rankin. Keep awake."

Hawkins figured he had less than an hour before he lost the cover of the darkness. He needed to be closer to the wall. With that in mind he started in toward the target again.

Hawkins found the ground underneath was leaking water from some source. He couldn't do anything to avoid it, so he kept moving. He managed to keep his hands clear of the moisture. The water seemed to extend across his path, and he was soon crawling through a meandering stream a couple of inches deep.

The armed man didn't return. Hawkins spent minutes observing the area, aware of the breaking dawn as it started to dissipate the dark. He was able to make out the lay of the land better now. The problem with that was his visibility to any watching eyes.

He made the outer wall of the monastery, drawing

himself in close against the rough stonework. There was ample cover where thick weeds and foliage grew to a height of a few feet up the wall. Hawkins stayed where he was for a few minutes, observing what he could from his restricted position.

Some yards along from where he crouched he made out the weathered formation of an archway. Sculpted stone that might indicate a door. He crawled through the foliage until he reached the archway. His guess had been correct. There was a wooden door set back in the arch. And at shoulder height was a metal grille set in the weathered timber.

Hawkins rose, his first instinct to take out his Beretta, safety off. He took a cautious look through the grille. As the retreating shadows revealed more, Hawkins found he was checking out a stone-paved courtyard. To his left was the front of the monastery building. To his right, a larger gated entrance to the courtyard. The one he had seen open to allow the visiting vehicle inside. There were three parked motor vehicles in the courtyard. High-end SUVs.

He also made out a pair of armed men standing near the main door, talking quietly together.

There was no way he could assess how many people were inside the building. That would have to be figured out when Phoenix Force made its entrance into the place.

Hawkins was about to engage his com set when his ears picked up a sound close by.

Too close.

At his rear, slightly to his right.

A muttered word in Turkish, followed by the click of a safety being disengaged. Hawkins picked up the scent of cigar smoke and knew his recon was over.

There was enough pale light now to let a shadow register on the stone wall as the newcomer moved closer.

Son, you better do something fast, he decided.

Hawkins spun right, the Beretta in his fist sweeping around as he came face-to-face with the man behind him.

His move caught the guy off guard. Despite having come up behind the Phoenix Force warrior, the dark-haired man quickly lost his advantage. His reflexes were sluggish and his subgun was pointed away from Hawkins.

The Texan didn't give him the chance to rectify that mistake.

The solid frame of the 92FS slammed across the bridge of the man's nose. Hawkins had put all of his strength into the move. He heard the audible crunch as the guy's nose collapsed under the merciless blow. He stepped back, tears starting to stream from his eyes as the pain exploded and blood spurted from his crushed nose. Hawkins didn't give the man a chance to recover. He slammed the pistol back and forth across the guy's exposed skull, splitting flesh and fracturing bone. Totally at the Texan's mercy, the Özgürlük soldier was driven to his knees, unable to offer any kind of defense or make a sound.

Holstering the pistol, Hawkins stepped around the stunned soldier. He grasped the bloody head in his hands and gripped it, then jerked it without a moment's hesitation. There was the merest crunch as the head was severed from the spinal cord. The guy shuddered and collapsed in front of Hawkins.

He wiped his bloodied hands down his front, then clicked on his com set.

"We need to move fast," he said. "I have eyes on the courtyard inside the walls. Three parked SUVs. Two armed guys in sight. Can't say how many inside. I just took down an outside sentry. If we're going to do this, the time is now."

"Acknowledged. We'll move out now."

"Make it fast."

Hawkins clicked off his com set. He crouched over the dead man and picked up the fallen subgun. An MP5, with a 30-round mag that had a second one taped to it for fast reload. Hawkins set the fire selector to 3-round bursts.

Hawkins checked out the courtyard again. No change. Two armed sentries. The open space between the building and the main gates was otherwise clear.

He leaned against the wall.

"Let's go, guys," he breathed.

CHAPTER THIRTY

General Demir Marangol watched the two weapons men working over the backpack device. This was his first viewing of the Russian-made SADM. Though he would never have admitted it to anyone, Marangol was nervous in its presence. The military man was no coward. He had been in combat situations, faced and killed enemies, but there was something about the B-54 designated device that left him with a feeling of unease. The drum-shaped black bomb sitting on the table a few feet from where he stood exuded menace. Marangol understood the potential within that object. Knew the awesome power it could create if detonated. It was the unseen that affected Marangol. The lethal and terrible effect of the radiation that was a by-product of its explosive power.

Invisible and unstoppable. The very nature of the beast made Marangol want to turn around and drive as far away as he could. He had seen military training films describing the effects of radiation poisoning; had seen the images of Japanese victims of the World War Two bombs dropped on Hiroshima and Nagasaki. Images of those victims were resurfacing now as he found himself in the same room as the Russian device. Courage notwithstanding, Marangol would have been happier far away from the bomb. Very far away.

Having the device in their hands was still something

he found satisfactory. It gave the organization a great advantage. That could not be taken away.

This would be Özgürlük's moment. If success came their way, then everything that had gone before would not matter. He would have been the first to admit things had not been going too well for them.

Attempts to remove the Americans had failed.

It would have been so easy to simply walk away.

But Marangol would not even consider that. He was a military man and his training had drilled into him a simple truth.

The war was not over until the last battle had been fought.

Despite the setbacks, Marangol refused to back down. It was not in his character to turn and walk away. The word *retreat* had no meaning for Marangol. Pride in his profession kept him on track. He would keep moving forward because there *was* no going back.

They still had their final shot to fire. In this instance it would be a shot the world would hear.

Marangol watched as Hakan Kaplan crossed the room to join him. The general had a deal of respect for the Özgürlük second in command. Kaplan was far stronger in many ways than Polat. Direct and not afraid to make decisions, Kaplan had the character that would have made him an excellent soldier.

As Kaplan approached, Marangol sensed he had something on his mind.

"Hakan, are you about to deliver troubling news?" Marangol said.

"In a word, General, yes."

He showed the cell phone in his hand.

"News from America. The device sent to Baltimore has been located by the authorities. There was a gun battle. Our brothers have all been killed or wounded. The bomb is now in the hands of the Americans. There will be no strike against the country."

Marangol allowed a half smile to edge his mouth as he took in what Kaplan was telling him. This was what happened when civilians were allowed to run such an operation. To keep the military involvement hidden as much as possible until the right moment, the bulk of the Özgürlük plan had been organized by Polat and his people. And now it was going off the rails.

He stared past Kaplan, watching the men at the table working on the device. Even they were delaying things with their final adjustments. For a wild moment Marangol wanted to rush in and snatch the bomb away from them and drive with it to the gates of Incirlik and detonate it himself.

Damn them all.

They were incompetent fools. And likely to tear the whole plan apart.

He contained the impulse when he realized Kaplan was watching him closely.

"Hakan, how much longer are those idiots going to play with that thing?"

"Another few hours, General. The timing unit is out of line and until they fix it the bomb cannot be set."

"This is madness. We obtained nuclear devices. One has been discovered in America. And now we are left in the hands of these idiots who are struggling to get the last bomb to work. Tell me, Hakan, do you not feel we are on a slippery slope to nothing here?"

"Not the way things were planned, General."

The door crashed open and one of the Özgürlük soldiers rushed into the room. He paused when he saw the nuclear device on the table, his face turning white.

"Is that—"

"Don't worry about that," Marangol said, cutting him off. "What do you want coming in here?"

Before the man could reply, the distant sound of auto-fire could be heard. Hard on that came a low, muffled explosion.

"Because of that," the man said. "There are intruders inside the walls."

CHAPTER THIRTY-ONE

Phoenix Force came out of the remaining shadows to cluster around Hawkins. McCarter took a cursory glance at the dead man. "Been a busy lad, then?"

"He was ready to spoil the surprise," Hawkins said.

He took back his subgun and hung it around his neck by the strap. He was still carrying the MP5 from the dead sentry. He led McCarter to the iron grille set in the side gate, allowing the Phoenix Force commander time to check out the scene.

"This bloke and the one who went back inside the compound? They all you've seen?"

Hawkins nodded. "If there are others around the perimeter they haven't showed their faces yet," he said.

"Constantine. Landis. Go check out the area. Don't want any surprises creeping up behind our backs."

Encizo and James moved off without a word, skirting the wall as they made their way toward the far corner of the site.

McCarter turned to the gate. He leaned his weight against it, feeling the aged wood flex as he applied pressure.

"Our way in?" Manning said.

"If we can open it without too much noise," the Briton said.

"These places were built to last," Kartal advised. "This one is centuries old."

"Is there a chance I'll be breaking a Turkish tradition if I damage this gate?"

"Only if you are superstitious," Kartal said.

"Good thing I'm not, then."

JAMES AND ENCIZO reached the farthest corner of the perimeter wall without encountering any resistance. Neither Phoenix Force warrior expected that to last. Crouching in the damp grass, they peered around the corner of the wall and saw two armed figures, lit cigarettes in hands, weapons slung loosely around their necks.

"Man, these Özgürlük are so slack," James said.

"That's what happens when you rely on rent-a-mob."

"Well, the hell with that," the black warrior said. "Let's do this."

James attached his suppressor to the Beretta. He stepped out from cover, the autopistol up and targeting before the Özgürlük pair could react. The 9 mm weapon snapped out deadly slugs. The head shots put the men down instantly.

"You've gotten better at this," Encizo said.

"I seem to be getting a lot of practice," James said.

They reached the section of wall that offered the easiest route into the monastery grounds and James activated his com.

MCCARTER'S COM SET clicked and James came on.

"Two," he said. "Huddled together having a sneaky smoke. Both down and out. I'd say we're free to go."

"Okay."

"We can scale the wall back here," James said. "Not as high as the rest and the stonework is pretty crumbled. Plenty of hand- and footholds. We can get inside and cover the rear in case there are any troops who might spoil your entrance."

"Do that. Give me a signal when you're in place."

McCarter clicked off. He told the others what had been decided.

"We still have to get through this gate," Manning said.

He had inspected it. There was no key access, so he had figured the gate was secured by bolts inside, most likely top and bottom. Getting through quickly would depend on how strong the bolts were.

"Easy way would be to blow the bloody thing off its hinges," McCarter said. "By the look of the weeds growing around this thing, it hasn't been opened for a long time. If that's the case, any bolts will probably be rusted solid."

"How about we shoulder it open?" Hawkins said. "Couple of us together should be able to break through."

McCarter grinned. "The optimism of youth," he said. "Bran muffins for breakfast and too many Rambo movies."

Manning slipped off the small backpack he carried. He reached inside and produced a small wrapped block of explosive and a slender stick fuse.

"He's like a baby with candy," McCarter said.

"An explosion will alert everyone inside," Kartal noted.

"Have to take what we can get," Hawkins said.

Manning crouched at the side gate, his fingers manipulating the malleable explosive compound, pressing it into place.

"He is good with this?" Kartal asked.

"The best," McCarter said.

As Manning stepped back, fingering the small detonator unit, McCarter felt his com set click.

"We're inside and—"

James's voice cut off as the crackle of autofire reached McCarter through his earbud.

"I guess sneaky time has been canceled. Do it," McCarter said.

He waved the rest to the side as Manning flattened against the wall and activated his unit. The explosion was small, more of a hard crack as the compound blew. When the smoke cleared, the wooden gate had gone, leaving only one twisted iron hinge hanging loosely from the surround.

"Let's move it, people," McCarter said, leading the way through the breached gateway.

From behind the building came more autofire. Voices were raised in alarm.

McCarter led Phoenix Force across the paved area and saw two armed sentries moving to intercept. The time for moving around quietly had passed. He cradled his MP5, turning the muzzle toward the advancing pair, easing back on the trigger. The burst of 9 mm slugs caught one of the men in the body. He faltered and dropped to his knees and was caught by Kartal as she kept in step with McCarter. Her burst ripped into his chest high, knocking him over onto his back.

Hawkins burned a 9 mm volley at the second guy, shredding his left shoulder and throat as he moved the MP5's muzzle. The sentry went into a jerky fall, blood spurting from his wounds.

"Keep moving," McCarter said, plucking a fragmentation grenade from his harness. He popped the pin, let the lever spring free and counted off the seconds as he continued moving forward. He lobbed the grenade under the closest of the parked vehicles.

"There she goes," he said, waving the others aside.

The grenade detonated with an echoing burst. The SUV jerked up off the ground as the blast impacted against its underside. Flame and smoke billowed. As the vehicle returned to earth the ruptured fuel tank ignited, adding a swell of fire that enveloped the totaled SUV. Glass cracked with the heat and fragments of metal rained down across the courtyard.

As they skirted around the rear of the wrecked SUV, Hawkins threw another grenade in through the shattered rear window of a second vehicle. It dropped inside the passenger area and when it exploded the force of the blast took a couple of doors off their hinges. The third SUV was enveloped in flame from the explosion, the paintwork bubbling and peeling, window glass cracking.

Armed figures rushed out through the main door, recoiling at the swell of heat from the burning wrecks. They spread apart, turning to face Phoenix Force as they advanced across the courtyard.

"Go," McCarter said.

The courtyard echoed to the rattle of autofire.

Brass casings rattled on the stone slabs as the exchange of fire increased.

Manning and Kartal found themselves almost shoulder to shoulder, their subguns matching the fire from the Özgürlük shooters. Slugs bounced off the slabs, sizzled by Manning and the NIO agent as they forced the pace, putting down two of the Özgürlük crowd. Though the Turkish extremists outnumbered the Phoenix group, superior fire and steadier nerves took their toll.

Hawkins expanded his distance from the group, coming around in a semicircle that forced the enemy to turn in his direction. It was what he had been waiting for. He stood his ground and burned 9 mm slugs into the Özgürlük zealots.

Hawkins maintained his position and placed his shots with precision. He took down two of the enemy with well-placed short bursts from the MP5, gaining body hits that dropped the pair in bloody heaps, and then he dropped to a crouch as he edged forward and took on the next shooter. Hawkins felt the passing of slugs from the other guy. Even felt one tug at his sleeve. His nerve held and he settled his aim and put a pair of slugs into the target's head. The slugs cored in and took off the rear of the guy's skull…

McCarter had sprinted forward, putting down the surviving Turkish extremist with a raking burst from his subgun, spilling the man facedown on the ground. With the way open, McCarter paused at the cleared doorway and threw his final fragmentation grenade inside the building. He dodged to one side, flat against the wall. He heard the crack of the detonation and felt the wall vibrate.

McCarter turned, signaling for the others to follow, and plunged in through the smoke curling from the open doorway.

CHAPTER THIRTY-TWO

"This mustn't happen. Not now!" Polat declared. His face was set in an expression of utter disbelief at the crackle of gunfire and the crack of grenades. "You must stop them."

General Marangol had brought a small contingent of his special soldiers with him, out of uniform but well armed. He caught the eye of the squad sergeant and gave a quiet signal. The soldiers, all loyal to the general and his cause, headed across the large room.

The two techs at the table looked around in alarm at the increasing sound of combat. Kaplan crossed over to speak with them, assuring them the matter would be dealt with and they should continue with their preparations.

He ignored Polat's protests, knowing that it was not going to achieve anything at this stage. They were under attack, and something told Kaplan the Americans were behind the strike. When Polat came to him, clutching at Kaplan's sleeve, he brushed the man aside.

"Kadir, we have no time. We must resist or we will lose this bomb, as well."

Polat caught the words and said, "Lose this bomb, as well? What has happened? You must be keeping something from me, Hakan. What?"

"Tell him," Marangol said. "Tell him about losing the American bomb."

"Is that true?"

Kaplan said, "Yes. I had a call. The Americans located the Baltimore bomb. They took it away from our people."

Polat was stunned by the news. He fell silent as he stared around the room. His expression showed a man suddenly facing defeat.

"Hakan, why did you not tell me immediately? Are you telling me it is all over?"

"I was going to tell you later. Because here and now is the most important concern we have."

Marangol said, "No more daydreaming, Polat. If we do not get out of this, everything ends here. I am tired of playing your foolish games. Wake up, you foolish man. Decide to give in, or fight for what you believe in."

"Hakan?" Polat's word came out as a wail of despair.

"The general is right. Here we win, or we die, Kadir. And I do not want to die today."

"But they are all around us. Can't you hear the guns? How can we escape from them now?"

"Dammit, man, we fight," Marangol said. "This is what freedom stands for. Our survival. Or have you forgotten that? Everything we have planned… All the people who stand behind us… If we fail here, we fail all of them."

Polat simply stared around him, his nerve failing him. His mind had been able to create the illusion of Özgürlük, but reality had become something he could not handle.

All his dreams beginning to shatter around him.

The bomb in America taken back. Lost.

Many of his people dead.

His threat factor being reduced piece by piece.

His brother, Amal, dead.

All he had left was the remaining nuclear device sitting across the room. Without the power it represented, Özgürlük could easily fade to nothing.

Somehow the dream had to be kept alive.

It could not be allowed to fade away…

CHAPTER THIRTY-THREE

James and Enzico had been on their way to rejoin the rest of Phoenix Force when they spotted the timber door set in the building wall.

"Sneaking in behind the bad guys. Isn't that a little underhanded?" James said.

"I would have to agree," Encizo said. "But what the hell. These guys are threatening us with a nuke, so I think being nice just went out the door, amigo."

They examined the door. It looked solid enough, but when they shoulder-rammed it the ancient timbers gave, splitting and caving in.

The Phoenix Force pair checked their subguns and pistols. Satisfied, they pushed their way through and emerged in a side passage that led in the direction of the front of the building. The stone floor of the short passage was layered in sandy dust and rat droppings.

"Ugh," James said as they move along. "This could do with a cleaning service."

A bulky shadow blocked the archway at the end of the passage. A voice muttered something that was not in English and the passage vibrated as a subgun opened up. Slugs cannoned into the wall. Chips of sandy stone exploded and the passage was filled with gritty dust. The whine of ricocheting slugs that threatened to hit them.

"Son of a bitch," James said forcibly.

His MP5 rose in concert with Encizo's, and they raked

the archway with twin bursts of rapid 9 mm fire. The hard bursts caught the distant shooter and slammed the stonework on either side. The guy gave a heavy groan as his body was peppered with slugs, blood and dark fragments of clothing erupting from him. He slumped to one side, then tumbled forward in an ungracious fall. As he struck the passage floor his subgun clattered down beside him.

Encizo clicked his com set and warned the rest of the team that he and James would be converging from the far end of the building.

"No shooting the reserve team," he said.

James followed Encizo as the Cuban skirted the walls of the passage, stepping over the dead shooter.

They emerged into a vast, open room. Sunlight drifted in through the high windows, many of them created from colored glass that cast dusty rainbow shafts across the tiled floor. Old wooden furniture and scattered debris lay in piles around the room.

The high-vaulted ceiling threw back the hammer of crackling autofire as the crisscross shooting continued.

High-velocity slugs pounded the walls and autoweapons spit out hot casings.

The two men working over the nuclear device abandoned their places and dropped to the floor, crawling under the table.

On the far side of the room, McCarter and his team had spread out and were returning fire from an armed military unit.

Entering the room from the opposite end, Encizo and James trained their weapons on the armed defenders, taking advantage of their sudden appearance.

It was Encizo who noticed the stone gallery that ran along the east wall, high overhead. There was an open archway at floor level, which must have given access to a steep flight of stone steps leading to the gallery.

What had caught the Cuban's attention was the sudden movement up in the gallery. The movement morphed into a pair of armed figures coming into view, raising the subguns they carried. They turned the muzzles down toward the floor space.

"Cal," he said, nudging James on the arm and directing his attention to the upper gallery.

They both angled their weapons up at the gallery and triggered long bursts of 9 mm slugs that pounded the lip of the gallery, flinging dust and stone chips into the air. Without pause they readjusted their aim and sent further shots at the two men. The 9 mm hail of lead caught the would-be shooters, drawing blood and toppling the pair.

James broke away and sprinted across to the archway. As he went through the door and turned to the narrow enclosed stairway, autoweapons thundered loudly in the confined space. James heard the slugs slam against the stonework, showering him with splinters. He felt a hot burn across one cheek. Warm blood streaked down his face. James dropped to a crouch, angling his SMG up the shadowed stairs, and fired at the figure framed at the top. He heard the guy utter a grunt of pain before he lost control and plunged down the steep stone steps, crashing to the bottom, his body hunched and bloody.

The subgun clicked on an empty breech. Pressed against the wall at his back, James executed a rapid reload. He moved only when the action had been completed.

Two of Marangol's men went down from Phoenix Force's opening shots.

With Phoenix Force attacking from the front, the military men were hit hard within the first minute.

Encizo added his autofire from the opposite side of the wide room, and the moment James took down his targets, he rushed back out to add his firepower to that of the others.

The seemingly endless volleys slowed and fell away to a sudden, numbing silence. The opposition was down, either dead or wounded badly enough to be removed from the fight.

Polat and Kaplan stood in awkward silence, shocked by the sudden, tide-turning event.

General Marangol held his position, his 9 mm pistol at arm's length as he faced Phoenix Force.

"I will not surrender," he said defiantly.

Kartal moved to face him, her own weapon held steady in her hands. A bloody patch showed on her left arm where a bullet had caught her. She ignored the wound. She spoke to Marangol in Turkish, and even without translation the tone in her voice was harsh.

"Demir Marangol, you are under arrest. For acts of treason against Turkey."

"You cannot touch me, bitch. I am *General* Marangol. You have no authority over me."

"You relinquished that title when you committed unlawful acts. Had people murdered and plotted to endanger life with your nuclear bombs." Kartal chose to speak in English. "I know you understand English, so for the benefit of these men acting, as I am, under the name of the president of Turkey, I demand you surrender your weapon and turn yourself over to me."

The smile on Marangol's face deepened. He seemed to find the whole scenario amusing.

"You are like a child who has found a dangerous toy, Agent Kartal. Do you believe I am afraid of that gun you wave at me?"

"You should be," Hawkins said, "'cause she throws a damn straight bullet."

"I do not recognize your authority. You Americans have no right to challenge me. You are foreigners in this country."

"When you decided to take your bloody scheme to the U.S., you became a legitimate combatant," McCarter said. "Did you really think we would ignore your insane plan? General, it is over."

"Never. Özgürlük will not give in to you…"

Marangol's anger got the better of him. He made a sudden move and tracked his pistol on his closest target.

Berna Kartal.

He pulled the trigger. His slug hit her in her left shoulder, the impact twisting her around as she stumbled off balance and went down on the stone floor.

Marangol clamped his other hand around his pistol and went to fire again.

T. J. Hawkins triggered his MP5 and emptied his partly used magazine into the man. The burst of 9 mm fire slammed into the general's chest. He took a step back, placing a hand over the wounds where his blood was already starting to pulse from his ragged flesh. He struggled to remain on his feet but failed, his body thudding to the floor.

Hawkins and James moved to Kartal's side, supporting her. James opened his med pack and began to tend to her.

"You," McCarter said to a staring Kaplan. "Do one good thing today." He thrust his sat phone into the man's hands. "Call an ambulance. Tell them where we are and don't screw it up. We've all still got plenty of ammunition and bloody good reasons to use it. Berna, if you can hear, make sure he doesn't try to screw around."

Kaplan took the phone and raised it. He was ready to speak when he shook his head violently.

"No—stop him!" he shouted.

Heads turned in time to see Kadir Polat holding one of the discarded subguns and pointing it directly at the nuclear device.

"Put it down, Polat," McCarter said. "This won't prove a bloody thing."

"It will for me." Polat's finger curled against the trigger.

"It will do no good if you shoot," Kaplan said to him.

Tears were running down Polat's face.

"These people are the ones who are responsible for Amal's death."

"That was not to be part of our plan, Kadir. Amal acted on his own. Yes, he thought he was doing something brave for the cause. But it failed…"

"He should not have died."

"But he did. Through his own actions."

"I was not there to protect him."

"Blaming yourself will not—"

Polat's scream of frustration filled the room as he jerked the subgun forward, his action almost catching them off guard.

A single shot echoed sharply in the stone room.

The 9 mm slug struck Polat in the forehead, punching a hole as it entered his brain and blew out the back of his head. He arched back, the subgun drooping in his grasp, then dropped without a sound.

"Will someone please call that ambulance now?" Kartal said from where she lay, her Glock still raised in her right hand.

"Do it," Encizo said. He moved and confronted Kaplan. "Do it, you son of a bitch, before I decide Agent Kartal had the right idea and you can join your friend."

Hakan Kaplan made the call without protest.

McCarter took the sat phone off him to make a call of his own.

CHAPTER THIRTY-FOUR

Barbara Price and Hal Brognola were taking time out to review the Özgürlük mission.

"Close one," she said. "But then, most of them are."

Brognola shook his head, his face giving away what was swirling around inside.

"There are times I think we get handed every bad deal going on in the world. All the sick and twisted schemes that get dreamed up by sick and twisted people. And every time some crazy fanatic threatens mayhem, I have to send those guys out. They fly off to God knows where and put themselves in harm's way again. Every time I tell them a mission is a go…"

"Nice to know I'm not the only one who has bad moments," Price said. "If I had worry beads they'd be worn down to the string. Hal, the guys do it because they believe it's all worth it. They work on the same principle Mack does. If they don't stand up to be counted—who will?"

"So young, so full of wisdom," Brognola said.

Price burst out laughing. "You think so?"

"I can't always be wrong."

"Gary passed me information from that UK guy, Doug Henning," Price continued. "The one they worked with in London," Price said. "The cops found the rental car Tak Kumad, Özgürlük's hired gun, used. They traced it from the key fob in his pocket. Checked via the rental company and got a trace on the LoJack system fitted to the car. It was in a multistory parking garage not far from Aziz Makar's office. Kumad had left a carryall in the trunk and they located a laptop inside it. Turns out to have been Makar's missing machine."

"Tell me they found something useful on it," Brognola said. "Manning and Hawkins in the UK was not a real part of the mission. They went there on thin information and it turned out Özgürlük was paying back a couple of conmen in their own ranks. Nothing to do with the main mission."

"These things happen," Price said. "The guys did stop an assassin, and in a roundabout way they got us that laptop. Which has provided a good deal of information."

Brognola smiled. "See, you just can't help it," he said. "You defend those guys like Perry Mason on a roll."

"Damn right I do, Hal. Every time."

"So what was on that computer?"

"Only lists of Özgürlük contributors. All prominent Turkish businessmen, politicians. Facts and figures on contributions that had been made to the organization. Kind of a who's who of anti-U.S. agitators. Now, Makar might have turned out to be a crook helping himself to Özgürlük's funds, but he did keep accurate accounts. Seems he was a good financial man. There were details of contacts. All the payments made to contractors. Suppliers. Payoffs to a number of people who were helping Özgürlük. All the way down the line."

"Sounds like a goody bag the Turkish president will enjoy getting his hands on," Brognola said.

"A number of arrests have already been made. Anyone with ties to Özgürlük is running for cover. By the sounds of it the organization is pretty well broken up. Have you updated the President yet?"

"Yes. He's in the know. Sends his grateful thanks. His only regret is he can't make his thanks known more publicly. Hard to do that when we're not supposed to exist."

"You on top of it all now?"

"Almost. It's been hard keeping up with all the angles since Phoenix located that bomb in Turkey. David called in a covert team from the Incirlik base to take charge of it. They took the device back to the base and put it under guard until one of our technical teams could disarm it."

"No protest from the Turkish authorities?"

"By the time they found out, it was all over, bar the cleanup. The Turkish president laid down the law about making too much fuss. He was just glad the matter was over."

"So Kadir Polat is dead. And General Marangol. What about Polat's brother in arms?"

"Hakan Kaplan? By now he'll be measuring curtains for his prison cell. He's going to be spending the rest of his life in a Turkish prison. And believe me, Barb, he won't find it as cozy as an American one."

"I would have imagined it would have been a terminal sentence."

"From what I've heard, the Turkish president decided keeping him alive in a prison cell would hurt a damn sight more."

"Time to close the mission down," Price said, standing to leave. "Oh, how's Berna Kartal? Almost forgot about her. She deserves better than that."

"She'll be out of action for a while. But her position at the NIO is safe. It appears that when the Turkish president heard about her contribution, he ordered she be promoted and given some top Turkish award. Apparently he's going to present it to her personally."

"Nice to hear someone came out smelling of roses." Price paused at the door.

"The NIO has been doing some in-house cleaning, as well. They found out a civilian assistant had been monitoring phone calls using their own network. A guy who was part of Özgürlük. He had been listening in to Cem Asker's calls and picked up his arrangements to meet Kartal. Gave Özgürlük time to set up the hit when he met her."

"That could have turned out nasty if Phoenix hadn't been around."

"They had to move fast there."

"So when will our unsung heroes be back?"

"Phoenix is on the way. Able got in an hour ago. I think you'll find them checking in their ordnance."

"How did I miss that?"

"Ms. Price, regardless of what you believe, you do not know everything."

"Okay, I'll give you that, but to be honest, what I don't know isn't all that worth knowing anyway." She smiled as she closed his office door behind her.

Brognola sat in his quiet office. He let the silence envelop him. Just for a while. Until it was time for the next round, which he knew would come.

As the peaceful aura started to settle, Brognola glanced at his watch. Still time to go home, maybe get a night's sleep in his own bed. That sounded like a plan. He pushed to his feet, grabbed his coat and headed for the door.

He was reaching for the light switch when the phone on his desk began to ring.

* * * * *

COMING SOON FROM

GOLD EAGLE®

Available May 5, 2015

THE EXECUTIONER® #438
THE CARTEL HIT – *Don Pendleton*

Facing off against a Mexican cartel, the Executioner races to secure the lone witness to a brutal double murder.

DEATHLANDS® #122
FORBIDDEN TRESPASS – *James Axler*

While Ryan and the companions take on a horde of hungry cannibals, something far more sinister—and ravenous—lurks beneath their feet…

OUTLANDERS® #73
HELL'S MAW – *James Axler*

The Cerberus warriors must confront an alien goddess who can control men's minds. But are they strong enough to eliminate this evil interloper bent on global domination?

ROGUE ANGEL™ #54
DAY OF ATONEMENT – *Alex Archer*

A vengeful fanatic named Cauchon plans to single-handedly resurrect the violence of the Inquisition to put Annja and Roux on trial… and a guilty verdict could mean death.

Bolan heard the clink of metal on metal as the *a la muerte* soldier took another step closer, his equipment giving him away.

The guy was muttering to himself as he edged around the twisted roots of the tree and moved along its length. He stepped into Bolan's field of vision, and when he tilted his weapon, Bolan caught the dull gleam of light as it rippled along the barrel. That gave him his target, and Bolan intended to make use of it.

In one swift motion, the Executioner sprang from his hiding spot, grasping the guy's throat with his left hand as he rose to his full height, his right striking hard at the midsection of the exposed torso. The Tanto's cold blade sliced through clothing and sank in up to the hilt.

He felt the man shudder as he slid the penetrating blade left to right to extend the wound. A harsh groan burst from the Mexican's lips. Bolan slid his left hand around to the back of the guy's neck, yanking him forward, pulling his body in closer to the cutting blade. He felt warm blood oozing from the stab site.

Bolan pulled the weakening man in against the log, leaning on him hard, feeling the tremors that followed the damage done by the knife. The guy let out a long, ragged sigh as he began to slip to the ground. Bolan kept up the pressure until all movement and sound ceased. He pulled out the knife and cleaned the steel blade against the man's shirt, then sheathed it.

He could hear faint noises coming from the headset the man was wearing. Bolan slipped the comset from the body, held the earpiece close and listened to the transmission. He identified two voices. One ordered the other to silence, then spoke in swift Spanish.

"Enrico, what is going on? Talk to me. Where are you?"

"I found him," Bolan said, keeping his voice low. "You want to come and see?"

There was a brief silence.

"You are not Enrico... Who are you?"

"The one you cannot find. The one who is going to send you to Hell."

Don't miss
THE CARTEL HIT by Don Pendleton,
available May 2015 wherever
Gold Eagle® books and ebooks are sold.

JAMES AXLER

DEATHLANDS®

The saga that asks "What if a global nuclear war comes to pass?" and delivers gripping adventure and suspense in the grim postapocalyptic USA.

Set in the ruins of America one hundred years after a nuclear war devastated the world, a group of warrior survivalists, led by the intrepid Ryan Cawdor, search for a better future. In their struggle, the group is driven to persevere—even resorting to the secret devices created by the mistrusted "whitecoats" of prewar science.

Since the nukecaust, the American dream has been reduced to a daily fight for survival. In the hellish landscape of Deathlands, few dare to dream of a better tomorrow. But Ryan Cawdor and his companions press on, driven by the need for a future less treacherous than the present.

Available wherever Gold Eagle® books and ebooks are sold.

GOLD EAGLE®

GEDL2015

SPECIAL EXCERPT FROM

The top of the food chain has never seemed so high...

Read on for a sneak preview of
FORBIDDEN TRESPASS
by James Axler

Ryan wanted the enemy to run, and preferably not stop until he and his companions had escaped.

He saw J.B. coolly step into the road and fire a medium burst from his Uzi. A man to Ryan's left screamed and clutched his paunch as a line of red dots was stitched across it. He fell howling and kicking to the ground.

Ryan shifted targets and fired. Another man fell.

The chill joined at least a dozen others fallen in the roadway. At the rear of the mob, which had lost momentum and had begun to mill about, Ryan saw a tall woman, just visible before the bend. She had raven-black hair and creamy skin. She looked shocked, and her eyes were wide.

It was Wymie, the woman responsible for all their problems—including the fact they were now fighting for their lives against what seemed like half the population of the ville.

"Fireblast," he said, and lowered his aim to shoot a young man trying to point some kind of flintlock at them.

"Why didn't you chill her, lover?" Krysty called from the cover of the nettles across the road.

"She's the leader," he called back. "She's beat. She'll spread her exhaustion to the rest once we chill or drive off the hard core."

Even as he said that, he saw it start to happen. The initial volley of blasterfire from his team, crouched in cover to either side of the thoroughfare, had dropped so many of the attackers they formed a living roadblock. Those behind, mad-eyed and baying for blood a heartbeat before, now faltered. This mob had clearly let self-preservation reassert itself in the face of their waning bloodlust.

They were done. It was all over but for the fleeing.

Then, from the corner of his lone eye, Ryan saw a skinny old man, standing by the side of the road, leveling a single-action Peacemaker at Ryan's head.

He already knew he was nuked, even as his brain sent his body the impulse to dive aside.

The ancient blaster and its ancient shooter alike vanished in a giant yellow muzzle-flash. It instantly echoed in a blinding red flash inside Ryan's skull.

Then blackness. Then nothing.

Don't miss
FORBIDDEN TRESPASS by James Axler,
available May 2015 wherever
Gold Eagle® books and ebooks are sold.